912666

FIC
Lew   Lewis, Roy

           A secret dying

A Secret Dying

ROY LEWIS

A Secret Dying

St. Martin's Press
New York

Library of Congress Cataloging-in-Publication Data

Lewis, Roy
    A secret dying / Roy Lewis.
        p.   cm.
    ISBN 0-312-08887-6
    I. Title.
PR6062.E954S4   1993
823'.914—dc20   92-33373
                                                      CIP

First published in Great Britain by HarperCollins Publishers.

First U.S. Edition: February 1993
10 9 8 7 6 5 4 3 2 1

A Secret Dying

CHAPTER 1

1

He was late.

There was a fresh, early evening breeze blowing off the sea, tangy with salt she could taste on her lips. The square-sterned fishing cobles were moored at the jetty, a few late visitors wandering along the tiny, curved harbour, among the litter of lobster-pots, ropes and nets. Beyond the harbour white horses danced on the wavetops, excited as she was, alive, tumbling hurriedly under a scudding, grey sky.

She turned her back to the breeze and looked back past the fishermen's cottages that lined the harbour. Some of them—like Lance's—had been converted into weekend retreats, and she cursed the fact that she had left the key he had given her in her other purse. But even so, she knew she could not have waited there for him, in the dim twilight of the two-roomed cottage, with the steady ticking of the old grandfather clock to madden her, remind her of passing time and the emptiness around her. The churning in her stomach, the excited surge of blood in her veins, would not have stilled. She could not sit and wait, patience was not a strong point when there was this urgency in her mind and in her loins.

Behind the village rose the rocky outcrop of the Great Whin Sill where stone had been quarried for centuries. The Sill ran out northwards towards Castle Point. There it lurched a hundred feet sheer out of the North Sea, a seaward defence for the fourteenth-century Lancastrian stronghold where John of Gaunt had built his gatehouse. She stared at the ruined walls, a mile distant, frowning. She shrugged in sudden frustration, needing to be active, turned away from Craster harbour and began to walk along the coastal path towards the stark, romantic ruins of Dunstanburgh.

Lance should have been here.

She needed him. The adrenalin still surged through her, she needed to talk, to tell him what she had discovered, to see the excitement rise in his eyes too. She marched now along the coastal path, her mind dancing with excitement as she skirted the broad green sward with the sea crashing greenly against the rocks below, to her right.

It was typical of a journalist.

His desire matched hers, she was sure of it, but the newspaper business was as demanding as any mistress. She understood how it was, but nevertheless the frustration welled inside her at the thought of what she knew, and how she would tell him.

Afterwards.

First, there was a hunger to be assuaged.

Triumph always did that for her, she thought to herself as she stood above the great cleft chasm of Egyn Cleugh. When she won, tasted triumph, it brought a sexual excitement in its train, and that excitement sharpened the hunger she felt for Lance. It was not new, of course: she was sufficiently objective to recognize that her sexual needs were, if not abnormal, at least powerful.

Kevin had been a mistake, an aberration.

She couldn't understand now why she had married him: the sexual satisfaction had never been there after the early months, and his refusal to quarrel had always been a source of frustration to her. When she and Lance quarrelled, the air turned blue, but the quarrel always culminated in a furious, violent love-making that left her exhausted yet fulfilled.

But now, when it was important he was here, he was late.

She heard the raucous cries of the gulls, wheeling and dipping in the chasm below her, watched the thunderous crashing of the tide surging into the cleft and its rhythmic thrusting tore at her, increased her need, so she turned her back against the dying sun and walked hurriedly back along the mile long coastal path, hurrying towards the village, and the Jolly Fisherman.

There was a faint haze of smoke in the air as she reached the harbour, drifting from the harbourside sheds where West Scottish herring were cured over whitewood chippings and oak sawdust. It had been one of her first assignments on the *Journal*: a tourist account of the kippering sheds of Craster. It was odd being here now, with the story in her head, a different woman, with a different man, and everything she wanted within her grasp.

She waited a little while longer, the salt breeze in her face, watching a black cormorant ride the waves, and beyond, a distant freighter making its way southwards across a grey sea towards the Tyne. Then she shook her head angrily and walked across to the Jolly Fisherman.

The odours of tobacco and beer reached out to her as she entered the room. The shirt-sleeved barman pulled her a half pint of draught cider. 'Mr Stevens not with yer this evenin'?'

'He'll be along later. When he comes, tell him I'm in the corner, over there.'

'Will you be wanting to eat?'

'Probably not.'

She was short with the man, impatient. A conversation with the barman was not what she wanted. She stared at the barman's thick forearms and the thought of Lance's muscular back suddenly came into her mind as a sharp, visual, almost tactile image. She could almost feel under her fingertips his dorsal muscles tensing and hardening as he thrust at her, and she turned away, afraid the barman could see the lust in her eyes. She sat down in the corner, hidden from the door, and her thighs quivered suddenly, uncontrollably, as she thought of the story, and how she would tell him and how they would soon be locked together, reaching high . . .

She sipped at the cider, to calm herself. She waited.

*

It was half past eight before he walked into the Jolly Fisherman. She saw him before he turned and caught sight of her. His crinkly hair was damp from the light drizzle that had come inland from the sea and his pale eyes glittered; his coat collar was turned up and the white, open-necked shirt emphasized the tan of his features, legacy of a two-week assignment in Corfu which had given them an explosive reunion on his return to Newcastle.

He came across to her, grinning, a pint of Guinness in his left hand. 'Sorry, Princess. But you know what it's like. The Old Man called a conference about yesterday's front page. He was not in one of his better moods.'

He sat down, sliding across the seat beside her. 'And what sort of mood are *you* in?' he asked, and leaned forward to kiss her in greeting. She grabbed the back of his neck, pulling his mouth hard against hers, and as she felt his thigh pressing against hers the liquid sensation in her loins increased, and she groaned.

He pulled away, staring at her, grinning again. 'Sorry I asked! Like that, is it? I knew you didn't like waiting—'

'We're wasting time.'

The grin faded, and something of her lust was reflected in his eyes. He had always matched her in a swift change to passion: they could be ablaze together in a matter of seconds, wherever they were. It was why she couldn't resist him . . . not that she had ever tried.

'I've just bought myself a pint,' he said in mock complaint.

'Leave it.'

'It's been a long day and a long drive from Newcastle,' he protested. 'The night's young—I don't need to be at my desk until two tomorrow and I know your schedule—'

'To hell with my schedule. I want you. *Now.*'

He stared at her, and took a long, tantalizing pull at his Guinness. 'Something's happened.'

'That's right.'

'A story?'

'*The* story.' She stretched her arms wide in an expansive, welcoming gesture. She laughed. 'It's all come together. I made it.'

'I thought I was going to make you, a moment ago.'

'That too. But this is something amazing, and if I can work it out, get it straight it's the kind of story that could fly me to Fleet Street—'

'Our Fleet Street's no longer there.'

'You know what I mean.'

'What the hell are you talking about?'

She stared at him, kissed him again, fiercely, and then touched her tongue to her lips, savouring the sensation of his lips. 'I want you.'

'I know that, Princess. When didn't you? But this story—'

'It can wait.'

'But I want—'

'No.' Her fingers fixed on the pint glass and drew it from his grasp. She pushed it to the far side of the table. Her face had darkened, her eyes seeming to glow in the dim light as she leant towards him. 'I don't care what you want, unless it's me. This is my night, my story, and I'm going to tell it my way. When you're locked with me, and I've got you trapped, and . . .' Her fingers wandered lightly along his thigh, touched him. His hand closed over hers and his eyebrows lifted.

'Oh. It's as bad as that, is it?' he grinned. 'Why didn't you say so before?'

She'd always liked that about him—his ability to laugh, make light of the passion that could make her nerve ends raw with excitement so that she could be blind, unthinking, careless. He always seemed able to keep something in reserve, to surprise her when exhaustion and satiation beckoned.

He squeezed her fingers so hard that she felt tears spring to her eyes. He rose from the table, still gripping her hand. The barman looked at them as they left, and then glanced

knowingly around the bar after the door closed behind
them. 'Looks like being a hard night,' he said, and someone
at the dartboard laughed.

She seemed insatiable.

She had dragged at his clothing as soon as they were
inside the cottage, not even giving him time to lock the
door. They had tumbled wildly into bed, and there was no
laughter at first—the passion was raw, and demanding.
She had shuddered to an early climax, but still said nothing
as she kneaded him back to life and they made love again,
more slowly, intense in the darkness that surrounded them,
relinquishing their hold on the outside world and its realities and losing themselves deliberately in the long, sliding,
riding of a sexual rollercoaster.

He was still inside her when the sound of cars in the
village had long receded and there was only the distant,
faint thunder of the sea on the rocks, drifting in through
the half-open window. They were sexually alive still, but
her insistent passion had left them physically spent, and
they lay there in the darkness, breathing lightly, waiting for
the surge they both knew would return, to come again.

'Well, Princess,' he whispered. 'What diet have you been
on?'

'Just you. It's inspirational.'

'That I don't believe. What's turned you on has something to do with professional greed. I ought to feel miffed.
You ought to want me for being me. But there's some fan-
tasy going on in your head that's turned you into an
alleycat. So what is it?'

'Why do you want to know?' she asked, stretching and
lifting her body against his in a languorous, deliberate
motion.

'Not so I could bottle it! But at least I could have warning
next time.'

'Hah! If this story breaks the way I think there'll be lots
of next times!'

'So tell me.'

'Isn't there something else you'd like to think about first?' she asked teasingly.

He grinned, bit gently at her lips and reached over to pin her wrists against the headboard, spreadeagled while he rose above her. 'I'm not just thinking about it, Princess, but until you tell me—'

The door cracked open like a cannonshot. It slammed against the wall and he left her, swung around in the bed to stare in panic behind him. He could make out little for a moment, then there was the dark shape towering in the doorway, haloed by the faint light that came in through the downstairs windows. There was something raised; he heard a gasp, she started to say something, but his own mouth was dry, his heart pounding in his chest.

'*Kevin!*' she cried out, almost croaking the name.

There was a brief silence, and then a sharp snapping sound came, a flash and something wet and sticky splashed on his face. He pulled away, dragging his arm from under her as she rolled, her face a dark, shapeless mask, a slow thick welling, glistening in the semi-darkness. He tried to throw himself out of the bed, tumbling sideways, the thick bile of fear in his throat but he was caught up in a tangle of sheets. The silence seemed to reverberate around him as he fell on his knees to the hard boards of the cottage bedroom, the rug skidding away under him.

He looked up, and the dark shape was standing there, the shotgun raised, levelled.

Lance Stevens gibbered in panic, choking on the taste in his throat and he raised his arms to shield his head, a vain protective gesture. The great wind came, pushing his arms aside, thrusting through them to his defenceless head.

He was aware of a brief, black flashing before his eyes and a thunderous sound before the darkness came, and the silence.

2

Simon Brent-Ellis, the Director of the Department of Museums and Antiquities—or the DDMA as he was known by his colleagues—was a tall, heavily-built man with white hair, albino eyes and a walrus moustache, stained at its tips from the cigars he habitually affected in the office, at home and on the golf course.

He had the feet of a policeman and hands to match, so his attempts at elegance were perpetually doomed as he clumped his way about the offices or in and out of the County Committee Rooms. He was inclined towards beige suiting, pink striped shirts and floral ties, and formal occasions led to no toning down of the colour clashes. It was rumoured that Chief Executive Powell Frinton, a somewhat conservative man, had literally choked when the new DDMA had wandered into his first management committee meeting some five years previously. The coffee stain had never been removed from his waistcoat. Discreet conversations with the DDMA had however produced no noticeable results for Powell Frinton—the DDMA was a free soul who took neither offence at nor notice of criticism, and continued on his own sweet way, confident of the political support that had placed him in office.

As the son of an ex-Lord Lieutenant and a regular visitor to Buckingham Palace Garden Parties, it seemed he could afford to annoy the Chief Executive with impunity, and as for competence at his job, it was undoubted. He was recognized as a first-class delegator of duties who did his own best business on the golf courses in the county. These, he stressed, were close to some of the finest Roman and Celtic sites in the county, and required regular and personal oversight from the DDMA himself. The councillors who played with him agreed, and his department was a relatively happy one for his regular absence.

He also had a wife, a formidable lady who chaired the Finance Committee and commanded considerable ward

support at election time. She was of the view that golf kept
him out of mischief. It was an attitude which he enthusiasti-
cally endorsed.

When the Chief Executive had persuaded Arnold Landon that he might find life rather more to his taste in the
DMA, Arnold had expressed his doubts. He had, nevertheless, allowed himself to be persuaded, and now he was not
sorry. He had enjoyed his work in the Planning Department, as far as he had been allowed to enjoy it, but he was
forced to admit that the pressures in the DMA were not of
the same intensity. The pace of life was more leisurely, the
activity more in line with his interests, and he had little to
do with County Hall politicians, like Mrs Brent-Ellis. They
were not the easiest people to deal with, as he had already
found to his cost on more than one occasion.

There had been some problems when he had transferred:
his fame, or notoriety, had preceded him. There were some
who were wary because of his expert reputation in the
antiquities line, until he was able to explain that he held
no formal qualifications, but had merely developed, as a
hobby, an understanding of stone and wood and of the men
who had worked in these materials over the centuries. His
expertise could therefore be dismissed essentially as an ami-
able eccentricity—neither dangerous nor threatening. And
once it was made clear he was after neither promotion nor
other people's jobs, he was accepted, tucked away in a dark
corner of the department and allowed to settle in.

Settling in, it seemed, meant having little to do for the
first few weeks. He then discovered that it was legitimate
to spend a few more weeks pottering through catalogues
and old County Histories, developing a 'feel' for the work
of the Department.

He also had a travelling allowance, and was happy to
discover he could legitimately spend time in visiting the
various protected historical sites and museums in the
country during his 'familiarization' period.

It was with a feeling of some alarm, therefore, that he

suddenly found himself summoned to the office of the DDMA himself. The bearer of the message herself showed surprise.

'Didn't think he was in this week,' she offered. 'And in any case, it's Wednesday.'

'So?' Arnold had queried, puzzled.

She sniffed. 'He don't come in 'fore Tuesday mornin', never arrives after Thursday evenin', and usually takes Wednesday off. Wednesday's committee day,' she added, as though that explained everything.

She led the way, swinging her pert bottom as they traversed the clerks' room where young, shirt-sleeved clerks stared and pursed their lips and sniggered, and processed Arnold down the grey-painted corridor to the DDMA's suite.

'Over to you, Miss Sansom,' she said gaily after opening the door.

It was rumoured that Mrs Brent-Ellis chose her husband's secretaries personally. This one had been in post eight months. She was Teutonic in appearance and gruffness. Her fingers seemed too thick to use a word-processor or file a document but her mannish clothing and severe hair style gave her an air of Prussian menace, so no one ever dared look at her typing or her files. It was said not even the DDMA did.

'You are expected, Mr Landon,' she intoned accusingly. Arnold almost thought she was going to explain she had ways of making him talk to the DDMA. He was somewhat relieved when she merely opened the inner door and waved him through, closing the door quietly behind him.

A thin blue haze of cigar smoke hung in the air. The DDMA sat half sprawled behind his wide mahogany desk, caressing his moustache and staring out of the window with a wrinkled brow. The window gave him a distant view over the town towards the north end of Morpeth, and eastwards towards Amble and the coast. The sky was mackerel grey and there was a hint of rain in the air. Perhaps the DDMA was thinking of his golf.

As Arnold advanced into the room Brent-Ellis waved his cigar in a vaguely welcoming gesture, offering Arnold a chair. When Arnold was seated, the DDMA sighed, and turned to face him.

'Dear boy,' he drawled. 'I don't believe we've met.'

'Er, not really, Mr Brent-Ellis.'

The albino eyes widened as though surprised at the name; recovering, they lidded lazily with the confidence of status. 'Remiss of me, not to make your acquaintance sooner. But there you are . . . a busy life, hey?'

There seemed little Arnold could reply to this sally, clashing as it did with quite different information current in the office. The DDMA was observing him carefully through the blue haze. 'So . . . the Chief Executive tells me you, ah, expressed a desire to join us. Because of your personal interests. Museums . . . and Antiquities.'

'The suggestion was made to *me*,' Arnold demurred.

'But you know a lot about the kind of things we're responsible for. Old buildings. Artefacts. Er . . . and so on.' The DDMA seemed momentarily dazed as his voice tailed off with the effort of reminding himself of the responsibilities of his Department.

Arnold shrugged. 'I know something about mediæval building systems, stones, fourteenth-century woodwork-ing—'

'Yes, all that sort of thing.' The DDMA's interruption was followed by a closer scrutiny, as though something else had been called to mind. 'Yes . . . Old Barns and things . . . I remember now.'

Arnold's heart sank. He had hoped that his unlucky penchant for getting into trouble was going to be left behind him by moving to a new Department, but it seemed it was too much to hope for. Powell Frinton would have warned the DDMA. It was only fair to do so, Arnold conceded to himself.

'Anyway,' the DDMA continued, 'I don't suppose you've ever had anything to do with the Tourist Board?'

'I'm afraid not.'

'So you don't know Ben Edwards?'

'I understand he's the Director, and I've seen him on television but I can't say our paths have ever crossed.'

'Bloody lucky you!' the DDMA muttered, almost to himself, then flashed Arnold a yellow smile edged with nervousness. 'He can be a pain in the backside, you know, a bit . . . aggressive, our Mr Edwards. Do you know Kevin Anderson?'

Arnold frowned. 'Yes. I met him the first day I was in this department. He took me to lunch, in fact. A pleasant young man.'

The DDMA was watching Arnold closely. He nodded. 'Yes. Haven't had much to do with him, myself. So don't know what makes him tick. He's gone on leave.'

'Oh?'

'Oh, indeed,' the DDMA replied and settled himself deeper in his chair, hunching his shoulders to express unhappiness. He observed his cigar reflectively. 'Chaps are allowed leave, of course—need it to recharge the batteries and all that sort of thing. But it's best to, well, you know, agree dates and kind of follow the rules, don't you agree? Not right to just up sticks and charge off.'

Arnold remained silent. It was none of his business if Kevin Anderson had not cleared leave with his superiors. But Arnold was surprised. Anderson was a quietly spoken, reserved sort of man who kept very much to himself. Married, about thirty-five, medium in build and controlled in personality, he seemed to have no particular friends in the office, though he had been quick enough to put himself out to help Arnold during his first days in the department. A good-looking young man with a pleasant smile, but haunted by an unexpressed anxiety, Arnold had concluded. It was as though he welcomed the opportunity to meet someone new, lay the basis for a vague friendship. Even so, Arnold had seen little enough of him during his time in the office.

'When a chap charges off like that, you see,' the DDMA continued, 'he can leave problems behind. Work un-finished. That sort of thing. Which is why I thought of you.'

Arnold raised his eyebrows. 'Me? In what context?'

'The work, man. What Kevin Anderson was involved with. The stuff he left unfinished. Seemed to us—to me—it would be sort of up your street. Quite.'

'What was Mr Anderson doing when he . . . took leave?' Arnold asked, puzzled.

Brent-Ellis took a long draw on his cigar, then puffed furiously at it for several seconds as he realized it had almost gone out. He inspected its glowing end with satisfaction, eventually, and smiled, waving the cigar in triumph at his creativity. 'Outside job, really. That's why I mentioned Ben Edwards. You see, the Tourist Board asked us to do a job for them. Brochure or something similar. Part of a series, I understand. To appear in book form also. Nothing wild. Thought we had the research capacity. Well, we do, don't we?'

Feeling challenged, Arnold nodded. 'I suppose so. What was the brochure about?'

'Pele towers and suchlike. Northumberland heritage. That sort of thing.'

'And Mr Anderson left it unfinished? Can't its com-pletion wait until he gets back?'

'Ben Edwards reckons not. Says he's got deadlines. Don't understand such thinking, myself, but there you are. Thing is, Mr, er, Landon, can you see your way clear to help?'

'In what way?'

'Finish the job for Anderson. Drop everything else. Do a Light Brigade, rush at it, get Edwards off my back.' The albino eyes were suddenly angry, darting redly about the room as though seeking escape. 'Can you do that for me, Landon? Get Edwards off my back?'

'I can try, sir,' Arnold replied, feeling almost relieved

that he would apparently have some real work to do at last. 'I've nothing particular on my desk at the—'

'Fine. Great. Splendid. Hell's flames, look at the time! I've got to be out of here!'

Miss Sansom opened the door as he rose from his chair, almost as though she and her employer had been synchronized. Arnold stood up, stepping aside as the DDMA blundered past in his beige suit. 'Er, where shall I start, sir?'

'Start?' The DDMA seemed bewildered, as though he had already forgotten Arnold and the subject of the conversation. 'Ah. Well. Yes. Er . . . get Anderson's files. Then go see the Tourist Board. They'll fill in the details.'

Miss Sansom gazed at the DDMA with an unconcealed admiration in her eyes as he clumped past her; the longing and pride was replaced by scorn as she switched her glance to Arnold, leaving in Brent-Ellis's wake. How could he possibly expect such a busy man as Mr Brent-Ellis to allow himself to be bothered with details? She snorted, adoringly, and slammed the door behind Arnold in the emphatic dismissal she reserved for the DDMA's minions.

A phone call to the Tourist Board gave Arnold the information that the Director, Ben Edwards, was not available in the Newcastle office, but could be contacted at Allendale, where he would be staying for the rest of the week at a conference.

'Allendale?' Arnold repeated, startled. 'That's some distance—'

'Are you speaking from the Museums and Antiquities Department, did you say?' the girl on the phone inquired.

'That's right. I—'

'Is it about the brochure?'

'Well, yes—'

'I hope it's ready!'

Arnold hesitated. 'I'm afraid it isn't. I've just taken it over—'

'Oh, my dear me, it's not ready!' Her voice was breathy

with panic. 'I don't know how I can possibly tell Mr Edwards . . . He expressly told me it had to be ready. Can't you go to see him at Allendale? He'll want a report, he's been on about it all week. The deadlines—'

The dreaded deadlines. Arnold thought back to his conversation with the DDMA. He had wanted the burden removed from his back. Arnold sighed. Perhaps it would be best if he went across to Allendale. It was a pleasant drive, after all, to the Northumberland borders.

After he had seen Kevin Anderson's files.

Arnold set off next morning. There was no need to go back into the office at Morpeth; he was able to take the high road skirting the spruce slopes of Redesdale, part of the Border Forest Park, and use the looping hill road towards Chollerford. He stopped at the George for an early morning coffee, enjoying the sheltered garden overlooking the river, and watching the martins swoop beneath the arches of the picturesque bridge, mirrored in the North Tyne waters. It relieved some of the anxiety in his veins.

At Chesters he took the old Roman road to Haydon Bridge and then struck out left towards High Staward with the spread of Hexhamshire Common to his left. He soon reached the signpost for Allendale Town.

From Roman times onwards the dales south of Hadrian's Wall had been explored by miners seeking lead, zinc and silver, and there were still old mine shafts and derelict cottages to be seen. Allendale Town itself, however, had long lost its importance as a lead mining centre and had been taken over by trout fishermen and skiers. Perched on a steep cliff fourteen hundred feet above sea level, the town commanded a wide view of the East Allen River. Arnold parked in the town and then made his way down the hill to take the riverside walk that passed the mouth of the Beaumont Level, the large tunnel that was once the entrance to a lead mine.

He knew Allendale Town well enough, for his father had

brought him here years before, pointing out their industrial heritage, and now he paid little attention to his surroundings; his mind was dwelling on what he was going to say when he kept his appointment with Ben Edwards at midday. His search through the files Kevin Anderson had left had been worrying. He had turned to the young man Anderson shared an office with and asked in surprise, 'Is this all there is?'

The young man had scratched a freckle on his nose. 'Far as I know.

'There are no other papers?'

The clerk had frowned, pushed out a pendulous lower lip and looked warily doubtful. 'Not for me to say. Kevin went out and about a fair bit collecting the material. But, far as I know, that's it.'

'But I understand there's a deadline from the Tourist Board.'

'Wouldn't know about that.' The young man's hesitation had been patent. Almost defensively, he added, 'All I can say is, Kevin hasn't been too good these last few weeks. Not himself.'

'How do you mean?'

The clerk shrugged. 'Dreamin' a lot, like. Starin' out of the window. Preoccupied. Usually got on with things, Kevin did, canny worker, like, but somethin's been bothering him and I guess he wasn't concentratin' on his work.' He gazed warily at the papers in Arnold's hands. 'Bit thin, like, is it, the file?'

That, in Arnold's view, was the least of the problem.

He had spent some time reading the material, and then he had made use of the few historical volumes on Northumberland castles in the office library. He became more despondent the more he read. Now, as he strolled along the riverside walk under the alder and birch at the stream's edge his mood grew no lighter. He could foresee an unhappy interview with the Director of the Tourist Board.

Precisely at eleven fifty-five he walked along the row of

rugged, golden-stoned buildings that radiated outwards from the broad, tree-lined square. As they petered out the desolate, mine-scarred moorlands rose high; it was on its view of these moorlands that the Allen Gorge Hotel prided itself. That, and its doubtful claim to be at the exact geographical centre of Britain. Arnold presented himself at the reception desk and asked for Mr Edwards.

'He's at the conference, isn't he?' The slim girl behind the desk consulted an expensive watch, making sure Arnold noticed it. 'They should be breaking just now. If you care to wait, I'll page him as they come out.'

Pensively, Arnold sank into one of the deep, brocaded armchairs in the reception area, surrounded by paintings of horses and dogs. He picked up a copy of *Country Life*, and edged his way through its advertisements. A door slammed at the head of the staircase to his left; voices reverberated down the hall, and men began to drift down the stairs, heading for the bar. The conference was breaking up. Arnold rose, just as the girl at reception called out. 'Mr Edwards? There's a Mr Landon to see you.'

He was of medium height, stocky, belligerent of eye and short of temper. His manner was urgent, as though he lacked time to do all he wanted, and his mouth was twisted with a wandering dissatisfaction, the rootless kind that found incompetence behind every arras. When he shook hands with Arnold there was a fierceness in his grip that suggested he saw every social encounter as a challenge. His voice was deep and vibrant and he kept it that way, consciously; his features were rugged, his nose prominent, but from the way the receptionist's eyes followed him Arnold guessed he would be a man attractive to women. Maybe it was the suggestion of raw, physical power; maybe it was the breadth of his shoulders. Maybe he'd bought her the watch.

'You want a drink? I do.'

Before Arnold could reply he had turned and headed for the bar. In spite of the people who had got there before him

he obtained service quickly. He brought Arnold a gin and
tonic even though Arnold had not asked for one, and he
gestured towards the terrace. Arnold followed him: the
Director of the Tourist Board was a man used to getting
his way.

Ben Edwards breathed deeply as he stood on the wide,
sunlit terrace, looking back towards the grey-green swell of
the moors. He sipped his own gin and tonic and then
glanced back at Arnold. 'Not talked to you before. Brent-
Ellis a few times. When I could catch him in. And even
then, it was a waste of words. You got the material, I trust.'

Arnold took a quick sip of his drink. 'Er, not exactly.'

'Not exactly.' Ben Edwards's eyes were flinty. 'What the
hell is that supposed to mean?'

'We've hit a problem.'

Edwards hissed like an angry snake. '*You've* hit a problem, not *we*. I already have other problems. This one's for
you to solve. What the hell are you talking about?'

Arnold took a deep breath. 'I'm afraid the material isn't
yet ready.'

'The hell it isn't!' Edwards stared at him and slowly
purpled. His shoulders bunched, muscles gathering under
the light grey suit he wore, and his eyes became sharp angry
points of light. 'Brent-Ellis told me it was all in hand. Why
isn't it ready? What bloody excuse is coming up now?'

'I'm sorry, Mr Edwards, but I'm new to this project,
and I'm not sure what's happened. All I can tell you is that
it'll be a little while yet again before I can pull the stuff
together—'

'*You!*' Edwards glowered at him, his dark eyebrows
almost meeting as he frowned. '*You're* getting the stuff
together? Why?'

Uneasily, Arnold explained, 'A certain reallocation of
duties—'

'Anderson's been taken off the project?'

'Well, yes, you see—'

'But he was supposed to have it ready last week. Why's he been suddenly hauled off the job?'

Arnold sighed. 'That's not quite it. He . . . he's taken leave at this time.'

Edwards exploded. 'He's buggered off on his holidays? What the hell goes on in that department? I made it clear to Brent-Ellis when I phoned him six weeks ago that this material was top priority. We're paying enough for the damn stuff, God knows. And now you turn up here telling me it's not ready, again, while Brent-Ellis is buggerin' about on some golf course and that wimp Anderson is hiding himself somewhere in the hills. Him and his damned fell-walking! Don't you lot up there in Morpeth understand how important this is, Landon?'

Calmly, Arnold replied, 'I just told you. I'm new to this project, Mr Edwards.'

Viciously, Edwards stabbed a finger towards Arnold's eyes as though a little gouging would bring his point home. 'Then I'll tell you all about it. Why the hell should I be involved myself personally in this business, you may ask? Do you think I usually spend my time messin' about with trivia? I'm the Director, for God's sake! And here I am, chasing up a piddling history of the pele towers of Northumberland! And all because of that crazy old woman in Cambo. You heard of Miss Alice Savage, Landon?'

'I can't say I have.'

'She's a nutcase, but she's loaded.' Edwards shook his head angrily. 'We always find ourselves strapped for cash at the Board—Government grants don't give us half of what we need. So when the chance of a windfall comes like the offer from Miss Bloody Savage, it's got to be bloody well grabbed, hasn't it? And if there's a condition to the gift —like she wants a book written on the Castles and Ghosts of Northumberland—OK, we'll go along with that, load of rubbish though it might be. And the best way to do it is to farm it out. So we get researchers, and we get a couple of idiot professors from Newcastle who've never heard of deadlines in their life, and we manage quite well until we find there's a problem over the pele towers and we're advised to go to your bloody department, and that bloody cretin Brent-Ellis hands it over to Mr Wimp himself, Kevin Anderson! I should have stopped it right there. But I didn't, and now we're waiting, the time's going past, the old lady's on her last legs, she could pop off any moment, and if that book isn't finished before she leaves this earthly hell most of the money goes to some damn dogs' home.'

'I don't quite understand—'

'I just told you. Miss Alice Savage has made it clear to us. If she sees the book—and the series of brochures that will make it up—available to visitors to her beloved Northumberland, she'll stump up at least forty thousand quid. But if she doesn't see it before she breathes her last we'll be lucky to see ten nicker under her will. It all goes to her canine friends—God save us from idiosyncratic octogenarians! That's why this is important. That's why the Director himself is doing the bloody pushing. And that's why your telling me the work isn't yet finished makes me madder than hell, Mr Landon!'

He glared accusingly at Arnold, the breath rasping in his chest, and then he finished his drink at a gulp. He slammed the glass down on the balustraded terrace wall, where it shattered, exploding down into the garden below. He ignored it. He marched back into the bar, leaving Arnold staring unhappily at his own, barely touched glass. There was a sour taste in his mouth, and it was nothing to do with the gin.

Edwards was back some two minutes later, fortified with another gin and tonic. It looked like a double.

'So,' he said grimly, 'when are you going to let me have it?'

Arnold hesitated. 'I'm not sure, Mr Edwards.'

Edwards controlled himself, but his mouth was ugly. 'Explain yourself.'

'There's not a great deal of material. Notes, mainly.
But—'

'Go on,' Edwards said in a warning tone.

'I . . . I think some of it will have to be checked. Maybe
redeveloped.'

'What the hell is *that* supposed to mean?'

'I'm afraid, in my view, some of the notes are . . . inaccurate in their interpretation.'

Edwards was silent for almost a minute. He stared at
Arnold thoughtfully. 'In your view, you say.'

'That's right.'

'And just who the hell are *you*?'

Arnold made no reply. There seemed nothing he could
say. And he was becoming resentful of Edwards's tone of
voice. The man still glared at him, but there was a conflict
of emotions in his eyes. He seemed to be weighing something up, calculating behind the anger. He clicked his
tongue behind his teeth suddenly, and took another mouth-
ful of gin and tonic. 'Inaccurate, I think you said. Anderson's work?'

Arnold made no reply. Edwards laughed bitterly. 'It
would have to be. Kevin Anderson! He always was a useless
wimp. I should have known better than to trust that bastard. I should have told Brent-Ellis to find someone else,
once I knew. And how the hell she ever came to marry
that excuse for a man . . .' He turned away in a violent
movement, his back to Arnold as he glared out across the
roofs of the town. 'Anderson! He's buggered off on leave
with the work undone. And useless! It figures.' He was
silent for a little while. 'All right, my friend, so you're the
bloody expert now. How long?'

'To finish it?' Arnold asked calmly.

'To do an accurate version. That Savage woman . . .'

'I can't be sure. I'll have to visit some of the sites. Conclusions in the notes—'

'Spare me the details,' Edwards groaned. 'The fact I have
to bother with this at all . . . I asked you *when*.'

Arnold shrugged. The DDMA had told him to concentrate on the brochure, cut free from anything else. Not that there was very much else. 'Three weeks?'

'I'll give you ten days.'

'I —'

'You heard me. Ten days.'

'It's very short. The research I'll need to do, the verification of some of the factual interpretations —'

'I don't give a damn about that. This contract went to your department six weeks ago. It's still not finished. Everything else is in—even from those intellectual nonagenarians in the History Department of the University, for God's sake! We've got publication deadlines. And the old lady is quivery on her pins—there's no telling how long she'll last. She certainly won't see out this damned summer. I can't take the chance of losing forty thousand just like that. I'm giving the go-ahead for print on the rest of the material. And your stuff will be on my desk in ten days.'

'I —'

'If not,' Ben Edwards interrupted in a steely tone, 'I'll raise hell in your department, and I'll have that incompetent bastard Brent-Ellis's head for it, whoever he might be married to!'

Get Edwards off my back, the DDMA had said. Miserably, Arnold considered what his own future in his new job might be if Edwards were to fulfil his threats. He sighed. 'I could try.'

'Not could. Will. And do.'

'That's easy enough to say,' Arnold protested. 'I'll need to draft in some assistance.'

'That's your problem. I couldn't give a damn.' Ben Edwards turned slowly. His high colour had receded, but he was the more menacing for his regained control. He raised his glass and drained it of the double gin and tonic. His eyes glittered, perhaps influenced by the quick alcohol intake. He looked tough, and stocky and determined with the sweep of the rugged fells at his back. 'You'll do and you'll deliver and we'll go to print in ten days' time. And one more thing, Landon . . .'

'Yes?'

'When that weak-kneed bastard Kevin Anderson returns from his bloody holidays I want you to take a personal message to him. Personal from me, to him.'

'I don't really know—'

'I'm going to have his backside in a sling, Landon. Take him on one side. Tell him that. He's crossed me just once too often, and that's a fact. You can tell him, when you see him.' He glowered viciously at Arnold. 'I'm going to have his guts.'

3

The small bookshop on the Quayside was a little too much off the beaten tourist track to be well frequented by visitors to Newcastle. Those who came to admire the Laing Gallery or Stephenson's High Level Bridge and the massive eighty-two-feet keep of the twelfth-century Norman castle tended to stay at that level. They were disinclined to wander down the steep flights of narrow steps, the chares that wound past seventeenth-century timber warehouses through the Black Gate to the quay itself.

There were many who thronged there for the Sunday morning open market, of course, but by midday even they had gone. Besides, Ben Gibson didn't open his shop on a Sunday.

It was a somewhat idiosyncratic bookshop, in any case, reflecting the eclectic tastes of its owner. Ben Gibson was a small, frog-like man and a former watchmaker; he was well known to Arnold, and counted as a friend. Recently stricken with a heart attack, he had made a good recovery, but during his time in hospital the shop had been tended by his niece, Jane Wilson. Of her, Arnold was rather wary.

It was not that he disliked her. In fact he admired her, for her intelligence, and the courage she had already demonstrated when they had faced danger together on the Durham moors. It was more that she disturbed him.

She was brown-haired and snub-nosed, thirty years of age, with a pleasant enough face when she smiled. She was inclined to be serious: she wrote rather romantic versions of history and tended to be passionate about her theories, but it was her occasional directness that unsettled him— that, and the fact that she tended to tease him. He didn't mind the teasing: it was just that he was never sure just when he was being teased. It kept him on the edge of his seat in her company.

Ben Gibson was amused by the relationship. He enjoyed it and cultivated it gently; he considered they had a great deal in common, even if Arnold was not yet aware of it. Jane was, but remained stubbornly defensive, particularly about her work which she felt Arnold regarded as superficial. It made her unsheath verbal claws from time to time. It amused Ben.

He was smiling now, as he sat in the back room of the little shop after closing time and observed while Arnold sipped his cup of tea and Jane watched him, a cat contemplating a nervous mouse.

'I've got a problem, you see,' Arnold muttered.

She sniffed. 'Clearly.'

Her tone gave him no assistance. Arnold looked at Ben but the bookseller just smiled.

'I wouldn't come to you—'

'That goes without saying.'

'—but the deadlines I've been given are impossible. The Tourist Board want the material within ten days, but I've got to inspect the sites and verify my own understanding before I can even look at the notes—'

'And you want me to do some research for you.'

'That's about the size of it,' Arnold said lamely.

'You've worked well enough together in the past,' Ben Gibson suggested in a gentle tone, 'even if you don't see eye to eye on the Arthurian influence in mediæval castle building.'

'Eye to eye? Mr Landon thinks it's rubbish,' Jane Wilson snorted, rising to Ben's bait. 'He cannot even see that Queen Eleanor's reading had a direct influence upon the building of Conway and Harlech—'

'I wouldn't exactly say—'

'You said *exactly* that!' As Arnold wriggled uncomfortably, Jane caught sight of the twinkle in her uncle's eye and realized she was being gently goaded. She relented, smiling briefly at her uncle. 'Still, that's yesterday.'

Ben Gibson leaned forward. 'What exactly is the problem? What's the commission you're undertaking?'

Arnold hurriedly told them about his interview with Brent-Ellis and his meeting with Ben Edwards. 'But quite apart from the fact that Anderson's notes are thin, they're ill-researched. He's taken as gospel various Victorian handbook theories that have long since been discredited.'

'You mean he's been careless in his reading?'

Arnold hesitated. 'It looks as though . . . well, it seems his heart wasn't in the work. Maybe he had other things on his mind—I don't know. Anyway, the problem is I can't really agree with Kevin Anderson's findings. To begin with, he's just gone ahead with the statement that there are a number of pele towers in Northumberland. But what's he talking about?'

'Pele towers,' Jane replied sharply. 'Everyone knows—'

'Aha! Knows *what?*' Arnold could not suppress the triumph in his tone, in spite of the frown it brought to her brow. 'Everyone knows Northumberland is famous for its pele towers. But there are many who'd argue it's an inaccurate term. Peles, as opposed to palisades, are mentioned in thirteenth-century documents, when erected as temporary fortifications in the English–Scottish border skirmishes.'

'So?'

'When they built the peles they employed a lot of carpenters and daubers and the peles were constructed rather like colonial blockhouses—heavy timbers laid horizontally, jointed at the angles and made fireproof with earth and clay.'

'I've seen enough Western films,' Jane remarked drily, 'to get the picture.'

'But that's hardly the pele towers that we see today, is it? What we see are sort of small keeps, houses which were necessarily fortified as a result of Scottish border raids. Even vicarages became small fortresses from the fourteenth century onwards—they used to crowd parishioners and cattle inside when the reivers' alarm was given.'

'But surely, you're being pedantic,' she suggested.

'I prefer the word *accurate*. Stone towers of three or four storeys, the kind that have survived here in the north, are not peles at all—they're more correctly described as tower houses. They've often got a barmkin, a fortified yard, for the cattle. The longer houses, of two storeys, where the upper rooms were used for domestic use and the lower ones for cattle and horses—they are properly called bastel houses. But Anderson cheerfully lumps them all together as pele towers.' Arnold hesitated, looking at Jane doubtfully. 'It's inaccurate.'

She glanced at Ben Gibson and nodded. 'Well, that may be so, but common usage—'

'Tourist Board brochures and books should be accurate,' Arnold interrupted stubbornly. 'At the very least, there should be some explanation along the lines I've expounded. Just to call them all peles—'

'So write the explanation,' Jane said cheerfully. 'Stick it in a footnote. You don't need me for that.'

Arnold rubbed his chin in an awkward gesture. 'It's a bit more complicated than that. Kevin Anderson's easy acceptance of pele towers as a generic term is also reflected in his acceptance of received wisdom regarding the building of some of these tower houses. Take Warkworth, for instance. The castle was built soon after 1380—there's heraldic evidence for that. The great tower house there is supposed to have been built by John Lewyn—regarded as the outstanding northern architect of the time. It's a square of about sixty-five feet in plan with a projecting bay on each side giving a cruciform effect and—'

'I think you can spare us the details, Arnold,' Ben Gibson suggested with a grin.

Arnold smiled, aware of the manner in which his enthusiasm could carry him away. 'Well, all right. But Anderson has lumped all these tower houses together, made the assumption that Lewyn was the man who built them. That's arguable.'

'Is it important?' Jane asked slyly.

'Important?' Arnold almost exploded. 'Of course it's important! To ascribe buildings to one architect when they're clearly built by another, well . . . you just can't do that sort of thing! Not in a brochure or a book issued in an official capacity—'

'So who do you think was involved in these other peles —sorry, I mean tower houses?'

Arnold hesitated. He lifted a shoulder, in doubt. 'I can't be sure. I . . . I have a theory. But it's been a long time since I visited some of these towers. I need to check . . .'

'Who do you think?' Jane pressed him.

'Henry Yvele.'

Ben Gibson frowned, and pursed his lips. He hunched forward in his chair, more wizened now since his heart attack but with a mind as sharp and lively as ever. 'Yvele?' He pronounced it Eevelle. 'I've read about him . . . We have some volumes on mediæval building here somewhere . . . He was a southerner. Didn't know he ever came north. Worked at Canterbury.'

Arnold nodded. 'He built the West Gate there, and the gatehouse at Saltwood Castle in Kent. But you must remember that the masons and architects in the old days were travellers—as were most of the craftsmen. The king would call them for royal buildings from all parts of the realm. And when barons got licences to crenelate, or build tower houses, they went for the best available. As for Henry Yvele—it's been suggested he was with John Lewyn in 1392, when the octagonal turrets that flank the entrance to Lumley Castle in Durham were built.'

'From which you deduce . . . ?'

'He wouldn't have come north just for Lumley. He would have spent time here; he'd have been working in the north after that. He took Lewyn's patterns and designs. He used them, but put his own styles to them. It's too easy to ascribe Tarset and Dacre and Langley to Lewyn. It needs looking at. That's what I need to do.'

Jane Wilson humphed and finished her cup of tea. She frowned at Arnold thoughtfully. 'I still think you're being pedantic. Theories are fine—I've got some of my own with which you disagree . . . So, while you're whizzing around these sites, doing your own thing with the stone and the ruins, what am I expected to do?'

'I thought you might be prepared to help by doing some book-hunting for me. Books and articles that I've not time to read—'

'Because you're out gallivanting.'

Ben Gibson giggled. 'Now, Jane, don't be hard on Arnold. Could *you* see a date in the way stone is carved?'

'I suppose not,' she answered grudgingly. 'All right, do you have a list you can give me?'

Arnold made no attempt to hide his relief. He fished in his inside jacket pocket and brought out a folded sheet. 'I've made a list here. The articles are mainly from the publications of the British Archæological Association. You'll need to check in the Calendar of Patent Rolls also —I've given the references. Then there's the books listed, by Addy, Braun, Colvin and Everett.'

She frowned. 'It's quite a list. This will disrupt my own research.'

'What research? You've just *finished* a book,' Ben Gibson

chided. 'You've started nothing new yet. This might even give you some ideas for your next work.'

'I'm not sure Mr Landon would approve of that,' she replied tartly. 'He thinks my books are rubbish.'

'I never actually said that,' Arnold muttered.

The next two days were happy ones for Arnold.

His father had raised him in the Yorkshire Dales and had given him a love for the history that lay around them. Together they had walked the dales, visited the old lead mines, the Roman signal stations, the crumbling abbeys and the ruined castles. They had scrambled through thick undergrowth to find a corbel stone; they had stroked ancient timbers, hard as iron, and inspected the ancient joints that carpenters had carved centuries ago.

Arnold had listened while his father explained how stone had been split and dressed, walls pinned, tie-beams and braces and collars fixed to support massive stone roofs. And all around them had been the magnificent sweep of the fells, their wilderness and solitude softened by winding rivers, rocky streams and hidden waterfalls where men had walked for centuries but left no mark on the earth.

And when Arnold had moved further north he had found another wonderland where the air on the Northumberland uplands was heavy with the sweetness of warm grass and he could have a job that called him to inspect ancient works and use the skills his father had first nurtured in him.

The two days were busy, but it was work he enjoyed.

He visited the vicar's tower house in Corbridge, mapping its ground floor, wall staircase and the principal room with fireplace and sitting windows and garderobe. He spent some time at Edlingham Castle and grieved over the buried vaulted basement before inspecting the clerestory windows and fireplace in the magnificent two-storey hall, and he checked dimensions against the brief notes Kevin Anderson had prepared.

He made further notes at Dacre Castle, with its unusual

plan of large and small towers, and at Langley Castle with its sheer walls and corbelled bartizans. His final call was on the way home, at Belsay. He hardly needed to visit for he knew it well, but he had always admired the splendid Northumbrian three-storeyed tower and as he inspected the two west wings, the vaulted kitchen and first floor hall with its traceried windows he was struck by the connections he could make with the tower house at Chipchase.

The use of the thick walls to accommodate mural chambers and oratories tended to confirm his theory that Henry Yvele had acted as mason here.

There remained only Tarset and Brunskill, for another day.

First, he thought it wise to call back to the office of the DMA in Morpeth, to make a report to the Director, if he was in.

Surprisingly, he was.

Miss Sansom actually simpered when the DDMA thanked her for showing Arnold into the office. Clearly, she found his moustache emotionally overwhelming. Brent-Ellis waved Arnold to a seat. He seemed relaxed, the inevitable cigar glowing as he contemplated Arnold with fatherly eyes.

'So, Mr Landon, how is it going? You must have managed to calm down the fiery Mr Edwards, for I've heard nothing from him for two days.'

'I saw him at Allendale. He's given an extension of ten days to deliver the material.'

'Kind of him.' The DDMA pulled at his cigar, and flicked some ash to the carpeted floor. He sighed. 'And you're going to make the deadline? I should hate to be forced into another telephonic conversation with the Neanderthal Mr Edwards.'

'I've made a start. I've been out to Edingham and spent two days at some of the tower houses—'

'Splendid, fine, glad to hear it.' Brent-Ellis nodded vigorously and stroked his stained moustache. 'And you've got

Anderson's notes to help you, after all. So there shouldn't be too much difficulty in finishing the job on time.'

'Well, it's not quite as simple as that. I'll need to—'

'Drop everything else, of course, I understand that. On the other hand,' Brent-Ellis paused, eyeing a note on his desk, 'since you're clearly going to be out of the office and wandering around the country, I wonder whether you could pick up another little task while you're at it?'

Arnold was uncertain. 'I'm going to be hard pressed to complete the brochure in ten days. As it is I've had to ask someone to help me with the research—'

'Ah yes, but where will you next be going on your peregrinations?' Brent-Ellis asked.

'I'll have to go to Tarset, and maybe Brunskill—'

'Well, there you are then!' Brent-Ellis beamed and leaned back in his chair triumphantly, as though he had solved a problem of some magnitude. 'That's the answer, isn't it?'

'The answer to what, sir?' Arnold asked, stiff with indignation at the thought of having to add to the burden he already faced, completing the research in ten days.

The DDMA picked up the note on his desk, held it between finger and thumb and peered at it vaguely. 'Far as I recall, Tarset isn't too far from Temple Barden, hey?'

'About seven miles, I would guess.'

'Well, there you are. While you're in the area perhaps you'd be kind enough, old chap, to call in at the Old Rectory in Temple Barden. Feller called Nick Dimmock. Called in by phone; they took a message. Acquaintance of my wife . . . vaguely. It was in her, er, blue period, as I recall. Yes, not the best of times. Tend to keep arm's distance, these days, very wise. Anyway . . . He's of the opinion maybe we could help him.'

'I'm not sure—'

'Well, take a look anyway. Can't have people ringin' in all the time with problems, can we? Shouldn't be difficult. Something to do with a painting.'

'A *painting*?' Arnold protested. 'That's hardly in my line.'

'Mine neither,' Brent-Ellis said cheerfully. 'Can't tell a Degas from a dugong. Absolute tyro. Still, if the public think we can help, least we can do is try, hey? Public servants and all that.' He smiled supportively at Arnold. 'Call in to see him, there's a good chap, while you're at Tarset and kill two birds with one stone.'

There seemed little Arnold could say in answer. The DDMA was already turning away and riffling through the pages of the *Journal*, lying open on his desk. 'Talking of which . . .' he muttered.

'Sir?'

'Reminds me of something . . . Ah yes, here it is.' The DDMA spread the centre pages of the newspaper out on his desk and leaned over, scrutinizing them. 'You been following this series?'

'What series?'

'"Ghosts of Old Northumberland". Interestin' stuff, some of it. Load of rubbish, of course, but interestin'. Poltergeists . . . rattlin' chains . . . spooky sounds in the night . . . Tarset's mentioned, and so is the Old Rectory. The White Lady of Tarset and the Grey Monk of Temple Barden.' Brent-Ellis sniffed. 'All so colourless, these ghosts, aren't they? Why can't we have a Red Huntsman or a Green and Yellow Parlourmaid or somethin' along those lines, hey?'

Arnold hesitated, waiting as Brent-Ellis pored over the article. He shuffled his feet, and half rose from his chair. 'Is that all, sir?'

'What? Oh yes.' The DDMA frowned, as though he had forgotten something. 'But hold on . . . what was I going to say? Somethin' reminded me . . . That's it! See the byline?'

Arnold twisted around to look at the newspaper. 'Lynne Anderson.'

'Rings no bells?'

'I'm afraid not.'

'Isn't that Kevin Anderson's wife?'

'I really couldn't say.'

'Believe it is. Journalist. Interestin', hey? But that wasn't what I wanted to say, really. This Dimmock feller—'

'Yes?'

Brent-Ellis drew on his cigar thoughtfully. 'Well, handle him with care. The articles by this Anderson woman reminded me. He's a bit . . . odd.'

'In what way?'

The DDMA regarded him owlishly, cigar poised to make a point. 'Far as I can gather, he sort of . . . believes in these things.'

'What things?'

'Ghosts!' the DDMA announced with a hint of impatience.

Arnold stared at him uncertainly. 'That's a reason for me to be careful when I meet him?'

'Well, it's not just *ghosts*,' Brent-Ellis replied uneasily, 'he's sort of into other things as well. My wife tells me— she was interested in séances and that sort of stuff for a while you know, in her blue period, but not now, she's into red now—she tells me he's sort of a member of various societies. Regards himself as a White Witch, or something. Got a sword. And a cape.' The DDMA paused, thinking as confused images crossed his mind of swords and capes and white witches. He grunted. 'Excuse for orgies, if you ask me. But, well, he's got friends in some powerful places, oddly enough, so I wouldn't want you to go stepping in it, putting your foot into any messy cowpats, that sort of thing.'

'Do you mean he dabbles in the occult?' Arnold asked warily.

'That sums it up neatly, I think,' the DDMA replied, frowning vaguely in Arnold's direction. 'Yes, quite . . . You'll go carefully with him when you visit, won't you?'

It was one request Arnold was more than happy to accede to. He'd already had enough of the occult to last him a lifetime.

4

Detective Chief Inspector Culpeper spent his holidays at Amble. Each August he drove up from Morpeth to the small seaport with his wife—their only son was now thirty and well settled at Guisborough in the Cleveland Police— and followed the same routine. They hired a small fishing-boat and would head out for Coquet Island, just a mile offshore. On the quiet evenings, as the eider ducks crooned on the island, his wife would have her binoculars out, bird-watching, while he fished, a pipe clamped between his teeth, and thought about nothing.

Driving past Craster Tower now, and under the arched stone bridge down towards the harbour, he felt a certain resentment. He hated the thought of this area being scarred by violent crime: he wanted to keep Amble and Warkworth, Seahouses and Craster havens he could retain in his mind —places of relaxation where he could escape the harsh realities of life in the police force.

John Culpeper was in his mid-forties now: a broad, thick-waisted man with straight grey hair, neatly parted, soft, autumn-brown eyes and a certain air of wistfulness, as though he wished life was not as vicious as he sometimes found it. He had started as a local bobby in the Durham Police, and had been based in a pit village: he had never quite got over an early assignment, a suicide who had placed his head on the rails before the coal trams came hurtling down the hillside. He still had occasional nightmares about it, thirty years on. It was always the police who had to clear up a mess like that. As they had to clear up this mess at Craster.

The police car nosed its way past the parking area on the right, overlooking the village, and drew up in front of the cottages. There were two other police cars already parked there, and a straggle of locals watching events from a short distance. Down at the harbour itself things were quiet: the fishing-boats were out.

There was still a living to be made even if death had visited the village.

Stiffly, Culpeper got out of the car. A young detective-sergeant came forward to greet him. Fresh-faced, keen and efficient, Sid Waters would go far, Culpeper guessed. But then, he thought as he glanced around at the blue skies above the harbour, promotion always meant movement, and he was happy enough to be in Northumberland.

'So, Detective-Sergeant Waters, what've we got here?'

'Murder, clear enough, sir.'

'The cottage?'

'This way, sir.'

Waters led the way into the cottage. It was crowded: police, the first of the photographers, fingerprint officer standing by for the go-ahead, forensic liaison officer, still waiting for the pathologist to show. It was a small cottage, and the stairs were narrow. Sid Waters stepped aside at the top of the stairs. The door into the bedroom leaned crazily on its hinges. The room was in chaos.

A tumble of bedclothes. A woman with her face shot away. A man, twisted in the bedclothes on the floor, hands and chest torn apart. The insistent buzzing of flies.

'Shotgun.'

Culpeper could see that. 'How did the killer get in?'

Sid Waters shook his head. 'No signs of forced entry. Maybe he was already in the house. Or the front door was unlocked. Or he had a key. No way of telling yet.'

There was a broken bedside clock on the floor. It had been knocked over in the turmoil. The hands stood near to twelve. Culpeper raised his eyebrows. 'It'd be pretty quiet around here at midnight. Anyone hear anything?'

'Not that we can ascertain, sir. We're not sure when it happened, of course. Maybe two-three nights ago. It was the local postman raised the alarm. He found the front door unlocked. Deadbolt, but it was off the catch. We've talked to people in those nearby cottages that are still lived in. I mean, several of them are now holiday homes. We're check-

ing on the ownership, so we can interview the people own-
ing the empty ones. The police surgeon is on his way;
fingerprints standing by; the photographer's taken some
shots.'

'You been a busy lad. Any thoughts?'

Detective-Sergeant Waters wrinkled his nose, and
shrugged. 'Not really. Except . . .'

'Yes?'

'They weren't married.'

The room was silent for a little while. Culpeper stared
woodenly at the two bodies in front of him. The passion
they would have felt was now a thing of the past; it had
been all for nothing, perhaps. His mouth was dry, his eyes
wistful as he turned away and clumped back down the
stairs. His stomach had begun to churn at the sickly scent
of blood and the buzzing of the flies. The air outside was
fresh and clean, the wind blowing in from the sea.

'They weren't married?'

'No, sir. We've looked at the contents of her purse. There
was a driving licence there. She's called—she was called
Lynne Anderson. She also had a card in her handbag—
NUJ.'

'Journalist?' Culpeper glanced at Waters in dismay. If
there was one thing worse for headlines than a murdered
policeman it was a murdered journalist. 'Hell's flames, we
can expect all sort of steam over this one, then! The newspapers really go to town if one of their own is faded.'

'Two, sir.'

Culpeper let out a gust of air. 'They're *both* journalists?'

'He's called Lance Stevens. His wallet was still intact.
Press card and photograph.'

'Bloody hell!'

'The motive was clearly not robbery. Wallet, purse
untouched, and as far as we can see nothing missing from
the cottage itself—no sign of disturbance except in the bedroom. Looks like the killer came in, blasted them both, and
left.'

'And no one heard anything . . .' Culpeper shook his head. 'So . . . you seem to have things in hand, as usual, Sid. Looks like a love-nest, this?'

'I would guess so.'

'Was she married?'

'She was wearing a wedding ring.'

'What about him?'

'Can't say. No wedding ring. But I've rung into Head-quarters—they're setting up an Incident Room, and Tom Lemming is making some inquiries about this guy Stevens.'

'Hmmm.' Culpeper stood in the doorway of the cottage. The small patch of garden at the front looked uncared for. He glanced around at the other cottages and across to the Jolly Fisherman. He sucked at his teeth thoughtfully. 'Right. I'll be back in a few minutes. I think I'll go have a chat at the pub.'

Slowly he crossed the green in the warm late-morning sunshine. There was a young couple sitting outside the pub, drinks in their hands, seemingly oblivious of the police presence in the village. Life could be like that: murder? What murder? Culpeper walked through the main entrance. The barman was shirt-sleeved, polishing a glass with a grey cloth.

''Morning,' Culpeper offered.

''Morning, sir. What can I get you?'

Culpeper hesitated. It was still a bit early. To hell with it. 'Small whisky'll do. And some soda.'

He waited while the barman turned to the optic and drew off a measure. Life was better in Scotland, Culpeper thought sourly: measures were larger there. He watched while the barman added the soda water, flicked a finger to signify when there was enough.

'So,' the barman said thoughtfully. 'You one of the bobbies?'

'You could say that.'

'Bad business.'

'Indeed.'

'Both dead, I hear.'

Culpeper nodded and sipped his drink. 'What's your name?'

'Fred—Fred Purchas.'

'Born around here?'

'Local man, aye.'

'Did you know the couple in the cottage?'

Purchas hesitated, then made a grimace, twisting his mouth doubtfully. 'Not know, exactly. Seen them in here often enough. Had a chat with him a few times . . . Mr Stevens.'

'You didn't know her?'

'Not by name.'

'So how long have they been coming in here?'

The barman leaned forward, elbows on the bar in front of him. He waved his hand to and fro. 'Well, he's been coming in for maybe two years. He bought that cottage, I hear tell, two years back, just before I started work here. Never joined in much with the locals, though, usually had company.'

'Company?'

'A woman, like.'

'Same one?'

Purchas grinned vaguely. 'Well, you know how it is. He worked in Newcastle, I understand, and he'd come up for weekends. Brought a bird for company most times. They never lasted long, though. Except this one. She was longer than most.'

'How long?' Culpeper asked.

Purchas pursed his lips. 'I'd say maybe two months. And . . . well, she was a bit different.'

'In what way?'

The barman hesitated. He picked up a glass and began to polish it. 'Not easy to describe. But there was a kind of edginess about her. She . . . well, the others, they'd come in with him and sit and have a drink, and all right, I guessed he'd take the woman back to the cottage and sleep late in the morning, if you know what I mean. But there was no hurry, you know? With her . . . it was different.'

'I don't understand.'

Purchas sighed. 'With her, she didn't seem to want to hang around drinking too long. She was . . . kind of eager. Looked like she couldn't keep her hands off him, couldn't get enough of him.' The barman sighed, as though wishing he knew a woman like that.

Culpeper was silent for a while. The barman waited. At last Culpeper asked, 'When were they in last?'

The reply came in a rush. 'Three nights ago. She got here first. She was edgy as hell. She got herself a drink, sat over there behind the door and wasn't pleased he was late, like. Anyway, when he did arrive he bought a drink for himself but he didn't get to drink it. She made it clear she didn't want to wait. They went off almost as soon as he'd arrived. Left most of his drink. If you ask me she had the hots that evening, and couldn't wait to get him to bed. You notice things like that sometimes. The look in a woman's eye. She had that look all right. They was out of here like rabbits. I tell you, she was hungry that night.'

Culpeper finished his drink slowly. He nodded. 'Her husband ever come in here?'

The barman's eyes widened. 'Husband? I wouldn't know. Didn't know she was married. Never even knew her name.'

'So you wouldn't know if he came in here that night?'

'Wouldn't have a clue.'

Culpeper nodded. 'Right. I'll send someone over shortly, so you can make a statement. Anything else you remember, you can give to him.'

He walked back in the sunshine to the cottage. Detective-Sergeant Waters was standing in the doorway. 'The pathologist's arrived.'

'Good.' Culpeper squinted up into the sun. 'It seemed our Mr Stevens had a succession of girlfriends—this one

was the last. We'll have to check each of them—see what
they have to say.'

'You mean maybe a jealous ex-flame? With a shotgun?'
Sid Waters's tone expressed his doubt.

'It's not been unknown.' Culpeper shook his head. 'I'm
going back to Morpeth now, and then I'll be going down
to the *Journal* offices in Newcastle. When you've cleared up
here get back to the Incident Room and cast a net out for
these ex-girlfriends of Stevens. We got a lot of legwork to
do. Keep in touch.'

'You going to get a trace on the husband, sir?'

Culpeper nodded grimly. 'Exactly that,' he said.

CHAPTER 2

1

Arnold spent the next morning checking the notes he had
made during the previous two days and getting them typed
into some literate form. He phoned Jane Wilson at the
Quayside bookshop and she was able to tell him she was
getting sent to her at the Quayside photocopies of a number
of the articles he had requested. A trip to Wetherby to the
British Library would be necessary to get access to some of
the books: they were long out of print.

'People don't seem to get over-excited about mediæval
buildings,' she asserted, 'so there's not much demand for
books about them.'

The worse for them, Arnold thought sourly.

He was still smarting over the extra task that had been
placed upon him by the DDMA. It was unreasonable, particularly when Arnold was going to be so hard pushed to
keep to Edwards's deadlines. Once he had got his notes
typed, however, he decided he had better hurry on to make
the last two visits he needed to do. As for Mr Nick

Dimmock, he'd have to wait for Arnold to make a brief evening call on his way back to Morpeth.

Arnold set off at midday. There was a stiff breeze blowing, and a hint of rain in the air, but inland the cloud was breaking up, with patches of blue sky showing, so he was hopeful that by the time be reached Tarset Hall the day would have brightened.

It was about an hour's drive from Morpeth. The road lay through Rothbury, so he was able to enjoy the winding drive along the river, climbing over craggy hilltops that gave him vistas of the misty hills with their flanks of open pasture. As he had hoped, the sky cleared and although the Cheviots remained cloaked in rain haze, the sun was warm and bright on the fields ahead of him as he came over the crags to Tarset.

He had never actually visited the Hall before, though he had passed the driveway and seen it from a distance. It had appeared in a guide book published some sixty years ago, but the article had concentrated on romantic and probably inaccurate associations it was claimed to have with mediæval legend and had barely touched upon it in architectural terms. Arnold was looking forward to seeing it at close quarters, even if he was in a hurry.

The driveway was flanked with rhododendron which had become badly overgrown, and the track itself was rutted, grass growing thick in the central area. He crossed a stream by a small stone bridge and noted that the bridge too was in a state of disrepair, but even so he was not prepared for the sight that met him when he came out from under the line of ancient beech trees and caught his first view of the Hall itself.

Tarset Hall had been built squarely, of a warm, reddish stone that would flush bronze in the setting sun. Arnold stopped the car some fifty yards from the house and stared. The central part of the hall was probably fourteenth- or fifteenth-century, but the gatehouse seemed to him to be a little out of place in its style: it would have been the remnant of an earlier, thirteenth-century tower house. The heightened walls had been carried by an arcade whose arches had long since been filled in to the detriment of the line, and although tower-like in appearance, Tarset Hall was nevertheless similar to many of the quadrangular mansions that Arnold had seen in the south. It would have been the kind of change that Henry Yvele could have wrought, if he really had taken a hand in the reconstruction—for that was what it would have been—of Tarset Hall.

But what disturbed Arnold was the state of the building.

The windows were shuttered, but those in the west wing were broken. The thirteenth-century gatehouse was crumbling at the cornices, some of the castellated front elevation had collapsed and there were gaps in the stone of the roof. The whole building had a sad, dishevelled look about it, as though it was ashamed at the state it had come to after earlier days of splendour, and the weeds grew rankly around the stoned drive and in the rubble that had been piled up against the west wing.

Arnold got out of the car and walked towards the pile of rubble. The stone was marked with the tell-tale clawmarks of mediæval dressing: there would have been a timbered walk here, rising up to the first-floor level and the clumsily bricked-up entrance to the solar room. The place was decaying from neglect, and a feeling of anger welled up in Arnold's chest at the thought that this magnificent structure, which had survived for more than five hundred years, should now be allowed to crumble in this manner.

He heard the front door of Tarset Hall bang and he turned. There was a man standing at the entrance. He carried a broken shotgun over his arm. He stared at Arnold for several seconds, and then slowly he marched towards him, stiff-backed, head up, deliberate. His gait was peculiar; he walked crablike, almost presenting his side view as though wishing to make available the smallest target possible. When he was some fifteen metres from Arnold he stopped. The gun still lay broken in the crook of his arm.

'I imagine you have some reason to be trespassing on my property?'

His voice was cultured but harsh. He was a little under six feet in height, perhaps fifty years of age. He was aggressive in his manner, but controlled: Arnold guessed that violence seethed not too far below the surface, nevertheless. He wore a hat pulled forward on his forehead but greying hair escaped into thick sideburns that ran down to his jaw. His eyes were angry under heavy black eyebrows. The anger could have been directed at Arnold, but perhaps it was an endemic anger, directed against the world at large. But there was something else about him that puzzled Arnold, as the man stood there at an angle, in half-profile, seeming to sidle forward and being the more menacing for the sideways approach. He was like the house. Where Tarset Hall had seen better days, so had this man; the façade of the tower house had crumbled, but its owner's clothing almost reflected it. The cloth was expensive and expensively cut, yet it had a faded, rusty look, dated, decaying like the house itself.

'I'm from County Hall at Morpeth,' Arnold said.

'That's a statement, not a reason.'

'The Department of Museums and Antiquities. We . . . we're doing some work on tower houses. For the Tourist Board.'

'I don't get many visitors, and those I get I don't welcome,' the man said harshly.

'I don't want to make a nuisance of myself,' Arnold replied in a quiet tone. 'I don't need to come inside. If I could have your permission to look around the outside of the house, check the thirteenth-century structure—'

'This house is fourteenth-century,' the man snapped.

'The gatehouse is older,' Arnold demurred.

'How can you tell that?'

'Its proportions. The difference in the stone used. The style in relation to the solar tower. It's of an older era: it's probably all that remains of the original tower house.'

The man stared at Arnold for several seconds. The sunlight was behind him and he now turned, to stare back at the gatehouse.

It was then that Arnold saw the scar, and realized the reason for the man's curious crablike walk as he had approached. The wound had been opened at the left temple. The scar had ridged redly, puckering the cheek in a way that suggested some portions of flesh had been removed. It ran along the edge of the thick sideburns, which had probably been grown to help conceal it in part, lifted the corner of the man's lip, making a travesty of his mouth and ran down the chin to the top of the throat. It must have been a horrific wound; now it had left the man scarred and bitterly conscious of his appearance.

He was turning back. 'You seem to know what you're talking about,' he said harshly. He stared at Arnold, aware of the shock in his face, and he grimaced, almost smiling in a contempt that was otherwise unexpressed. 'All right, then,' he said abruptly. 'You can take a look around. You'll excuse me, of course,' he added mockingly. 'I have other things to do.'

He turned abruptly and marched back to the house, the shotgun still cradled in his arm. Arnold wondered whether he would have threatened to use it. He had the feeling threats came easy to this man—and they would not be empty threats, at that.

For the next hour or so Arnold wandered around the house. He had been right about the gatehouse: when he came to inspect it more closely and checked its dimensions he was certain it had been part of an older building. He was able to climb on the rubble and get a better view of the west wing with its turret also: his guess was that before it had begun to collapse there would have been a newel staircase there, the turret corbelled out to give an octagonal chamber above. The window tracery was interesting: it closely resembled the quatrefoils at Dacre, where Arnold was now convinced Henry Yvele had left his mark. In his typed notes at Morpeth he had already drawn conclusions about a Lewyn–Yvele collaboration. It now seemed he was obtaining confirmation.

'What exactly is it you're looking for?'

Arnold turned, startled. The owner of Tarset Hall had returned, now without the shotgun. He stood staring up at Arnold, his hat shading his face, hands locked behind him, straight-backed.

'It's for a Tourist Board book. Tower houses. But I'm checking on architectural influences as well. I think a man called Henry Yvele worked on your house here.'

'You can really tell who built this house? How? No document I've seen gives that information.'

Arnold shrugged. 'It's experience. I . . . I've looked at many such houses. Mediæval structures. You can make an educated guess at their age and who built them, from the timbers used, and the way they were jointed. The joints changed over the centuries, new masons following old practices but improving on them. The particular stone used, and the location of its quarrying can give you clues to the age of a house. The clawmarks, the way the stone was dressed and split, the systems used to pin the stone slates, the layout of the chambers and bedrooms and solars, the use of vaulted cellars, corbels, hammerbeams, wind-braces, fan-vaults—'

'You sound like a Catholic convert,' the man below said drily.

'I beg your pardon?'

'There's none so enthusiastic about their faith. You're like that. You display the enthusiasm of a self-taught expert.'

Arnold shrugged. The man was perceptive, and perhaps too near Arnold's emotional bone in his comment. 'I don't really regard myself as an expert,' he said lamely. 'I'm not qualified—'

'But I imagine you could tell me a great deal about Tarset

Hall, and far more than the self-proclaimed experts with their paper qualifications.' The owner of Tarset Hall stood staring at Arnold for several seconds, then abruptly turned on his heel. 'When you've finished doing what you have to outside, come in and talk to me.'

It was in the nature of an order, but Arnold was disinclined to reject it, if it gave him the opportunity to look around the interior of the old tower house.

'So tell me why it was built this way.'

They were standing in what would have been the great hall. It had been divided into four ground-floor rooms at some time, with its upper floor extending its eastern bays with an arcade supporting the twin roofs. Dust drifted down in the sunlight that shone through the broken windows of the west end, as it would have drifted for centuries.

Arnold nodded. 'This kind of tower house really continued the tradition of the Norman keep: it was necessary in those turbulent days in the north.'

'Border raiders?'

'That's right. The wars between Scotland and England, and then the reivers. The lord—at that period it was de Bohun and his successors—would have had a standing army of professional soldiers—not large in number but more reliable than the old feudal levies. They were farmers, drawn from the land with their limited forty-day obligation. The mercenaries were different. He'd have to provide quarters for them.'

'Not at the castle?' the owner of Tarset Hall queried.

He had introduced himself, after offering Arnold a tour of Tarset Hall, as Major Rodney Manners, ex-Paratroop Regiment, and to save questions had explained that the scarred face was a legacy of the Falklands War. He had made the statement flatly, seemingly without emotion, yet Arnold detected a flicker of bitterness in his tone, a buried resentment of some kind that still moved in the man. Tarset Hall had been in the Manners family for three generations, but he was the last of the line. He did not explain whether he was married or not, but he made the point, again with an odd emphasis, that he had no children. But there was a clear pride in his ownership of the house, and he was keen to learn what Arnold could tell him about it.

Arnold shrugged. 'There have been excavations at Tarset Castle, but they're pretty inconclusive. The castle was torn down in the fifteenth century, and a lot of the stone removed for other building purposes so it's a bit difficult to determine the full extent of the buildings. Of course, some men-at-arms would have been kept in the castle, but it's really quite surprising how few retainers were held like that. Harlech Castle, for instance, withstood months of siege with just thirty-five soldiers in the garrison.'

'So Tarset Hall would have been used as lodgings?'

'I would guess so. It was common for the lodgings to be separate from the owner and his family to ensure privacy, but also protection against possible treachery and mutiny in his stronghold.'

Major Manners laughed shortly. The sound had an unpleasant ring. 'I know what you mean. Where money is the key, rather than devotion to the family, loyalties can slip. Desertion to rivals can occur very easily.'

Arnold looked at him uncertainly. There was a bitterness about the twist of his mouth that could have been the result of the horrific scar, but Arnold seemed to detach an underlying anger that was personal, and reflected in the man's words.

'The lord may well have kept private accommodation for himself in the gatehouse,' Arnold went on.

Major Manners was aware of the military implications. 'A strategic position for defence?'

'That's right. But I suppose it could have its inconveniences—the necessary room for portcullis machinery, for instance, so usually they later moved into the tower itself and the first-floor hall.'

'Mmm.' Manners reflected on the situation, staring

upwards to the tower hall. He walked across to the windows that gave him views over the hills. 'It would give him a strong and commanding position as well as privacy. I see that, militarily.'

'Excavations at the castle itself show an oblong plan with projecting angle turrets. There's a reflection of that here in the hall.'

Together they paced through the building. The thrust of the questions emanating from Major Manners were largely military, but he was also interested in what Arnold had to say about the structure itself, the vaulted storerooms on the ground floor, the tiny chapel, the kitchen, buttery, pantry and bedchambers on the second floor.

'One of the reasons why I think Yvele worked on this fortified tower house,' Arnold explained, 'is the height of the building. Some of the tower houses have lofty towers, which are regarded as French-influenced. That kind of structure is much more common over there, in Aquitaine and elsewhere. Yvele was more consistently stubborn in his English tower—he kept his structures lower, though he did go for the double tier of battlements, as you have here at Tarset.'

They made their way back to the east wing of the house. Arnold had made some notes for his own use while he had been wandering around the house with the Major and he pocketed these now as Manners led him into the small sitting-room at the back of the house and motioned him to a chair. 'You'll not refuse a whisky. All that talking, you should need one.'

Arnold didn't need one, but it would have been churlish to refuse when the Major clearly intended drinking. He shrugged and nodded. He looked around at the shabby furnishings of the room; there was the same dishevelled appearance here as in the rest of the house. The carpets were expensive but threadbare; the curtains grimy; an ancient damask hung crumpled and dirty near the fireplace, with its shattered lintel and there was a general air of shabbiness about the room.

Major Manners had turned, two glasses in his hands and he must have caught something in Arnold's glance, realized what Arnold was thinking, for his eyes darkened. He handed Arnold his glass and sat down in an easy chair opposite him. He was silent for a few moments, then coldly he growled, 'Do you think I don't care?'

Arnold wriggled uneasily. 'I'm sure you—'

'This is my home, and was the home of my ancestors. Do you think I don't care the place is falling down about my ears?'

'You clearly have a great interest in the hall, and—'

Manners sneered, almost self-accusingly. 'It's simply not enough, though, is it? Loving a house isn't enough. You have to work at it, keep it in a sound state. It's like loving a woman. You have to show you care, stay in constant attendance, watch it carefully, maintain it properly. But it still isn't enough. You need time and you need money— with a house or with a woman.'

Arnold hesitated, startled by the anger and bitterness in the man's tone. 'I know that the upkeep of a house like this is ruinously expensive. It's why so many have been made over to the National Trust—'

'This has always been my home, and I mean to keep it,' the Major insisted fiercely. 'And I thought . . .' He drained his glass quickly, rose, and refilled it. He sat down, staring into the glass. 'I've tried,' he said after a short silence.

Arnold did not know how to respond. In the event, it was unnecessary. The Major suddenly broke into full, bitter spate. It was as though he had rarely had the opportunity to express his feelings; or possibly it was that since Arnold was a stranger, the normal inhibitions disappeared and he could expose his innermost thoughts and feelings. 'It was always a struggle—for my parents, for my grandfather. But it got worse. And when I claimed my inheritance I was still a young man. For me, the Army was to be my career, and I thought . . . promotion, honours . . . but somehow it never happened. At my age, a major! I deserved better. My service record was good, I'd done my stint in Ireland, I'd seen action overseas . . . but I had enemies, you know?' He sneered, unpleasantly. 'It's my tongue, you see, and my temper. If you're plain spoken, if you don't pander to those who need flattery, there can be a block on your prospects. That's how it was with me. Even so, it almost came right.'

He raised his head, stared at Arnold as though daring him to contradict, or criticize, and the scar was purple on his cheek. 'I made a good marriage. I left it a bit late, perhaps, and she was considerably younger than me. All right, perhaps my motives were mixed. But we were . . . suited. I always thought so. And she was the daughter of Brigadier-General Metcalfe. I thought with their money, when we had a son . . . I could have restored Tarset Hall, provided another Manners to claim this inheritance and maintain the line . . .'

He fell silent, an angry gleam in his eyes as he contemplated the failures of the past.

'But then the Falklands came.'

Arnold stayed quiet. He had the feeling Manners had almost forgotten he was there, and was reciting a litany that would have been repeated over and over in his head, in the privacy of this room, even proclaimed to the stone walls themselves in the dark hours the man experienced.

'The bitterness of it all is that when I bought this—' the Major's fingers strayed to his scarred features— 'I didn't really mind. Odd, that. But it was like a badge, the recognition that hadn't come my way. Shrapnel, the burning . . . They got me out of there to military hospital, the plastic surgeons had a go and they patched me up but it's hardly a success story, is it? And besides, I got tired of them messing about with my face. I called a halt to it. You can take just so much. And by then, I could see what the powers that be, the top brass, the politicians, really thought of me . . . and others like me.'

He glared at Arnold as though holding him responsible. Arnold wriggled uncomfortably, and sipped at his whisky. 'Falklands veterans—' he began. 'Do you know we were barred from the victory parades?' Manners interrupted him fiercely. 'Can you believe that? They wanted all the pride and the boasting and the glory for that day, but they didn't want the reality, the scars to show. So I was kept back. I was left to fester in private. I wasn't allowed to be seen, when they honoured the Falklands veterans. That was when I got out.'

He took another hefty pull of Scotch. He leaned his head back against the brocade of the armchair. 'And that was when my beloved wife left me, also. We'd been married just eight years. I always thought we got on. But we'd been apart for three of those years. And this wound . . . you'd think a Brigadier's daughter could have handled that sort of thing. But she couldn't. There was another man, of course. A younger man.' He sneered self-deprecatingly. 'A more caring man, maybe. And the Brigadier . . . he was no help either. I think he thought I complained too much. Perhaps I did. But I had reason, dammit! I had reason.'

He finished his drink and rose again, steady-legged. 'Another?'

Arnold shook his head. He had barely touched his whisky. He watched quietly as Manners helped himself to another stiff shot of Scotch. He guessed that steady drinking, afternoon and evening, would be a part of the retired Major's life. 'You live here alone, now?' he asked.

'No wife, no servants, no dogs, no money . . . just this house. But if I had the money, do you think I'd leave the place like this? My father . . . family . . . generations . . .'

He sat down again. He stared at Arnold and shook his head. 'Not many people come here to see me. And no one who can tell me about this house, the way you've done.' He grimaced unpleasantly at Arnold. 'So there you are. You've succeeded in touching raw nerves, haven't you? You wheedled out of me the fact that I love Tarset. You know

I hate to see it decay. You know that it's become the most important part of my life. And you know I'm helpless to do anything about it. But maybe you're wrong, my friend. Maybe you're wrong. Who knows . . .'

'Major Manners, I've not deliberately—'

'Our family, we had money, you see,' the Major interrupted him. 'This BCCI bank collapse, it makes me laugh. The fuss that's going on. You think it's the first time people have suffered from incompetent financial advisers, from fraudulent banks? My grandfather was Indian Army and he lost most of the family money in a bank collapse. My father never recovered the position—but he tended to gamble, thinking retrieval of family fortunes lay that way. Me, I don't gamble—but if I did, my bet would be that I will find some way to make Tarset Hall live again. Or die trying, anyway.'

'I'm sure you will, sir.'

They both sat silently for several minutes. The silence grew oppressive, but Arnold hardly knew what to say. He recognized an obsession when he saw one, and the Major's commitment to the house was fierce, if hopeless. Struggling to make conversation, Arnold delved back into the recesses of his mind for anything he might have read about the tower house. Major Manners would be uninterested in small talk; his life centred on Tarset Hall.

'I seem to recall Tarset has been mentioned several times in articles. It's quite a well-known tower house,' Arnold suggested lamely.

The Major's eyes glittered. 'Well known for the wrong reasons. I've seen some of the bloody stupid stuff that's been written. Stuff and nonsense. And if you think I'm going to try to raise money by pandering to the sensational stories that ridicule what the house stands for, you're damned wrong!'

'I didn't mean—'

'There was that damned woman here a few weeks ago. Writing an article on ghosts! I caught her wandering about, wanting to get the atmosphere to write about the Tarset haunting. I gave her short shrift, sent her packing. I can tell you quite categorically there is no ghost here at Tarset Hall. It's one of those bloody Victorian fantasies. It went along with their fascination with ruins—I mean, they used to build ruins in their gardens, for effect! My grandfather, my father, none of us have ever experienced supernatural happenings. The Grey Monk of Tarset is a load of rubbish. Half the old houses in Northumberland are reputed to be haunted. Chipchase, the Lord Crewe Arms, the Brunskill ruins, they're all supposed to have their spooks and spectres. But it's all old wives' tales.'

Arnold hesitated. 'I'm sure you're right, Major Manners.'

'All right, that damned young woman might have recirculated the old story about the Grey Monk for the sake of selling newspapers, but that's her problem, and if her gullible readers want to believe it, that's up to them. But I won't have them beating their way to this door to gawp and gape!'

'I can't say I've read much about such a story but—'

'And then there's the story of the de Bohun treasure. There's a wild claim that the secret lies here at Tarset, and I've had the odd idiot who's come creeping around with divining rod and measuring devices and ranting ancient runes, but I've given them the toe of my boot. I've looked into it myself, when I was younger and more impressionable, but it's all rubbish. There is no "treasure": the de Bohun connection with Tarset or Temple Barden is pure fiction, and I'll have no truck with any of it.'

He snorted angrily. Arnold finished his drink. He felt uneasy. The Major's outburst had a dark, passionate side to it that disturbed him. The man's anger was somehow unreal, a dredging up of violence in a situation that called for none. Perhaps he had lived at Tarset too long, and dwelled too much upon its past.

'I'll have to leave you now,' Arnold said. 'I need to start making my way back to Morpeth.'

'Of course.' Some of the Major's training and politeness came back to him. He struggled to his feet. 'Hope you found what you want here at Tarset. And I . . . I'm grateful,' he added with a certain grudging reluctance, 'for what you've been able to tell me about the house. Perhaps I'll be able to have a copy of whatever is printed, in due course.'

'I'm sure that can be arranged,' Arnold said and turned towards the door.

At the front entrance Major Manners stood with his head raised, staring at the clouds gathering to the west. The breeze had strengthened, and it touched his greying hair, lifting it at the temple, where the wound started. His eyes were blank, his thoughts shuttered. He stood there as though he was waiting for something to happen.

The ridged scar on his face stood out in a purple slash, puckered and unpleasant. Slowly he lowered his head, and looked around him at the weed-ridden drive, the ravaged gardens at the front of the house. Pain came back into his eyes, seeping up past the cold indifference.

'No,' he said harshly, 'Tarset Hall is what it is, a dying house, a shadow of what it used to be, and should be. And die it will, unless I can rebuild it. But there's no buried treasure here, and as for ghosts . . .' He glared bitterly at Arnold. 'I've seen death on the hills above Port Stanley. I don't have to believe in ghosts.'

2

As Arnold drove away he had a hollow feeling in the pit of his stomach. He had not enjoyed his encounter with Major Rodney Manners. He could feel an immense sympathy with the man, could understand the way he felt and knew what he suffered with the decay about him. And yet there was something in the man's attitude which caused the hairs to rise on the back of Arnold's neck: the commitment, the hatred, the fierce anger that lay in the Major overcame the sympathy he had generated in Arnold, and it was with a sense of relief that Arnold took the turning down the lane towards Temple Barden.

Not that he was looking forward to discussing an old painting. It was completely out of his line, and he was conscious that all he would be able to do would be to mouth generalities that would fool no one. And he had a fair idea of where the brickbats would fall later, if he didn't come up to scratch and this Mr Dimmock made a complaint in the wrong quarter, like Brent-Ellis's wife. If she was sufficiently incensed to attack her husband, Arnold knew where that particular line could end.

The Old Rectory lay at the end of the lane, at the edge of the village of Temple Barden, and fronted by a narrow yard which Arnold guessed might once have housed the beginnings of a street market. For he was surprised to see that the house was considerably older than he had expected; moreover, it had certainly not been built as a rectory in the first instance, but would have been a manor house, or possibly a rich merchant's house with its three arches at street level, and the window on the east wall, which could have been a Norman doorway, originally.

Arnold parked the car in the lane and got out. There was a man standing in the doorway of the Old Rectory, shirt-sleeved, staring at Arnold.

'Don't get many strangers down this lane. Are you from County Hall?'

'That's right. My name is Arnold Landon.'

'Nick Dimmock.'

He held out his hand as Arnold walked forward. His grip was hard, his fingers long and thin. He was a tall man, towering over Arnold by several inches, and he was built like a lath, but one of tempered steel. His body was lean and muscular, the body of a committed runner, and his bearded face was long and thin. He had dark eyes that seemed to glow in the contrasting paleness of his cheeks, his nose was dominant, deep lines running from the base of his nose into the dark hair of his beard. The hair on his head sprouted thickly about his ears, but was thinning on top—the beard would be a compensation, a public demonstration of his virility in spite of the thinning crown.

'You'll have come in response to my call to the department?'

'That's right. The Director asked me to come and see you.'

'Mr Brent-Ellis.' Dimmock's mouth twisted in a faint grimace which suggested he held positive views about the Director of the Department of Museums and Antiquities. He stared at Arnold for a moment, contemplatively, then looked around him. 'You like the house?'

'Indeed. It's old . . . possibly twelfth-century.'

'Oldest in Temple Barden. It's a King John House.'

Arnold could not stop the smile that came to his face. Nick Dimmock caught the smile and it made him nervous; he ran a hand through his thinning hair and looked at Arnold suspiciously, wondering what he had said that was funny.

'So?'

Arnold wiped the smile from his face, and made a deprecating gesture. 'I'm sorry. I didn't mean to be rude.' He looked around him. 'It's just that the appellation "King John's House" was applied to many ancient buildings with which he had no concern.'

'How do you mean?'

Arnold shrugged. 'Mediæval people, if they could not assign a name to the person who constructed a house, tended to assign it to King John.'

'Why?'

Arnold looked at Dimmock quizzically. 'The Devil was commonly supposed to amuse himself by building earthen works and mounds. Devil's Dyke and so on. He didn't bother with houses. He left houses to King John.'

'I don't see the connection.'

Arnold laughed. 'King John, the wicked John Lackland, seems to have caught the mediæval imagination. He had a very bad press. He was regarded as next best thing to the Devil, so where there was a mound it was the Devil's work, but a house . . . that was John's.

Dimmock grunted sourly. 'I still don't see it as particularly amusing.'

Arnold shrugged. 'Well . . . it's just the thought that a "King John House", with its connotation with devilry, should end up as a rectory.'

Dimmock grimaced. 'I see.' It was clear he thought some response was necessary. He struggled to bring a smile to his saturnine features; after a moment it became genuine, grew broader as a thought struck him. 'Ah well, Mr Landon, perhaps the joke will appear even better to you then, when I show you what you've come here to see.'

'The painting?'

'Shall I lead the way?'

Dimmock turned, and entered the house.

It had been ruined.

Arnold had seen many mediæval houses which had been allowed to retain their original features, and some that had been 'improved' by the various generations who had lived there. In centuries past, changes had been wrought with a certain sensitivity in most instances, with traditional values still being imposed. The Old Rectory was different: the oldest house in Temple Barden had been the subject of a modernizing that had destroyed all the features that the original owners might have been proud of in their day. The ground floor had clearly been gutted, reconstructed and turned into a Victorian nightmare. The rooms were high-ceilinged where they would have been low; enlarged where they would have been intimate, and windows, lintels, fireplace had all been removed and replaced. It was a disaster.

Arnold sighed. Dimmock looked at him for a moment, perhaps guessing what was going through his mind and then suddenly sat down at the foot of the stairs, crossing his long legs at the ankles. He folded his arms, and contemplated Arnold for several seconds.

'They knocked it about a bit, over the years.'

'To ill effect,' Arnold agreed.

'Just the ground and first floors, mainly.'

'I'm relieved.'

'You're interested in old houses?'

'It's a hobby.'

'As well as work? That's encouraging. And unusual, if you know about paintings as well.'

Arnold licked his dry lips. He shrugged. 'I can't say I'm exactly an expert on old paintings.'

'Brent-Ellis sent you!'

'Ah . . . we're a bit short-staffed at the moment. And I happened to be passing Temple Barden. It—ah—it was felt I could sort of make a reconnaissance. Take the problem back to the office, if you know what I mean. For a more considered judgement. Later.'

Dimmock was not impressed by the lame excuse. He glowered at Arnold, unhappy at receiving the wrong man. He frowned, and tapped the toes of one foot against the other in a gesture of frustration.

'Have you heard of the Shroud of Turin?' he asked abruptly.

Surprised, Arnold nodded. 'Of course.'

'Tell me about it.'

Arnold hesitated. He had read a certain amount about the famous relic, which had received considerable publicity of recent years, with the Vatican allowing scientists to carry out carbon tests on the ancient cloth, to try to determine its provenance. He shrugged. 'It's a mediæval forgery. It's supposed to depict the image of the dead body of Christ.'

'Including His face.'

'That's right. The mediæval world was persuaded that the Shroud had been wrapped around the head of Christ.'

'Persuaded? You sound as though you disbelieve the

story. That the Shroud actually covered Christ after His death.'

'As I said—it's a forgery. If the cloth had covered His face the image would have been different—it would have resulted in distortions, because a real face is three-dimensional. The face on the Shroud, of course, is a flat bas-relief.'

'A miracle?'

Arnold shrugged.

'Some Christians believe.'

'I don't doubt it. But there's also the evidence of the blood on the Shroud. Scientists have discovered it contains traces of red ochre.'

'Environmental accident?'

'Or a skilled mediæval painter, simulating blood.' Arnold pursed his lips. 'And then there's St Augustine.'

'What about him?'

'Apparently, he used to lament that no one knew what Christ looked like. In the early Middle Ages artists painted Him like a clean-shaven youth. Then, quite suddenly in the thirteenth and fourteenth centuries images of Christ took on, quite precisely, the venerable appearance He presents on the Shroud.'

'Artists can be wrong.'

'Of course. But which school of painters was right—the clean-shaven or the bearded? One has to remember, the fourteenth century was a time of widespread holy relics— and widespread forgery. It was a way of making money, of bringing people to a church or an abbey. I mean, no fewer than three churches claimed to have, at the same time, the corpse of Mary Magdalene.' Arnold took a deep breath. 'But for me the clincher is really logic. The most devastating evidence is the thirteen-hundred-year gap between the death of Christ and the emergence of the Shroud.'

'You mean where was it all that time?'

'Precisely. I would have thought that if the Shroud was really the cloth that had covered Christ, this holiest of relics would have been known throughout Christendom—but for more than a thousand years it was unknown. It just appeared, it seems, in Europe, in the twelfth century.' Arnold shook his head. 'No. It was a forgery. It was prepared, and used, to win men's hearts through mystical images. Maybe it wasn't originally intended as a confidence trick; maybe it wasn't even shown as the actual Shroud; maybe it was intended as a painting, a representation, and known as such. But later followers might have come to blur the distinction, and start to worship it as the actual Shroud.'

'You mean things got out of hand.'

'It can easily happen. If people want to believe hard enough, they will. People got carried away. I understand, for instance, that the Church knew about the Shroud in the Middle Ages, and several times banned it from being displayed or used in religious ceremonies. It was becoming too venerated, getting between the people and the Church itself. Which is probably one reason why it disappeared for a hundred years—and only emerged later as the Turin Shroud. It had become a proscribed article.'

Dimmock scratched at his beard. Arnold could not see his eyes in the semi-darkness of the stairwell. He waited. Dimmock nodded. 'I hear what you say—and I don't disagree. There's the confusions, too.'

'Confusions?'

'I've done a bit of reading about it all. Mediæval writers kept repeating the mistakes made by earlier translators. I understand the original writings spoke of grave cloths, anyway. The Shroud, sure, but also the *sudarium*.'

'The what?'

'The cloth that was used to bind Christ's face; it was reputed to have been stained with his sweat and blood. They bound up the jaw after death in those days, just as they've done through the centuries. Apparently the *sudarium* was sealed up in the wall above the main gate into Jerusalem for a time. Until the Crusaders came.' He sighed. 'Still

... do you know who the most important family in this area used to be in mediæval times?'

Arnold thought for a moment. 'The Percys, I suppose: they had large landholdings in Northumberland.'

'What about the rest of the North?'

'The Cliffords, for a long period. And there was also the—'

'The de Bohuns. You know much about them?'

'Not a great deal,' Arnold admitted.

Dimmock laughed. His voice had a deep timbre, confident. 'Well, they were the usual kind: thick-brained idiots, most of them, trundling around in iron carapaces, thumping the hell out of each other. And endowing churches. Oh yes, they had a fear of the hereafter. They raped and cheated, pillaged and murdered in life, but bought heavenly redemption by willing their assets to the Church.'

'To the annoyance of their heirs, one imagines.'

'Who had to start the conquering bit all over again to regain the family fortunes. That's right. But that religious aspect . . . well, the story goes that the de Bohuns were a bit more closely involved than most. Strong Crusading tradition. And as a Norman family, they had landholdings in France. There's even a theory that they were responsible for hiding the Shroud in Aquitaine for a long period, when the Church wanted it destroyed because it had begun to interfere with religious practices—was dragging too much veneration in its train, so to speak.'

'There are plenty of theories. Is this one of yours?' Arnold asked sceptically.

Dimmock shook his head. 'No, no, there's a great deal been written about it. But, more to the point, it's been said the hiding-place for the Shroud at one time was here in England.'

'So?'

'So what if someone uncovered some evidence to suggest that there was a link between the Shroud . . . and a place like Temple Barden?'

Arnold was silent. 'I'm not sure . . .'

Dimmock leaned forward and the light from the doorway touched his face, animated, excited now, his eyes glowing with enthusiasm. 'Think of it. The Shroud was lost for hundreds of years. It emerged in Europe, and then disappeared again. But how did it get to Europe in the first place?'

Slowly, Arnold said, 'It's been suggested it was "rescued" by the Crusaders and brought back with them.'

'By the Knights Templar, yes. But Church pressure made them keep it hidden—or maybe it was just seen as loot, at first. But anyway, when it was hidden in Aquitaine —and before its re-emergence in France, and later its appearance in Turin, what if it was kept here in England? Think how fascinating it would be to scholars, to tourists, to so many people, to think that in a village like Temple Barden there could be a clear link with the Crusades, the men who brought back the Shroud, the knights who protected it for hundreds of years!'

'I'm not quite certain what you're driving at.'

'Follow me.' Dimmock sprang to his feet. He hastened up the worn stone of the old stairs to the first floor. Here the devastation had been less: the modernizers had restricted most of their vandal activities to the lower part of the house although some walls had clearly been removed. On the main landing Dimmock opened a dark, oaken door and beckoned Arnold through; they climbed a tight, twisting dark staircase until they reached another oaken door at the top of the stairs. It led into a small, narrow room.

'Do you know where we are?'

Arnold shrugged. 'I would guess this would be a chamber constructed under the eaves, above the main chambers which would have been placed directly above the ground-floor mediæval service rooms—the buttery and pantry.'

'That's about it. And timber-framed.'

The room was empty of furniture, and the far wall had

been partly demolished. Dust hung thickly in the air, dancing in the dim light at their entrance.

'Look at this.'

The demolished wall was typically mediæval: roughly hewn stone blocks with an infilling of rubble. Though an inner timber frame had been inserted, the old wall had been used as a support for a main beam of dark, iron-hard oak, running probably the length of the upper storey, but the top two-thirds of the structure had been pulled down, with part of the ceiling removed. The laths had been broken away, the crumbling plaster still in place along part of the length. There was a dark space there, perhaps six feet by four.

'That's where we found it,' Dimmock exclaimed triumphantly.

'Found what?'

'The painting.'

Arnold stared at him. 'I don't understand.'

Nick Dimmock clenched his fists: he could still get excited about the find. 'This room's not been used for years. The previous owners used it as a junk room, and there's evidence it's been cluttered with lumber for generations. In a rambling old house like this the larger rooms have tended to be used—but you could hardly swing a cat in here, so it's mainly been used for storage purposes, probably for hundreds of years. Anyway . . .'

He stood up on tiptoe, peering into the space in the ceiling. Faint light shone through the slates of the roof: though the house was three storeys high, at the rear it sloped sharply, and here they were close to the eaves at the back of the house. Dimmock gestured with a predatory finger. 'It was in there. I decided to clear out some of the junk in here. I was going to clean up that wall over there, remove the partitioning and the timber frame, and extend the main gallery. But the workman who was in here called me up—he said the ceiling was in a bad state and needed to come down. He began to take it down, but then he had a surprise: we realized it was a false ceiling. The lath and plaster you now see was a second, older ceiling, a few inches above the other, with a small gap in between.'

'What was the purpose of that?' Arnold asked, puzzled.

'That was my question! And then when we started chipping away we realized there was something on top of the ceiling. It was heavy, wrapped in cloth. We cut the ceiling away around it, and there it was. A *painting*, of all things!'

'You mean it had been secreted there?'

'At some stage in the dim and distant past someone had placed the painting in protective coarse cloth and hidden it face down on the timbers of the ceiling, then constructed a false ceiling below it to complete the secrecy. It was never intended to recover that painting in the short term: it had been put in a hiding-place where it would be safe for a long time. A very long time. The question that burns me, of course, is—how long?'

'What does the painting depict?'

Dimmock turned and glared at him. 'I made a mistake. I let people know about it. There was some newspaper publicity, but it died down after a while. It seemed unimportant. But then I started thinking. Reading. I left the ceiling as it was. I had the painting inspected. Valued. But you know what experts are like—particularly art experts! It's old all right. They agreed on that. Mediæval, some of the experts say. Others say it's rubbish. And they're in the majority, it seems. And they all say it's non-assignable. They don't know what school it is, who painted it, or what. So they're inclined to dismiss it. A curiosity, that's all. No great value—a thousand or so, maybe. But I'm not certain, and I don't trust experts. I got it locked up here in a special room. Wired with alarms. Just in case. Not taking any chances. Don't know what it's worth, but who can tell? But I thought if someone from your department could look at it, link it to what you might have in the County Archives . . . There's other ways of dating a painting, don't you see?'

'External evidence, you mean?' Arnold asked.

Dimmock stared at him. 'What evidence?'

'The painting's environment.'

Dimmock was silent for a few moments, his breathing harsh in the narrow room. 'I was thinking of documentation, tracing its history, going through the archives for some mention of it, getting its provenance sorted out. But—environment . . . ?'

Arnold pointed to the ceiling. 'You say you found the painting there. Experts disagree about its age. Well, if the painting was secreted above a false ceiling, there's one thing you can certainly be sure of. It's bound to be older than the ceiling itself. So, if the ceiling was built in 1900 the painting's got to be older than that.'

'And if the ceiling was erected in 1400?' Dimmock muttered, almost to himself.

'Then the painting is fourteenth-century—or earlier.'

Dimmock took a deep breath. 'All right, but the problem is, how can we find out how old the ceiling is? I mean, ceilings are ceilings.'

'It's not quite like that,' Arnold said gently.

'You could date a ceiling?'

'It's possible. You see, if the false ceiling was inserted some inches below the lower one we'd need to check the timbers and their jointing, the lath construction, the materials used in the making of the plaster, and we'd need to look for other clues in the room itself, constructional issues which could help date the room, within the overall pattern of the house.'

'But is that possible?'

'It's certainly feasible, Mr Dimmock. You see, the master masons of the eleventh and twelfth centuries left a tradition behind them: the masons' lodges passed on secrets and skills of the trades one to another. But no craftsman is happy just to copy the work of his master. He tries to improve upon it—and probably does so. And then his work is copied, for a period, until another dissatisfied craftsman improves upon the work he's been copying. So by looking at timber, and joints, and stonework, and interior decoration, and internal constructions, it's quite possible to date something fairly accurately. And with a house as old as this, there'll be records in the County Archives which can also help us. The manorial rolls, for instance, may well give us information about what work tenants might have been allowed to do inside this house centuries ago. The nobility,' Arnold added, 'were careful owners. They kept good records. Or at least, their Stewards did. After all, they had to keep their masters in armour.'

Dimmock was silent for several minutes. He stared at Arnold, and then looked long at the damaged ceiling. He shook his head. 'If you're right—'

'You haven't told me what the painting depicted.'

Dimmock stared at Arnold for a moment, then crooked a finger at him and led the way back into the gallery and down the stone stairs. At the front of the house was a sunny room with leather settee, a large amount of bookshelving stacked with elderly-looking volumes and a desk. Clearly, Dimmock used it as a study for his research. Dimmock walked across to the desk and unlocked the drawer. He drew out a large, imitation-leather-bound photograph album. It was full of photographs of the painting he had been talking about: there were shots of the painting as a whole, and of every square inch of it. Some close-ups concentrated upon the eyes, others on the hair. There was a series that stressed the nose, another that explored in detail the upper lip and its curvature. Some of the photographs were obscure, and Arnold was unable to relate them to the overall painting itself. Nostrils, teeth, irises of the eyes, detail of the beard, all were recorded, dwelled on, identified. At the back of the album was a large photograph, folded three times, of the painting as a whole, reproduced on a thin cloth-like material.

'This is what it really looks like,' Dimmock said almost reverentially.

Arnold felt a twinge of excitement. It was a representation of what would have been a panel painting, the kind that commonly were hung in churches in mediæval times, as reminders to the brethren, representations of divinity, and objects of veneration. If the flesh could not be present, the image was there to inspire.

And this painting was inspirational.

The eyes were deep-sunk and hollow, pleading in their tenderness and pain. The heavy lids seemed almost transparent and the dark shadows under the eyes tended to emphasize the ethereality of the image. The nose was clearly delineated, high-bridged, the top lip down-curving to the full lower lip. The beard was painted in detail, forked at its tip, and the hair on the head was long, drawn down to the shoulders. The background was hazy, as though deemed unimportant, but there was a vague outline of cross bars, a fretwork. Arnold stared at it and something moved in his chest.

'Well?' Dimmock demanded huskily.

'It's a head of Christ,' Arnold replied quietly.

Dimmock gripped his shoulder with fierce fingers. 'No. In a way it's more important than that. It's a replica of the face on the Shroud!'

They sat in the sunny room, Arnold on the leather settee, Nick Dimmock perched on the edge of the desk, his long legs swinging. He had locked away the album, after giving Arnold one photograph, but there was still a sense of excitement in the air. 'The problem is the Government,' Dimmock said angrily.

'How do you mean?'

'Old houses like this are expensive to maintain. I'm not a rich man. When I bought this house I had a decent job —a small printing business—but I was forced out by high interest rates, poor cashflow. But I'm still a businessman at heart, and I don't fancy working for someone else. My nest egg is depleted and the Government doesn't help.'

'With the house, you mean?'

'That's right. No grants from English Heritage for the oldest house in Temple Barden! Too many civil servants, that's the real problem. So a man has to do what he sees best. For a while I thought about the ghost.'

'Ghost?'

Nick Dimmock smiled thinly. 'Didn't you read that series of articles in the *Journal*? Lots of old houses in Northumberland boast a ghost. Here it's the Lady in White. She's reputed to be a maidservant who was raped by the rector two hundred years ago. He was panicked by her screams and in the struggle he strangled her. He buried her in the grounds of the Old Rectory and told people she had left the area to go elsewhere, to a better position. She had no relatives—she was an orphan—so there was no hue and cry. He got away with it—or thought he had. He married, and then the nightmares started. He kept seeing her still dressed in her white nightshift. He fell down the stairs one night and broke his neck. The White Lady wasn't satisfied. She had been denied the justice Society should have given her —and she was buried in unconsecrated ground. She still roamed the house. Still does, they say.'

'Have you seen the apparition?' Arnold asked drily.

Dimmock laughed, a short barking sound. 'Oh, come on, this is all a Victorian fairy tale! You know what they were like. Any old manse was bound to have a ghost and if it didn't have one, they'd invent one. Local colour, that sort of thing. I've never seen her. And no one can point to where she's buried in the garden. But if people want to believe it . . .'

'You've not discouraged the story.'

'Why should I? The thought was, if people want to come here and have a *frisson* at the thought of the Lady in White, well, let them—at a price. But I soon realized there wasn't much money in that! Not unless I turned the place into an inn or something, like the Lord Crewe. People would then come and stay, in hopes of seeing the ghost. But pubs are not my style. No, my salvation doesn't lie with the mythical raped maidservant.'

Arnold hesitated. His glance strayed to the desk where Dimmock had locked away the album. 'You think—'

'The painting could be a different matter. Don't you see it, Mr Landon? If I can prove that there's a link between the Shroud of Turin and this painting, if I could prove that here lies the key to the missing years of the Shroud, the painting could then prove to be of immense value, the Old Rectory could become a Mecca for all who are interested in historical research, the occult, religion—'

'I think you've got your religions mixed,' Arnold suggested.

'All right, Mecca, Christianity . . . but remember, the Shroud came from the Holy Land. And the representation here, it could provide the link to determine its provenance.'

Arnold was silent for a while. Dimmock seemed lost in his own thoughts. Clearly, he felt that his own financial salvation lay in developing an interest in the painting. Arnold himself had felt a quickening of interest, if only in the historical aspects of it all.

'You said you have the painting here at the Old Rectory.'

'That's right.'

'May I see it?'

Dimmock hesitated. He stared at Arnold, as though worried that he might have allowed a nefarious impostor into his house, but after a moment he swung his legs down and headed for the door, pride in his possession overcoming his nervousness.

He led the way to the back of the house, to a low door of stout construction, which had been locked and padlocked. Dimmock switched off the alarm system and fiddled with the padlock. He opened the door and led Arnold inside.

The room was dark, narrow and airless. Dimmock switched on the light—there were no windows.

The painting was hung on the plain whitewashed wall. It was in a simple wooden frame. Arnold stared at it and again felt the tingle in his veins that he had experienced when he had looked at the photographs in Dimmock's study. There was a feeling of power and of pain and of torment in the features that he saw, and yet the painting itself—about five feet by three in size—was dark, and discoloured, and difficult to make out in the harsh reflective light.

Arnold stepped closer to inspect the painting, shading his hand against the reflections on the paint. He looked at the background, tracing the vague outline of the trelliswork, and the curious arrangement of bars in the corner. There was also something else, tucked away in the bottom right-hand corner of the painting. It looked like a shield, with some markings on it. They were difficult to make out.

'So,' Dimmock muttered after a little while, 'do you think you can help me?'

Arnold thought about Mrs Brent-Ellis and the Director himself. Pressure had been brought, and Arnold would have been resentful if he had been forced to do something outside his competence and interest. But perhaps this was different. Dimmock's motives were his business, but the challenge afforded by the dating of the house and the ceiling and the ancient beams of the roof was an interesting one. He nodded. 'I can try.'

'You'll take a look at the ceiling?'

'And in the archives,' Arnold added.

Dimmock stared at him for a long moment and then to Arnold's surprise he stiffened, punched the air with a clenched fist and let out a strangled cry of elation.

'And then we can say to hell with the White Lady of Temple Barden—and all those bloody art experts, to boot!'

It was, Arnold thought, early days to get excited, but he smiled, infected with Dimmock's enthusiasm. He waited outside the room while Dimmock locked up behind him and then he took his leave.

3

The following morning Arnold arrived at the office in Morpeth and left a message that he was going to the library in Newcastle to undertake research in relation to Nick Dimmock's painting. He had been specifically asked by Brent-Ellis to do the work, and he had little else on his desk that was urgent, so he decided to take the opportunity immediately to find out what he could about Temple Barden and the Old Rectory. He would be able, at the same time, to start work on the errors he had discovered in Kevin Anderson's brochure on the tower houses.

The recipient of the message, Miss Sansom, glowered when he handed it to her. She was wearing her dark suit like a uniform. Arnold wondered whether her leisure wardrobe included jackboots.

He had a standing arrangement at Newcastle that he could use one of the carrels in the stack room of the library for his research: the staff there knew him well and he had free access to the volumes in the stack room, most of which had not had their pages turned in twenty years.

He began by collecting from the shelves the old volumes that consisted of extracts from local newspapers of the day together with learned articles and gossip. *Havelock's Records* gave him the first mention of the Old Rectory: there was also a pencil sketch of the building itself, together with an account of the White Lady.

The writer claimed it was a seventeenth-century legend but gave no sources. There was no suggestion or hint about the painting or the Shroud. Arnold hadn't expected any. The ceiling had been up there a long time and the painting had been secreted well before the seventeenth century, in his view.

The article on the White Lady was one of a series in *Havelock*, so Arnold decided to check back through the others in case there were any hints in the series itself. There were none. The articles ranged over the Lord Crewe Arms and similar locations, and included, he noted wryly as he remembered Major Manners's attitude, Tarset Hall. He read about Tarset, out of interest.

It was a general account which dwelt on the historical antecedents of the Hall and its connection with Tarset Castle. Arnold's view that the Hall had been a lodging for men-at-arms from the Castle was suggested in the article; it also commented upon the ownership of the Hall in previous centuries. There were sketches of the armorial bearings of the Cliffords and the de Bohuns.

The Victorians had a soft spot for that sort of thing, Arnold mused. Picture books about *Great Beauties of the Day* tended to feature society ladies with wealthy backgrounds; *Arms of our Ancestors* showed heraldic devices of the leading families in the belief that the masses were interested. Perhaps they had been. Arnold wondered if the publishers had ever made any money, beyond that they received from subscribers.

He glanced idly at the de Bohun and Clifford arms in the sketch; it was not a field in which he was personally interested, though he had come across armorial bearings often enough in his investigation of old houses.

There was a postscript to the account of the Tarset Hall ghost which touched upon another issue, over which Major Manners had become almost virulent in his comments.

THE TARSET TREASURE

Readers of our latest publication will perhaps have been surprised that no mention was made, in our correspondent's account of the Tarset Hall Ghost, of that equally legendary story: the Tarset Treasure.

It has long been believed that several hundred years ago, at the time of Richard III, or even earlier some writers aver, a fabulous treasure was housed at Tarset Castle. This treasure, which was claimed to have been 'beyond the wildest dreams of avarice and worth the ransoms of a hundred kings' has never been detailed as to its content or nature. Furthermore, no one seems to be certain how it had been amassed, since the owners of Tarset Castle were never among the leading families in the land. Legend is silent as to its provenance, or indeed who held title to the treasure.

Stories of its secretion at Tarset have nevertheless long been bruited abroad. Unfortunately, with the destruction of Tarset Castle itself, the legend languished, for who can deny that if the location is destroyed the treasure must of itself be destroyed also?

Suffice it to say that with the razing of the Castle the mystery of the Tarset Treasure increased. Many attempts have been made over the centuries to discover its whereabouts, but all were unsuccessful. Whether it was spirited away by its owners, whether it remains buried beneath the ruins of Tarset Castle, or whether it was simply a mere chimera no one at this modern day can say. But it remains to tease the mind and the imagination and remind us of our heritage and our link with the past.

Arnold grunted to himself.

The article said nothing; it merely repeated, without detail, the kind of hoary old myth that would have been current in a hundred places and a hundred countries, ever since men began to worry about hobgoblins and fairies. Somehow, there always seemed to be a pot of gold involved, a fantastic treasure at the end of the rainbow. He could understand the violent scepticism of Major Manners. Nick Dimmock, on the other hand, with other values and other motives, might well have been tempted to pay more attention and seek to maintain the legend had it applied to Temple Barden Old Rectory.

By lunch-time Arnold had had enough. He replaced the books on the stack room shelves, dusted himself down and walked out to the entrance of the library. He hesitated for a while, considering whether he should visit one of the restaurants near the Bigg Market but decided against it; he went out into the sunshine and the subtle classical curve of Grey Street, where crowds were bustling around the entrance to the Metro, and walked down the hill towards the Quayside. He bought a couple of ham sandwiches and turned in at Amen Corner to sit in the quiet church square, enjoying the warm sun. It was just one o'clock when he walked down Castle Stairs and made his way to Ben Gibson's bookshop on the Quayside.

Ben Gibson himself was seated just inside the door on a high stool, an old volume in his hands, half-rim glasses balanced on the end of his pug nose. The shop was empty: it was never particularly busy, but that suited Ben. He had worked most of his life as a watchmaker: the bookshop was his retirement interest and his passion. He was not in business to make money.

As Arnold entered he looked at him with undisguised pleasure, and welcomed him with a smile. 'So, what brings you here, my friend?'

'I'm doing some work at the library,' Arnold explained. 'And I thought I'd call in to see if Jane has managed to get hold of the books and articles I need to finish the brochure for the Tourist Board.'

'I believe she has, I believe she has,' Ben Gibson rumbled. He twisted his froglike frame on the stool and called to the back of the shop. 'Jane? Those books arrive for Arnold this morning?'

Jane Wilson appeared in the doorway to the stack room. She was somewhat tousled and there was a smudge of dust on her nose. She was not in the best of tempers. She snorted. 'And when Mr Landon arrives, we must all run! Yes, Ben, they came in and I unpacked them but I haven't sorted them yet. He'll have to wait.'

Ben winked at Arnold. 'He's in no great hurry. He'd like a cup of tea with us, though, while he waits. Can you manage that?'

Arnold winced. He waited for the uproar. It didn't come,

but the silence was worse. Jane Wilson came back into the doorway and glowered at Arnold as though he was responsible for all that was unpleasant in her life. Then she turned her baleful glance on her uncle. Enjoying himself, Ben smiled blandly at her. Arnold could not stand the pressure. 'I know where everything is. I'll make it for the three of us.'

She appeared in no way mollified as she disappeared once more into the stack room.

Arnold made the tea in the back room and after a few minutes Ben Gibson came in to join him. 'No punters around, so I've locked the front door. Give us a chance for a cosy chat. You told Jane the tea's ready?'

She must have already realized it because she entered as he spoke, carrying a small pile of books and a file of photocopied material. She dumped it in front of Arnold, spilling his tea as she did so. 'You used to being waited on hand and foot?' she asked unfairly.

'I'm grateful for the trouble you've taken,' Arnold replied in a mild tone. He poured the tea that had been spilled into his saucer back into the cup. 'Your tea's already poured.'

She sat down without a word, still glowering. Ben Gibson looked at them both fondly. He seemed to enjoy the fact that they seemed to get on so poorly. It was as though he was hugging to himself a secret he knew, that they didn't. 'Well, then, Arnold, so what's all this excitement I hear about up at Morpeth?'

'Excitement?'

'Haven't you seen the papers this morning?'

Arnold shook his head. 'I didn't really have time. I went straight into the office, and then came down to Newcastle. What's happened?'

'Two people murdered,' Jane Wilson said shortly.

'Up at Seahouses.'

'I thought you said Morpeth.'

'Ahah!' Ben Gibson exclaimed. 'The woman, apparently, was *from* Morpeth. No names given out yet, but it looks like it was a lovers' tryst that someone burst in on. The police are being very cagey about it all in their statement, and the newspaper seems oddly edgy, champing at the bit sort of thing. Least, that's the impression I got. There's a leading article—seemingly unconnected, but you know how these things are worked—about the public's right to know.' He sighed. 'So you can't enlighten us, as a local denizen?'

'I'm afraid not.'

'Ah well.' The little bookseller sipped his tea. 'So how is the research getting on?'

Arnold shrugged diffidently. 'I've visited most of the sites now. I haven't started writing up my notes, but once I've gone through the material Jane's obtained for me I should be able to make a start.'

'Addy, Colvin and Everett are there,' she said, gesturing towards the pile of books on the table. 'The photocopies are from the articles in the British Archæological Association journals. And there's some bits from the Calendar of Patent Rolls. But Braun is out on loan. You'll have to wait for it.'

'That's plenty to go on.'

'Maybe Jane can give you a hand with the writing of the brochure itself,' Gibson suggested cheerfully.

'Uncle—' she warned.

'That won't be necessary,' Arnold said hastily. 'I'll be able to get on with it at the weekend.'

'So what were you doing in the library? They won't have these books,' Jane asked.

Arnold sighed. 'I'm afraid I've been saddled with another commission. And one I'm out of my depth in.'

'What's that?' Ben asked.

'A painting.'

'A *what*?'

Arnold explained.

When he had finished they were all silent for a little while. Ben Gibson was frowning, lost in thought. A light had come into Jane Wilson's eyes. 'It sounds very romantic,' she said quietly.

'Right up your street, hey, Jane?' Ben Gibson teased.
'Can't you work this theme into your next historical novel?
Or are they romantic novels? Or social histories? Just what
do you classify them as, niece?'

She ignored him. It was badinage she'd suffered from
often enough. She stared fixedly at Arnold. 'This painting
—and the false ceiling. Why do you think it would have
been hidden like that?'

'Religious persecution,' Ben Gibson announced abruptly.

'Persecution? But what's wrong with keeping a religious
painting? And particularly one which would seem to be
similar to most of the depictions of Christ at that time.'

'Ah well.' Ben Gibson nodded his head sagely. 'It's the
other connotations that Arnold mentioned that might be
the clue. You did say this Mr Dimmock is excited about a
connection with the Holy Shroud of Turin?'

'Well, that's his theory,' Arnold replied. 'All I'm going
to do is check on that ceiling and the building itself to try
to date the period when the painting was actually hidden.
He's given me a photograph of the painting, but I don't
think there's anything I can do with that. Not up my street
at all. But I can work on the date of its location.'

'Surely you could guess, even now?'

'Oh, I don't know—'

'*Arnold!*' Ben Gibson interrupted reprovingly.

Arnold grinned. 'Well, I could make a guess, but I'd
have to do a lot of checking to confirm it. But if you were
to press me now—which you are—I think that ceiling could
have been fourteenth-century.'

'So old!' Jane exclaimed.

'It's possible.'

'And Mr Dimmock talked of the de Bohuns, and the
Knights Templar.'

'That's right.'

'So there you are: religious persecution,' Ben Gibson
exclaimed, with a peremptory wave of his hand.

Jane sighed. 'Explain.'

Ben Gibson folded his arms and gazed at her fondly. 'You always loved stories when you were a little girl.'

'Uncle—'

'I'm sure Arnold could tell you as much as I about the Templars. But if Mr Dimmock thinks there's a Shroud connection with this painting, he must surely be thinking of the demise of the Preceptory—around about 1312—as part of the Papal purge. The Knights Templar, you see, had become too rich and too painful for Pope Clement of Avignon—'

'Avignon? Oh, of course, this was the time of schism in the Church of Rome.'

'Correct, my girl. Don't interrupt. I was saying . . . too rich to tolerate.'

'The King of France also wanted the money,' Arnold suggested.

'That's right.' Ben Gibson held up his cup of tea as though it were a chalice.' Philippe the Fair, King of France, envious of the wealth and power of the Templars, carried out a series of dawn raids—an exemplary planning operation for the time, never bettered even under Stalin. He succeeded in rounding up almost every leading Templar in the country. He accused them of heresy. Of worshipping false gods. Of bestiality. Of rape and seduction. You name it: the usual calendar used by venal, powerful people wishing to get rid of their enemies in an aura of godliness and sanctity.' He smiled. 'It was even said that the Knights Templar actually worshipped—horror of horrors—a man's head.'

Arnold smiled. 'Or to be more accurate, a picture of a man's head.'

'That is so. *Imagine* the heresy!'

Arnold glanced at Jane. She was listening intently.

'There's a modern theory that this was just another way of explaining the Shroud,' Ben Gibson continued. 'You know—it was not a picture of a man's head so much as the image of the head on the Shroud itself, which was gradually revealed by raising the cloth from a casket built for the purpose. Some writers argue that the casket was the origin of the legend of the Holy Grail, by the way. But no matter. At dawn on October 13, 1307, more than a thousand senior French knights were rounded up and their leaders were burned at the stake. Religious persecution. The same thing happened throughout Europe: the Knights Templar, the soldier monks of Christ, were suddenly bad news—*persona non grata*.'

'A few escaped, of course,' Arnold said.

'Tipped off, some believe. And that's what our friend Mr Dimmock will be relying upon in the long term. Because if he thinks the Shroud itself was brought to England—to Temple Barden no less—it would have to be by a knight who escaped the October terror, who had lands in France, who came to England, and when hell rose here too, hid the Shroud until times had become gentler. But it's all a pretty weak theory—unsupported by evidence.'

'What about the painting?' Jane asked.

'Who knows?' Arnold replied. 'It could mean something, or nothing.'

'Could I see the photograph?' Jane asked.

Arnold nodded. He fished in his briefcase and took out the photograph that Dimmock had given him. He glanced at it briefly himself, struck again by the pathos in the eyes, and then handed it to Jane. She looked at it for a while in silence.

'Where did the Shroud come from in the first place?' Jane asked.

Arnold shrugged. 'It's a mediæval forgery, it seems. But it's been traditionally linked to earlier claims—there are stories that suggest great religious significance was attached in Eastern Turkey in the tenth century to a cloth bearing the features of a man. As vague as that. The cloth was reported to have been brought to the City of Edessa— modern day Urfa—from Jerusalem, centuries before. It had been hidden for a time in Jerusalem, then was rediscovered in a niche above the gate. In 944 the cloth was captured by the Byzantines and taken to Constantinople. There the Crusaders "rescued" it in 1204.'

'And after that?'

'Nothing. A silence for one hundred and fifty years—and then stories began to circulate about the Holy Shroud.'

'And this painting in Temple Barden?'

'Could—just *could*—be a representation of that Shroud. But it's all very hazy, don't you agree?'

'But very romantic,' Ben Gibson repeated with a smile, and was rewarded by another glower from his niece.

'And what does Mr Dimmock hope to get out of his researches?' Jane asked.

'A small business, it seems. He believes that if he can prove the painting was a representation of the Shroud, and was hidden at the same time as the Shroud could have been at Temple Barden, he could encourage myriads of visitors to the Old Rectory.'

'You think that possible?'

'I wouldn't have thought so. But who knows? With the right kind of marketing, the right kind of publicity—'

'I thought you were a serious man,' Jane remarked coldly. 'Why are you lending your skills to such a project?'

'Now there's a question!' Ben Gibson exclaimed.

Arnold shrugged. 'It's part of my job, it seems. My duties haven't exactly been outlined to me yet, but since it's the Director who has given me these two commissions person-ally—the brochure and the painting—I'm hardly in a position to refuse.'

'Hmmm.' Jane studied the photograph for a while in silence. Then she asked,' Could I hang on to this for a while?'

Arnold shrugged. 'Be my guest. I don't think there's much I can glean from it. If you have any friends who are knowledgeable about mediæval art, perhaps you could find something out. I'll be concentrating on that ceiling and that room—after I've come to grips with Kevin Andrews's brochure.'

After all, he considered, it was for Brent-Ellis to confront an irate wife; Arnold had no desire to he hauled in front of an angry Ben Edwards again.

'And what about these?' Jane asked, nodding in the direction of the British Library books. 'How long will you want to hang on to them for your research?'

Arnold shrugged. 'I'm going to be pushed for time. Ben Edwards, the Director of the Tourist Board, is pressing for his brochure. I'll have to work on these over the next few days and I hope to finish by the weekend. You can have them back then.'

'And your theory about Henry Yvele?'

Arnold glanced at Ben Gibson. The little man smiled: he had caught the slight emphasis upon the word *theory*. Patiently, Arnold replied, 'I think I'm right. Kevin Anderson simply took the received wisdom of Victorian writers. But they're inaccurate. I've looked at Chipchase, Langley, Tarset Hall and while I can't be absolutely certain, there's enough there to lead me to believe that Yvele did work on these buildings, that the tower houses were the result of, at the very least, a collaboration between John Lewyn and Henry Yvele and so I should be changing the thrust of the brochure as it's presently planned. I've got to take a look at Brunskill yet, but I think it'll confirm my thoughts.'

'Arnold Landon wins again,' Jane Wilson said softly.

Arnold sighed. He was never certain why she had this edge about her whenever she spoke to him. Maybe it harked back to their first meeting, at Harlech, when he had been disparaging about her books, not knowing who she was. Maybe she simply disliked him.

'Well, children,' Ben Gibson said brightly. 'Another cup of tea?'

After leaving the Quayside, Arnold spent another two hours in the carrel in Newcastle Library. As it grew near four o'clock he finally packed up, and went up to the multi-storey car park. He was always nervous about leaving his car in Newcastle streets: ram raiders from North Shields made a practice of stealing older cars from Newcastle for use in their assaults upon shop windows. Once used, the cars were abandoned with their noses smashed through the plate glass, while the raiders made their escape in fine-tuned Fords which they housed in lock-up garages between raids.

Arnold drove back north hurriedly, feeling it necessary to call in at the office before it closed, just in case the DDMA wanted to speak to him. When he arrived at the office car park he realized he need not have bothered: Brent-Ellis's car was not there. He was probably away on some golf course or other.

Arnold went up to his office. There were two messages on his desk: one was from Ben Edwards's secretary. It was simple enough. A reminder that Mr Edwards was still waiting for his report. Its brevity contained a warning, and Arnold felt his stomach turn. He did not care for Mr Ben Edwards. The second, surprisingly, was from the DDMA himself.

Arnold was still reading it when the door to the office opened, he looked up and saw a man he had met on several occasions previously, but one he had hoped he would not have to meet again.

Detective Chief Inspector Culpeper.

'Well, Mr Landon, and how are you?'

Arnold moistened his lips. 'I—I was just reading this memo from the Director. It says you want to see me.'

'That's right,' Culpeper beamed. 'Always pleasing to meet old friends.' He pulled forward a chair and sat down, unbuttoning his jacket to ease his paunch, and he looked around him, his wistful, autumn-brown eyes noting the barrenness of the office. 'So you've made a move, then.'

'Yes.'

'I got the impression life wasn't exactly smooth for you in the Planning Department.'

'It was all right.'

'You saw off two Directors in your time.'

Arnold felt a faint stir of resentment. The men he had worked for had caused their own downfalls. 'That was nothing to do with me.'

'Oh, of course, I wasn't insinuating otherwise.' Culpeper grinned and took out his pipe. 'You mind?'

Arnold shook his head.

Culpeper tamped some tobacco into the bowl of his pipe. 'Filthy habit, anti-social and all that, but there you are. Man of my age . . . so what do you think of your new boss, then?'

Arnold shrugged non-committally.

Culpeper grunted. 'Bit odd, seems to me. I mean, is he ever in his office? I interviewed him today, and saw some of his staff—they pack in early here, don't they? All gone home bar you. And that Miss Sansom. Wouldn't want to meet her in a dark alley. But your Director, seems he was keen to get away even earlier. Appointment, he said. I'd finished with him, and he couldn't help much. Referred me to you, really. Before he shot off like a startled rabbit.'

'Me?' Arnold could not keep the surprise out of his voice. 'Why should he refer you to me? What do you want to see me about?'

Culpeper scratched a match, applied it to his pipe and puffed vigorously. When he was satisfied, he squinted at Arnold through the rising blue smoke. 'I wouldn't have bothered you, since you've only been here in the department for a few weeks, but Brent-Ellis mentioned your name, so . . .'

'But why?'

Culpeper was silent for a little while, observing Arnold sadly. At last, he said, 'You're a friend of Kevin Anderson, I gather.'

'A friend?' Arnold frowned. 'Hardly that.'

'What, then?'

'Ah—I don't know really. When I took up my new job he popped in here several times; he helped me get orientated, if you know what I mean. We had a drink in the pub a couple of times. But I hardly know him.'

'What *do* you know about him?'

Arnold shook his head. 'Very little, really. He's a pleasant young man. Married, I understand. Lives here in Morpeth. But beyond that—'

'Did he tell you where he was going on leave?'

'I didn't even know he *was* going on leave. No one—that is—'

Culpeper drew on his pipe, thoughtfully. His eyes were suddenly sharper. 'You were going to say?'

Arnold grimaced. 'I was going to say that it seems he took his leave rather suddenly. I didn't know anything about it but there was no reason why I should. It's just that the Director called me in and told me that Kevin had taken sudden leave, without permission it seems, when he was in the middle of a project—and I had to take over the work he'd left undone. It was urgent,' he added lamely.

'And did you see Mr Anderson before he left on leave?'

'I'm not even certain *when* he went.'

'Did you see him last Friday?' Culpeper asked patiently.

Arnold wrinkled his brow in thought. He nodded, slowly. 'Yes, that's right. He came in the office and had a cup of coffee with me.'

'Did he usually join you for coffee?'

'No.'

'Did he have any particular reason for joining you on that occasion?'

'I don't think so, but I don't know, really. Inspector, what's this about?'

Culpeper inspected his pipe for a moment. 'What was he like when he called on you that morning? His manner, his demeanour, like.'

Helplessly, Arnold waved his hands. 'I don't know. He

—he came in, something about some papers—' But it had seemed like an excuse, now that Arnold thought about it. He recalled feeling that Anderson was at a loose end, wanted to sit down with someone, have company. 'He was sort of—preoccupied, as far as I recall.'

'What did he have to say?'

'Very little.' Arnold shook his head. 'In fact, I can't recall anything he said. He came in, sat down, had a coffee, said very little. He wasn't here more than ten minutes, if that.'

'Did he seem nervous, edgy, out of sorts, like?'

'I can't say so. He was thoughtful, I suppose, and silent. But in my experience he was always quiet.'

'Did he talk about his wife at all?'

Arnold stared at Culpeper. 'No. I wouldn't have expected him to. I keep telling you. We weren't close friends.'

'It seems he was as close to you as he was to anyone in the office.'

'That can't be so. I hardly know him.'

'It's you he chose to come and talk to when he was troubled,' Culpeper suggested.

Arnold shook his head. 'Was he troubled? I'm not aware that he was. I don't know what you mean. I've never been someone he could confide in if he had something on his mind. We didn't have that sort of relationship. I would guess he was a lonely man—'

'He was married.'

'Yes, but you know what I mean. Here at the office, maybe he had no friends, little contact with others, for whatever reason. I was a newcomer, maybe he thought he could make a new start, begin a relationship. I don't know. But talking of his wife, he never did that.'

'Hmm.' Culpeper stared sadly at his pipe. It had gone out in spite of his efforts. He fished for his box of matches, struck another and relit the pipe. 'Well, the news will be in the papers tonight, so I suppose there'd be no harm if I tell you. I've just got back from Seahouses.'

'There's been a killing there,' Arnold said.

Culpeper nodded. 'Two. One of them was Kevin Anderson's wife.'

Arnold was still. He felt cold. He stared at Culpeper, his fingers rigid as they gripped the edge of the desk in front of him. He was eventually aware that Culpeper was looking at his fingers, and he made a conscious attempt to relax. 'Who was the other person killed?'

Culpeper shook his head slowly. 'It wasn't your friend Kevin.'

'He wasn't my friend.'

'From all the signs, and inquiries we've made locally, it looks as though Mrs Anderson was having an affair. The cottage at Craster belonged to a journalist called Lance Stevens. From all accounts he was a bit of a lad. Had a string of women up there over a period of years. But the latest was Mrs Anderson. Latest, and last.'

'What happened?'

Culpeper sighed. 'They made it easy for the killer. They'd been at the pub. Seems like Stevens was late and she'd been waiting for him. Impatient. They left quickly. They were so eager to get to bed back at the cottage they didn't even lock the door. They were in bed when they died. The killer came in, walked up the stairs and discharged a shotgun at Mrs Anderson. Then the gun was turned on Stevens. Quite messy.' A shadow touched his sad eyes. '*Very* messy, in fact.'

'When did it happen?'

'Couple of nights ago. We'll get precise times when the pathologist's had a chance to deal with it. What we do know is that it all happened in the late evening. And after her husband left this office last Friday.'

Arnold stared at the Detective-Inspector. 'You're not suggesting—'

'I'm suggesting nothing at this stage. But the facts are that Mrs Anderson and her lover are dead, and your friend Kevin has taken leave of absence, without getting permission from the Director of the department in which he works. Moreover, no one seems to know where the hell Mr

Anderson has gone. Now it's imperative we get in touch with him. Where did he say he was going, Mr Landon?'

'He said nothing about leave at all. His conversation was . . . limited. He said nothing of importance—'

'What would you regard important?' Culpeper said quickly.

Arnold sighed in exasperation. 'I meant nothing significant. It was small talk—the kind of talk you can't even remember afterwards. The weather. The job. I don't know. His visit to this office was just—unremarkable.'

'I can't agree. It seems it was the last chat he had with anyone before he went on his . . . holiday.'

'You can't seriously believe—'

Culpeper's features were lugubrious. His pipe had gone out again. 'I haven't formed any beliefs about this case yet, Mr Landon. I said it's imperative we get in touch with Mr Anderson. If only to tell him what's happened to his wife. Maybe he doesn't know. I gather he's a bit of a walker, isn't he?'

'I wouldn't know,' Arnold said stubbornly.

'Yes. That's right. You don't know him very well. He just comes to talk to you before he disappears. Coincidence. Well, I hear from others in the office that he's a fell walker. His wife didn't go with him much, it seems. Maybe she preferred indoor pursuits. But it could be, you see, that he's gone off innocently enough on the hills, could be miles from anywhere, out of touch, no newspapers, no radio, and maybe he doesn't know that his wife's dead, murdered.' Culpeper hesitated. 'Did he say anything to you about this character Lance Stevens?'

'I've never even heard of Lance Stevens. And I can't imagine why Kevin Anderson would want to talk to me about him.'

'Aye. Well . . .' Culpeper rose, walked across to the window and opened it. He tapped out the ashes from his pipe, let them fall to the car park below. He stared out across the roofs of Morpeth, moodily, for a little while, then turned to look back at Arnold. 'Aye, we'll leave it like that, then, for the moment. Mrs Anderson's had her face shot away and her lover was also killed. Mr Anderson's disappeared, no one knows where. He came to see you before he left—but you've no recollection of the conversation you had. He seemed preoccupied, but he never had much to say for himself anyway. Is that about it, Mr Landon?'

'That's all there is, Detective-Inspector Culpeper.'

Culpeper stared at him thoughtfully, with sad eyes. 'I reckon, bonny lad, that if anything else occurs to you, you'll be letting us know.'

'There's nothing else I can say, Inspector.'

'And when Mr Anderson gets in touch—'

Arnold bridled. 'I've told you. We're not particular friends. There's no reason why he should get in touch.'

Culpeper held up both hands, palms facing Arnold. 'Aye, you said that. So if he gets in touch with you, like, I imagine you'll be letting us know.'

'It's unlikely he'll contact me.'

Culpeper sighed. He had a funny feeling about this one. 'Aye. But you never know, bonny lad. You never know.'

CHAPTER 3

1

Jane Wilson didn't mind working with her uncle. She had always been fond of him, and he had been good to her, treating her as a daughter rather than a niece. When he had suffered his heart attack she had been only too pleased to come along to the Quayside and help run the business. It began as an act of affection, but she quite enjoyed the atmosphere as well.

She regarded herself as an independent woman. She had taken a degree in sociology at university, but had quickly found that it was not regarded as a particularly marketable product in the matter of employment. She had drifted from one job to another, working as a personal assistant, spending a period as a clerk in local government, then as a researcher in the House of Commons library, but it was during a slack period, and out of a sense of boredom, that she had written her first novel.

She had been on holiday in Scotland, near Oban, at an isolated farmhouse near Taynuilt and had read an historical novel that so incensed her with its incompetence and inaccuracy that she determined she would write a better one in a matter of weeks. She regarded herself as being fortunate, thereafter: the publishers to whom she'd sent it announced they liked it, subject to certain revisions—which she was glad to put in hand—and from that point onwards she realized she had discovered what she wanted to do.

A stream of historical novels had followed. They were successful—not so much as to move her into the bestseller lists, and none had been filmed, but successful enough to provide her with a steady income and a regular fanmail. The latter was flattering, but hardly necessary to her ego; the money was most welcome. The best part of it all, however, was the freedom and independence it gave her, and the chance to do something she really enjoyed doing: historical research.

She had been able to surround herself at home in Framwellgate Moor with erudite and rather less than erudite books about the Middle Ages. Her library was crammed with historical biographies and accounts of royal personages; they jostled side by side with social histories and historical journals. She had a reasonable collection of items from Selden, and had indulged herself with some eighteenth- and nineteenth-century treatises. But her main interest lay in the Middle Ages: it was a time so different from that in which she lived, though the passions and motives that inspired the characters in her books differed not a great deal from those that moved people in the twentieth century.

Perhaps that was what made her books so successful. Readers liked the potted history she provided, but were also able to identify with the individuals who peopled her pages. Her fanmail exclaimed she brought the past to life. If that was really so, she was happy, for the past lived for her. Hours spent poring over dusty volumes were well spent for Jane; the writing itself was arduous, though she could lose herself in it, and she never failed to feel the spark of excitement when the new book arrived in its pristine dustjacket from the publishers.

So the Quayside bookshop was in fact a bonus. It was an idiosyncratic collection of volumes, relying much upon Ben Gibson's own interests and tastes, but they were not far distant from her own, and she was able to pursue some of her own historical research while she actually worked in the shop. She constantly came across volumes she could use and spent a great deal of time merely browsing in the shop, during the many quiet times that occurred there.

The other bonus was meeting Arnold Landon.

There were times when she was not sure it really was a bonus. They had met at Harlech, in circumstances that were not conducive to friendship, and there were certainly times when he infuriated her. On the other hand, she recognized in him a true original, an eccentric whose passion for wood and stone had rounded his character, developed his mind, and sharpened his intellect. She was certain a great deal of the information he held in his head was of little practical value, yet he had the capacity to surprise her with the breadth and extent of his knowledge. He also possessed a remarkable understanding of people—perhaps because, like her, the past lived for him and he realized that the person who does not know the past cannot fully understand the present. His reticence, shyness and lack of forcefulness annoyed her; she felt there were occasions when he should be more positive, but perhaps that was a reflection of her own innate independence of mind rather than a true criticism of his personality.

Her own life had been enriched by knowing him, but she would certainly be the last to tell him so. As for Ben Gibson, she sometimes suspected he knew exactly how she felt, and was amazed by the knowledge. And yet, basically, how did she feel? It was a question that confused her, and she pushed it to the back of her mind.

She had not objected to helping Arnold over the issue of the brochure, and his account of the painting at Temple Barden had interested her. Ben had been right: it was an opportunity to seize. Her books were often sparked by incidents or issues that came to her attention—sometimes modern issues that could be woven into an historical framework. And this one—the mysterious painting, the Crusader background, the romantic violence of the Knights Templar and the thunder of their fall—it was a theme that she could use, if only she could do more work on the background, and let her imagination wander, then people it with real historical characters.

It was what made her books sell.

'I called in at the *Journal* offices as you asked me,' Ben Gibson said as he shuffled through to the back room. 'They were able to give me photocopies of the articles you asked for. Lynne Anderson.' He squinted quizzically at Jane over his half-rim glasses. 'She was the woman who was found murdered at Seahouses. I hope that's not the reason for your interest. Ghoulish, if it is.'

'You know me better than that,' Jane replied. 'No, it's just that when Arnold told us about the Temple Barden painting, I realized I might be able to use it, fictionally.'

'So our Mr Landon *is* of some use after all, then,' Ben remarked, grinning.

'Occasionally,' Jane replied primly. 'Anyway, when he mentioned that some articles on the tower houses and their ghosts had already appeared in the *Journal* I thought I

might as well have a look at them. Save some research time
—if I can avoid the journalese.'

'*Ghosts of Old Northumberland*,' Ben read aloud as he
thumbed his way through the sheaf of photocopies. 'Trashy
enough title. So what's she got here? Chipchase, Langley,
the Lord Crewe, the Grey Monk of the Old Rectory and
the White Lady of Tarset—she did a fair bit of chasing
around, anyway. But all old hat stuff, I would guess.'

Jane nodded. 'Monks, howling dogs, rattling chains,
walking ladies in white and prowling monks in grey. There
might be something there, anyway. Is this the whole lot?'

Ben Gibson shrugged. 'It's what's been published up to
now. I asked them whether the series had been finished.
Apparently not. She was still to turn in material on Brunskill and Warkworth, but it would seem that they won't
deal with those now, in view of the circumstances.'

'Are they not going to get someone else to finish the
series?'

'I don't think so. It's had a five-week run, and the impression I got was that they'd been thinking of cutting it off
soon anyway—Lynne Anderson had been trying to push
them for further space but they'd been reluctant. It'll be
killed now—along with the author.' Ben paused. 'There
were two of them up at Seahouses. It's all the gossip up at
the newspaper offices. It seems the man's been identified
as one Lance Stevens, a reporter on the *Journal*. Lynne
Anderson was a freelance, they met on the paper and an
affair started.'

'With two journalists killed I can imagine the newspaper
will be throwing the headlines about.'

'That's right. It seems Stevens was working on some
information he'd picked up about the riots at North Shields
and Tyneside recently. He was going to do a piece on the
Meadow Wells estate, and the criminal families that were
dumped there. They suggest up at the offices that it could
be one of the gangs felt he was getting too close, so decided

to put an end to it and make an example of him. And then there's the husband.'

'Is he suspected?' Jane asked.

'Well, he's incommunicado, apparently. The police want to interview him. There'll be a piece about it in the *Evening Chronicle* tonight. Incidentally, he works up at Morpeth—and guess in which department.'

Jane widened her eyes. 'Not in Arnold's!'

'The very same.' Ben shook his head. 'I wonder if Arnold knew him?'

'I hardly think so. He's been in the department only a matter of weeks.'

'Mmmm. Anyway, fetching these articles for you led to an interesting half-hour's gossip. I hope the photocopies themselves are equally as interesting for you.'

Jane grimaced. 'Well, I'll read through these in due course, and see if there's anything that I can use.'

Ben was still looking at one of the sheets. 'There's the Tarset Treasure,' he suggested. 'Sounds sufficiently women's magazine mystery for one of your books.'

Jane ignored the friendly barb. 'What was the treasure?'

Ben scanned the article carefully. 'Hah. It's a booboo. Can't say. Our deceased author backs off from describing it: says it's worth a bomb, but can't say what, or where, it is. Not much detail because there isn't any detail in the records. The article spends more time really on the ghost story—the White Lady. Seems she was a maidservant—'

'Spare me,' Jane groaned theatrically. 'It's got to involve rape and murder.'

'You've guessed!'

'Couldn't anyone? The hallmarks of Victorian melodrama.'

'Cup of tea?'

'I wouldn't say no.'

The afternoon sun was slanting through the narrow windows of the bookshop, and dust danced in the beams as Ben Gibson passed through to the kitchen at the back. Jane sat with her chin cupped in her hands, staring out towards the window. There was the muted sound of traffic from the Quayside, lorries rumbling past to the site at Pandon where luxury flats were now being built on the river frontage, with a view down the curve of the Tyne and across to the Gateshead bank. She liked the atmosphere down here; the river still held the past on its banks, the great shipping companies, the coal staithes that had served the Victorian south, the mercantile houses that jostled their tall, splendidly-built shoulders one against another, the house from which the coal merchant's daughter had fled to marry her lover, destined to become Lord High Chancellor of England.

She looked down again to the photograph that Arnold had left with her. It fascinated her. The Quayside that stretched below the twelfth-century Norman keep held its eighteenth- and nineteenth-century echoes but this photograph stirred other, more ancient leaves. The face that stared out from the photograph was a depiction drawn across centuries, and the unknown artist had put all the pathos and passion that he could into the portrait.

Yet it wasn't only the face that interested her. The background was shadowy and ill-formed, a curiously inarticulate statement. Possibly, the state of the painting had deteriorated, been varnished over and lost its original colours, but somehow she doubted it. Rather, she was left with the impression that the artist made the background deliberately hazy, vague, unformed so as to emphasize the importance of the Christ image in the foreground.

There were some details to be seen, but they were difficult to make out.

Ben Gibson shuffled back in with the teapot and two mugs. 'No saucers,' he said.

'I don't drink out of saucers,' she replied.

'You miss one of the greatest pleasures in life. You poring over that photograph still?'

'Mmmm. Ben, do we have any books on heraldry?'

He spread his hands wide in an expansive, proprietorial gesture. 'In this emporium of good taste, all things are possible. Second stack, top shelf on the right.' He stirred some sugar into his mug, and glanced over her shoulder at the photograph. 'What you after?'

She pointed with her finger. 'You see, just here. There's a sort of faded coat of arms in the corner here. A motto. Can't really make out the words, and the armorial bearings themselves have been either varnished almost into oblivion or they were never prominently painted anyway.'

'I see them. Just. Odd thing to put in a religious painting, really.'

'Put there to please the patron, maybe,' Jane suggested. 'And then there's this peculiar barring just here. Like a sort of trellis. What's that supposed to mean?'

'Trellis?' Ben Gibson wrinkled his nose in thought. His heavy-lidded eyes were half closed, so that he looked more like a little frog than ever. 'Trelliswork. That rings a bell . . . Now what is it?'

Jane sipped at her mug of tea and watched her uncle as he dredged back into the cluttered recesses of his mind. She smiled; she was very fond of Ben, and she in no sense resented his teasing. And in spite of his age, his mind was sharp. His eyes opened wide suddenly, and as he caught her smile, he returned it.

'Ahah!' he said.

'What does that mean?'

'Something very interesting. Particularly for the owner of the Old Rectory.'

'Tell me.'

'You remember when Arnold was here, we were talking about the Knights Templar. And the matter of the Holy Grail was mentioned. The fact that mediæval literature might have confused the Grail with a casket that held the blood and sweat of Christ. An interleaving of legend and history and faith. Now I've read somewhere . . . yes, that's right. The theory goes something like this . . .'

Jane waited while Ben collected his thoughts.

'The winding sheet in which Jesus was wrapped was spirited away. It was discovered to contain His image—the thing we see on the Shroud of Turin. It was therefore saved, venerated, and occasionally exhibited in Eastern Turkey for the faithful to worship.'

'A practice which in due course the Church of Rome objected to,' Jane murmured.

'That's right. But of course, cloth is a relatively delicate thing. It can wear, be damaged—indeed, there are some signs that the Shroud of Turin was at some time or another affected by fire. However . . . since the cloth could quite easily be damaged on display, it was necessary to construct a casket in which it could be secreted. Folded.'

'That makes sense.'

'The method of folding was also important.'

'Why? For preservation purposes?'

Ben Gibson shook his head. 'Not only that. Think of it. If you have a shroud, which contains the image of Christ, and you want to display it—in its totality—how would you do it?'

'You'd have to hang it in a prominent place where it could be seen by all the congregation.'

'Would you position it before the worshippers come in to view it?'

Jane shrugged. 'I suppose so.'

Ben Gibson beamed fondly at her. 'When you write your books, do you tell your story straight through, chronologically? And do you reveal all the facts at once?'

'Well, no, because for dramatic impact and to maintain the interest—'

'You reveal it bit by bit. Exactly. Dramatic impact. But it wouldn't be very dramatic if the Shroud was just hanging there when people began to file 'in. Besides, the early accounts suggest that worshippers saw Christ actually rising, as it were from the tomb!'

Jane frowned. 'You mean they revealed the Shroud, slowly, bit by bit?'

Ben Gibson grimaced and lifted his shoulders uncertainly. 'We can't be sure. But it seems that the cloth could have been folded, with one end supported, maybe by a wooden bar which could be hoisted aloft. The first part of the service would be held—then gradually from the casket would emerge the head of Christ. The Shroud, hauled up gradually by pulleys.'

Jane stared at Ben. She could visualize the scene: a darkened temple, chanting voices, incense drifting in the air, an illuminated altar and the slow emergence of the features of Christ, as though rising from the tomb. A shiver touched her—she could imagine the sensation that would have been experienced by the worshippers, in the overcharged, electrical atmosphere of the darkened, mystical temple.

'As the service proceeded the cloth would be further unfolded and not only the head, but also the body of Christ would appear until finally He would be there, erect, suspended in full view of the worshipping throng.'

'Marvellous.'

'A fine piece of theatre,' Ben said drily.

Jane frowned. 'But what are you driving at?'

'The casket. The box in which traditionally the Shroud was folded. It has always been depicted as being made to a particular design. And the accounts that have come down to us speak of just that design.'

Jane glanced from Ben to the photograph and back again. 'A trellis pattern.'

'Exactly so.'

Jane stared at the photograph. The trellis pattern was vaguely delineated but could be made out. It was placed in one corner of the painting, but it served no artistic purpose that she could envisage. On the other hand, it could be there as a symbol or as a message. It could mean that the painting was to be regarded not simply as another painting of Christ, but as a direct link with the Shroud that had been

exhibited over the centuries as the image of Christ, formed
of His blood and His sweat and His pain.

'As you suggested, Ben, this would be of great interest to
the owner of the Old Rectory,' she said.

And there was still the puzzle of the armorial bearings
painted faintly in the right-hand corner. Jane collected the
books on heraldry from the shelf Ben had pointed out. She
took them to a far corner of the bookshop, near the window,
where she could work undisturbed. For the next few hours
she thumbed her way through the records until her mind
was spinning with gules and bar sinisters and argents. She
remained none the wiser.

The doorbell to the shop tinkled from time to time, and
she was aware of the low murmur of voices as Ben dealt
with the odd customer who visited the shop. The light was
beginning to fail when she finally closed the last of the
three books. Ben was locking up. She rose, stretched aching
muscles and took the books back to their prescribed shelves.

'Any good?'

'Not really. 'She'd answered before she realized who had
spoken. She turned in surprise. It was Arnold Landon. He
stood there awkwardly, one of the Anderson photocopies in
his hand. 'What are you doing here?' she demanded.'
'You're never away from the Quayside these days.'

'Just finishing off some work in the library. I called in
when I'd completed it, and Ben told me you'd been looking
at the heraldry materials.'

She was oddly reluctant to admit her interest in the story
he had told her. She sniffed disparagingly. 'Well, I've
wasted an afternoon on it all and got nowhere—nothing I
can really use in a book.'

Arnold hesitated. 'I got here half an hour ago. I didn't
want to disturb you. Ben's suggested the three of us should
go for a meal this evening, to the Red House.'

She shrugged. 'Suits me.'

'I waited until you'd finished with the books. In the

meanwhile I looked at those articles from the *Journal*, the ones by Lynne Anderson.'

'Yes?'

'There's some sketches of heraldic devices there.' He glanced at the sheet in his hand. 'I've seen them before, though, in the library. They've been copied from *Havelock*. Mrs Anderson clearly took her researches seriously: she must have read the old accounts of Northumberland ghosts in *Havelock* and elsewhere, taken what illustrations she wanted, then visited the sites themselves to get background information and interviews from the owners. I wonder— this is the coat of arms carried by the de Bohuns. I haven't got a copy of the Temple Barden photograph—I left it with you. Is it the same coat of arms?'

He was holding out the relevant article. Jane stared at it for a moment and then went back to her desk to retrieve the photograph. Together they bent over it, scrutinizing the faint image on the painting and comparing it with that in the newspaper article.

'Difficult,' Arnold murmured.

'Wait a minute.' Jane went back to the shelves, drew down one of the heraldic books and riffled through the index. 'The de Bohuns.'

She turned to the relevant page. There was a full colour depiction of the ancient armorial bearings. They stared at the picture.

'It's similar,' Jane said slowly.

'But not the same.'

The phoenix on the crest was the same, its jaws gaping, wings spread. The black dragons supporting the shield with their forked tongues and tails and glaring eyes were the same. The crested helmet surmounting the shield in the sketch was very similar in design to that shown in the heraldic book.

'But these were fairly common features,' Arnold suggested.

'That's right. Standard stuff in lots of armorial bearings.

I suppose they all employed the same artist for many of the arms. And later ones copied from previous arrangements. It's the detail of the shield below which usually differs.'

'And it does here.' Arnold traced the pattern of the design of the shield. There were similarities but they were not immediately striking. 'Of course, over the centuries one would expect certain changes. Artists would embellish . . .'

'But there's something in particular that's missing,' Jane pointed out.

'The bars.'

'That's right.'

The arrangement of horizontal bars on the de Bohun shield was missing on the shield in the painting. It gave an entirely different perspective to the shield itself, and made the two undeniably different. Yet both Jane and Arnold felt that the similarities between the shields were such that if the bars were to be replaced the armorial bearings would be a close match.

'Let's try it,' Arnold suggested.

Using the sketch in the newspaper article, he drew a rough series of bars across the relevant part of the shield. The results were not impressive.

'Stick to wood and stone and don't try art,' Jane advised.

'Doesn't look too good, does it?' Arnold admitted.

'But . . .' Jane wrinkled her brow. 'They could be the de Bohun arms, if only the bars were in place. Talking of which—' She picked up the photograph and inspected it again. 'What about these bars here?'

Arnold had noticed them previously. The faint tracery of bars in the background to the Christ head, seeming to serve no artistic or practical purpose. If they had been transposed, on a different scale, and placed on the shield, they could just possibly have fitted to make the shield on the painting a representation of the de Bohun arms.

'But why would anyone want to do that?' Jane questioned. 'What's the point of removing the bars from the de

Bohun shield and have them floating around elsewhere in the painting?'

Arnold shook his head. 'Hardly artistic licence. Maybe ignorance. I don't know. Maybe we're trying to force something here. The shield is most probably someone else's heraldic device, one we've not come across yet, or maybe it's just a piece of fiction. I can't see what purpose—'

'Symbolism, my dear boy,' Ben Gibson rumbled just behind them. 'The trouble with young people today—and measured against me I count you in that category, Arnold —is that they don't seem to realize everything doesn't have to be clear-cut and in black and white to mean anything. You should know better, Arnold: meanings can be derived from symbols, like Christianity from the Fish. Is there a fish in the painting?'

Arnold stared at him, and then at the painting itself. 'No, not at all.'

'There is on the menu at the Red House,' Ben announced cheerfully. 'And that's what I'll be having this evening. And then, over dinner, if you wish I'll give you a history of symbolism.'

2

By Saturday afternoon Arnold reckoned he had obtained all the information he was likely to need to complete the brochure for Ben Edwards. There were still some points he would have liked to spend more time on, to confirm his thoughts, and he would have liked to pay a visit to the ruins at Brunskill but with the kind of pressure Edwards had placed on him time was against it. Moreover, he had had a second interview with the man and did not relish a third.

Edwards had suddenly appeared in his office late on Friday afternoon.

He came barging into the room without bothering to knock. Arnold was alone, and he looked up in annoyance at the interruption to see the stocky, belligerent frame of the Director of the Tourist Board standing impatiently in front of him.

'Hello, Mr Edwards,' Arnold greeted him reluctantly.

Edwards was uninterested in such civilities. 'Have you finished the brochure?' he demanded.

'You gave me ten days,' Arnold protested. He gestured ineffectually at the pile of notes on his desk, the drawings scattered on the floor beside him, where he could look at them while he wrote. 'I'm still pulling the stuff together.'

'Time is money, damn it! I had to come in to County Hall for a meeting, so I stopped here to find out if by any chance you'd finished ahead of schedule. It seems I've wasted my time. Just what the hell is holding you up?'

'I explained to you when we met at Allendale,' Arnold replied stiffly. He did not like the aggressive Ben Edwards. 'The work Kevin Anderson did was incomplete. And inaccurate. I've verified that now. I have my notes ready, and I'll be able to work on them further at the weekend. Once I've rearranged them. That's what I'm doing now. With luck—and without too many interruptions—I should be able to let you have the typescript by Monday or Tuesday. It won't be the world's best prose—'

'I don't give a damn whether it's Hemingway or Shakespeare as long as I can tell that Savage woman the brochure's finished and she can release the funds she's promised us.' Edwards glared at him, breathing heavily, then fished in his pocket for a moment, to draw out a pack of cigarillos. He lit one, with no regard for any objection Arnold might make.

There was a tremor in his hand when he struck the match; vaguely, Arnold stared at him in a certain surprise. He was now accustomed to Edward's belligerence, but he had not expected to see signs of strain. Edwards was clearly under some pressure, a feeling of tension: perhaps the brochure was even more important to him than Arnold had assumed.

Or maybe there was something else on his mind, bothering him.

To break the uneasy silence, Arnold said, 'I think I'm going to be able to prove that the tower houses were at the very least heavily influenced by an architect—or master mason as they called them in those days—called Henry Yvele. Traditionally, some of these buildings have been regarded as the work of John Lewyn, but—'

'This'll be in the brochure?' Edwards interrupted sourly, cutting Arnold short as though uninterested in detail of his research.

'Of course.'

'That should please Miss Savage. If we can claim it's original research, maybe she'll be inclined to stump up more than the forty thousand.' He eyed Arnold uncertainly, and picked a flake of tobacco from his lower lip. His thoughts seemed to be elsewhere, wandering away from the brochure, yet dragged back to it. 'It is original, this research?'

The question was almost automatic, delivered in a flat monotone; it was as though Edwards was not really interested in the answer, for his eyes were vacant, his manner edgy. Arnold was silent for a moment. He nodded. 'It's been regarded as debatable, but I think I can prove—'

'Good,' Edwards said, a certain crispness returning to his tone. 'I shall make the point to Miss Savage.' He drew on his cigarillo, squinting at Arnold through the blue smoke, and his mouth twisted unpleasantly. 'But I still expect that bloody deadline to be kept. I can't take any chances.'

Arnold made no reply. He had already made the promise.

A short silence grew between them, the smoke haze growing about Edwards's head as the man stood there staring at Arnold grimly. Arnold was even more of the view that Ben Edwards seemed to have come to this office for some reason other than the brochure. His dismissive manner, his harping on issues that had already been agreed upon, suggested he was under some kind of pressure that was bothering him, making him behave in an uncharacteristic, irresolute manner.

Ben Edwards continued to eye him grimly for a few moments, and drew on his small cigar. He bared his teeth, forced the smoke through them and turned away towards the window. With his back to Arnold, he suddenly asked, 'Have you heard from Kevin Anderson?'

Surprised at the sudden turn in the conversation, Arnold said nothing. Edwards looked back over his shoulder: his eyes were sharp, cold anger accumulating in their depths. 'Well?'

'I wouldn't expect to hear from Anderson.'

'Why not?'

'He's on holiday —'

'I understand he's a friend of yours.'

Arnold sighed in exasperation. 'I don't know how that *canard* got about the office. I hardly know the man.'

Ben Edwards glowered. 'He didn't make friends easily. He was a silent son of a bitch, withdrawn, deep. Difficult to get anything out of him. But to a friend —'

'You seem to know him better than I do,' Arnold observed quietly.

Edwards's mouth twisted in a sudden, bitter anger. 'You could say our paths have crossed.' He paused, as old hatreds and old losses washed over his mind. 'You could even say we had certain things in common. But the story I get here in the office is that you and he struck up a friendship. He used to come in here and have a coffee with you.'

Arnold's exasperation almost boiled over. Why on earth was this regarded as important by so many people? Arnold shook his head. 'There were a few occasions, but —'

'What did he say about Lynne?'

Arnold sat stock still. There was an urgency in Edwards's manner that underscored his normal belligerence, gave it a fragility that suggested nervousness and uncertainty. Arnold stared at the man; the tremor was back in his right hand. Arnold shook his head. 'Lynne—that was his wife? He never mentioned her. I didn't even know her name, until it was reported in the newspapers.'

'You know she was murdered!' The words rushed out, viciously, overscored with anger. And yet there was something false about the vehemence, as though Edwards was forcing it, even playing some theatrical game, acting a part for Arnold's benefit, rehearsing a passion he did not really feel.

'So I understand.' Arnold thought of Detective-Inspector Culpeper's visit, but made no comment about it.

'The bastard killed her, you know. Her, and the man with her. He must be crazy—what did he expect her to do? She was a red-blooded woman, too much for him to handle. So he pulled the trigger on them both. And then went off like a rabbit to the bloody hills.' Edwards's tone was bitter. 'He can't stay out of sight for ever, though. They'll get him. I always said—'

He broke off, and puffed angrily at his cigar. Arnold waited. Edwards squinted suspiciously at him. 'I suppose you knew nothing about this man they found with her, either?'

'How could I?' Arnold grew annoyed. 'I keep telling you and others, Kevin Anderson was an acquaintance, not a friend. He didn't confide in me—he told me nothing about his wife, nor anything else of consequence—'

'The bastard didn't confide in anyone, I guess. But he must have known, must have guessed she was having an affair with that bastard Stevens.' Edwards made an exasperated stabbing gesture with his cigarillo. 'What the hell got into her? A wastrel like that—she must have known she was the end of a long line. And if Anderson had known about it, you'd have thought he would have wanted to talk—'

Determinedly, Arnold continued. 'He came in here to have coffee with me because I think he felt ill at ease with other people in the office. Maybe they knew more about him than he wished; maybe there had been rumours about his wife, I really don't know. But my impression is he came here because he was lonely and troubled, and wanted just to sit and have an inconsequential chat, perhaps to take his mind off things. But all that's mere supposition: I don't know what I say is right, I'm merely guessing. And that's with the benefit of hindsight. The fact of his wife's death . . . the exposure of her affair . . .' Anger crept into Arnold's tone. 'But he never really talked to me; I can't even remember what we talked about. It was nothing. It was unimportant. It was small talk. And I wish people would stop asking me about it, or implying there was a friendship between us. There wasn't. There was *nothing.*'

Edwards had reddened at Arnold's outburst. He stared at him as though he was seeing him in a new light. There was doubt in his eyes, a greater uncertainty as though he felt he had made some kind of mistake in coming in to speak with Arnold. His edginess increased; his hand was still shaking.

Arnold took a deep breath. 'I don't understand your interest in the murder of Mrs Anderson and her lover, Mr Edwards. But I can't help you in any way. Is there anything else you want from me?' Arnold waited, coldly. When Edwards made no reply, he went on, 'Because if there isn't, I'd appreciate your leaving me to get on with your brochure. It's *your* deadline, not mine. And if I can't have peace to continue with it, I'll not get it finished in time.'

Ben Edwards glared at Arnold uncertainly. He frowned, the pugnacity washed out of him for the moment as he struggled with thoughts he was unwilling to express. Recovering, some of the steel came back into his voice. He dropped the half-smoked cigar to the carpeted floor, contemptuously and ground it beneath his heel. His lip twisted as he stared at Arnold, almost daring him to object. 'You'll get it finished, Mr Landon. You'll get it finished, or I'll have your bloody head!'

He strode from the room, banging the door behind him.

And Arnold was none the wiser as to why Ben Edwards had really been motivated to visit him here in the office. He had the feeling it had nothing to do with the brochure he'd promised for Monday.

Rather, it was more likely to do with the murder of Lynne Anderson and her lover Lance Stevens.

There was a book in it. Jane was convinced of that now.

She had pored over the heraldic arms, and the photograph of the painting and she had been stirred. Slowly, she had let her imagination take over the images, wind them into a theme, of love and death and chivalry, a lost inheritance, the clash of arms, a young girl's emergence into womanhood and the man who fulfilled her dreams. An outcast, presumed illegitimate, unrecognized by his lordly father. A secret marriage: the turbulent years of Henry II, the faithless, murderous housekeeper, the wrongly outlawed villein who nursed the secret of the household from the deep recesses of the wild greenwood.

Yes, there was a book in it.

But she was not yet clear how she could work in the theme of the painting and the Holy Shroud, if she was to use them at all. She had become accustomed, in planning her fiction, to being roused by an event or a building or a person, fired to the preparation of a narrative, only to find that later the original impetus faded into the background as new ideas and fresh themes took over from the original charge.

But location was important. When she had written her earlier novels, they had been well received for the careful m..nner in which she had depicted the backgrounds. Critics —and her fanmail—suggested that is was the people and the backgrounds that breathed life into her historical romances. So she had always made a point of visiting the scenes she wrote about.

It had been on such a visit, to Harlech, that she had first met Arnold Landon.

She sniffed.

Despite his protestations, she felt he had a certain view of her work that annoyed her. She had no pretensions to intellectual stature or to being a great writer; she was merely a competent hack who enjoyed her work.

And historical research was important to her. If Arnold felt her research was of a lower order than his because of the use to which she put it, that was his problem. It rankled with her, but it also made her more determined to ensure that he would never be able to find historical fault in her books.

Not that he read them, anyway. She was almost sure of that, even though he had certainly known her name when they met.

'So, you off out, then?' Ben Gibson inquired when she took down her anorak and put it on over the light sweater she wore.

'You'll not need me in the bookshop this afternoon,' she replied. 'I'm going to take a drive; have a wander around some of the tower house sites Arnold's visited.'

'Checking on his work?' Ben Gibson asked mischievously.

'Doing my own research, for my own reasons—and nothing to do with Mr Landon,' she replied in a positive tone. 'I should be back in time for a meal this evening—but not before eight, I should think.'

'Drive carefully.'

She did.

She was not a good driver; inclined to be rather too careful, she drove slowly, to the annoyance of others. Their annoyance often pushed her to increase her speed, and that made her nervous. And yet, once she was out on the open, secondary roads west of Newcastle she was able to relax, winding her way through spreading farmland and rising hills, looking north to the lift of the Northumberland hinterland, watching the looping road flex ahead of her through banks of ancient trees, oak and birch and elm, crossing narrow stone bridges once travelled by the packhorse traders, heading deep into the age-old hills and mediæval villages that grew in her mind's eye as she began to lose herself in the past.

At Temple Barden she parked on the hilltop, and sat looking down at the village. She could see the Old Rectory that Arnold had described, and she wove it into her imagination, uncertain yet of the part it would play, but teasing, threading it into a skein of ancient intrigue.

Arnold had also visited Tarset Hall, so she drove there, not to follow in his footsteps but to obtain a view of the location he had described to her and Ben over dinner. When she reached Tarset, she balked, however. She was disappointed that the house was not visible from the road. She made no attempt to enter the driveway, but parked the car in the main road and looked up the drive. Arnold had told them about the house's state of dilapidation, and about its owner, but she did not feel she could simply drive up to the house to gawk.

After a little while she got out of the car, curious. She stood at the entrance to the drive and stared about her. High in the trees above her head a blackbird was in full throat, a joyous sound: birds would have sung in these woods for a thousand years, the undergrowth would have rustled to the passage of deer and boar and badger, lovers would have walked here and perhaps in the moonlight—

The harsh, violent noise of the car horn made her leap to one side in alarm.

Lost in her reverie, she had not heard the approaching Land-Rover until the driver had sounded the horn. It had come to a stop, turning into the driveway, and was now parked there just feet behind her, ready to drive on up to Tarset Hall. There was a man behind the wheel, glaring at her. She stood to one side, pressing herself against the tree bole to make way on the narrow track leading into the driveway.

'Sorry,' she called out sheepishly. She waved, in apology. The man behind the wheel made no reply.

He stared at her fixedly, frowning. Then, slowly, he opened the door of the Land-Rover and stepped down. His hair was grey under his hat; the lividity of the scar on his cheek made her catch her breath. From Arnold's description she recognized the owner of Tarset Hall at once. He stood a little way from her, one hand on the door of the Land-Rover. He was stiff-backed, and surly.

'You lost?'

Jane shook her head.

'This leads to Tarset Hall.'

'I know.'

'It's private property.'

'I know that too. I . . . I was just listening to the birds.' At the inanity of her remark, and incensed at her need to explain herself, she began to bridle. 'I wasn't going up to the Hall. And I've no desire to trespass.'

Major Manners's brow was thunderous. She gained the impression he did not like women. 'Are you from the newspaper?'

'Newspaper?'

'Like that other woman. The one who came here looking for ghosts and treasure and all that rubbish.'

Jane shook her head. 'No. Certainly not. I was just . . . I was just enjoying the drive, soaking up the scenery.' She took a deep breath, taking control of herself. 'It's a lovely part of the world. And not all of it is private property.'

He grunted, somewhat taken aback. He stood there, eyeing her uncertainly, his brow still knitted in an angry frown, and then he turned suddenly, climbed back into the Land-Rover and slammed the door.

Jane remained with her back against the tree bole, waiting for him to drive past her along the track. He made no attempt to do so. Instead, he sat behind the wheel, staring ahead of him fixedly, as if he was no longer aware of her presence. Jane waited, and then, after a few moments she walked past him, trudging back towards her own car. He paid no attention to her as she passed; it was as though he had dismissed her from his conscious mind as he sat there in his Land-Rover, staring ahead of him up the track.

Jane crossed the road to the far verge where her own car was parked. She looked back. The Land-Rover sat there, half turned into the driveway, the exhaust fumes pumping from its rear, the engine turning over rhythmically, the driver making no attempt to move on up the track to the Hall. Then, as she got into her own car Major Manners seemed to make up his mind. Instead of driving on into the track he began to reverse.

Jane watched as he pulled back into the main road and drew almost alongside her. He turned his head to look at her, and his eyes seemed to burn with a suppressed violent panic she could not comprehend. He opened his mouth to say something to her, then thought better of it. He clearly did not care for trespassers at Tarset Hall.

But she had had no intention of trespassing.

She shrugged. The gears clashed as he put the Land-Rover into first. The scar showed livid against his darkened skin. He drove on, past the entrance to his home, and vanished around the bend ahead. In a little while she saw the Land-Rover climb the hill ahead of her and vanish over the brow, among the trees.

Her heart was pounding. She could not explain to herself why she had been frightened. The man had every right to ask what she was doing at the entrance to his home. But his attitude was odd; the coiled ferocity in his glance had shaken her. He was a man with problems—but they were none of her business. She started her own car and drove slowly on, heading in the same direction the irascible Major Manners had taken.

At Barden village, three miles further on, she stopped. She felt vaguely shaken by her brief encounter with Major Manners, and though annoyed with herself for what she saw as a display of feminine weakness, she parked in the narrow main street of the village and entered the only tea-shop for afternoon tea. The village was a small one, its only claim to fame being the pretty little stream and stone bridge that bisected the tiny huddle of houses; it had probably been a mediæval aberration in the first instance, in view of the ancient importance of its sister village at Temple Barden, perhaps a landowner's desire to enlarge his self-esteem by encouraging farmworkers to live there. But life had largely passed it by and the teashop was dingy and ill-frequented.

The owner was pleasant enough, however, a round-faced, ample-bosomed woman who served a good pot of tea and reasonably fresh scones. She was also sufficiently sensitive to move back behind her counter when it was clear Jane had no desire to indulge in small talk, so Jane was able to sip her tea, calm down, and move again mentally into the ancient realms she had been exploring in her mind. She sat there, and dreamed, and plotted, and sipped a second cup of tea.

It was well after five when she left the village. She drove west, climbing into the hills until she found a track that took her left, through a copse to the crest of Reivers Crags. She parked, and walked the sandy track to the top of the crags themselves.

In the far, hazy distance she could make out the outline of the Cheviot hills shimmering in the late afternoon, tipped by the dying glow of the sun with a bronze sheen. Nearer to hand the green and brown patchwork of fields, white-dotted with sheep, broke up the landscape, emphasizing the swell and roll of the land, and then directly below her, stationed on the rocky outcrop that commanded the valley below, was the ruined pile of Brunskill Castle.

The Victorians had tried to build ruins like that. Gaunt, stark walls that overlooked a valley rich in eerie, mist-drifted woodland. Stone pillars among which jackdaws nested, vast unglazed windows through which kestrels and swifts swooped, dark, fire-hardened beams where bats could hang. Shadowed hallways where owls flew silently at night. There was a haze about Brunskill, the distancing of the ruins from their modern existence by a shadowy veil of history. The eleventh-century structure had been battered and smashed in the fifteenth, but its ruins retained a dignity, and an eerie menace that reflected the powerful structure it had once been, and the influence it had exerted over its surroundings.

She looked at it and saw it as a sleeping giant, a hall of kings who merely slumbered, to come again. And perhaps they could come again, in her imagination and in her book. Jane sat down on the crag and stared and dreamed and wondered.

Gradually the light faded.

The Cheviots lingered a while, ghostly, and distant until they withdrew into their hazy cloaks. The woodland darkened and the fields faded. Distant winking lights began to sprinkle the valley below Brunskill. The ruined walls themselves grew black and menacing, powerful, defiant fingers raised to the sky, but Jane was able to clothe the walls with damask again, restore the ruins in her mind's eye, people the darkening sward with men and horses, recall the trample of feet, the jingling of curb chains, the echoing calls of command. The darkness grew about her but the air was warm, the light breeze soft as it whispered old stories through the copse below her and she almost imagined she could hear voices, pick out ancient chants, bring back long-lost religious fears and fervours that had stirred men down there in the ancient castle.

Suddenly, she was cold.

At one moment she had been lost in a dream, mental images coursing through her brain, identifying the man who would stride through her pages, seeing the pride of the woman who would dominate his life and actions, staring at the imagined landscape in which their destinies would be interwoven towards the climax of their existence in the dying pages of her novel.

The next moment it was different: the half-heard voices had faded, the breeze was chill, mediæval chants had gone, and she was alone on Reivers Crags, the darkness was about her with a cold hand, and something had disturbed her, broken her reverie.

She started, sat up more stiffly.

She looked about her, shaken in an unaccountable fashion. She was uncertain what had disturbed her—perhaps an animal, the harsh cry of a gliding owl in the predatory darkness. Her skin was cold, tingling, and the hairs on the nape of her neck had risen.

Slowly she stood up, easing her stiffened joints. Her brow was furrowed, her heart beating unevenly. She looked down the hill from the crag, towards the ruins of Brunskill. The regal power, the menace of arms she had recognized earlier had changed: now there was an eeriness about the ruins that seemed to spell corruption and danger and the dark fingers of stone that reached up to the sky seemed clawlike, the horrid detritus of a half-destroyed evil. Even as the thought crossed her mind, she saw the flash of light among the ruins.

She froze.

It was the light that had disturbed her, brought her back to the reality of the cold hillside and the lonely crag. Among the broken stones of the ancient pile of Brunskill Castle someone moved secretly, flashlight in hand, hidden by darkness and careful of intent.

Chilled by an unreasoning fear in her veins, Jane stepped back from the edge of the crag. Her heart had begun to hammer, and though she told herself there was nothing to fear, that if someone wished to prowl through castle ruins a hundred feet below her that was their business, and no danger to her, she was still shaking when she turned and began to make her way back to the car.

It was the kind of terror she had felt sometimes in her childhood, she reasoned, when dark creakings in the old house could make her start up out of sleep at night, sweating and shaking with an almost hysterical fear.

But then she had been a child, gripped by an over-active

imagination. Now she was a woman, playing up her own fears when she had been lost, dreaming of a fictional past she wished to create. But she was still trembling as she walked back down towards her car.

Her feet rasped on the sandy track as she made her way carefully along, stumbling occasionally in the dark as she struck uneven patches of ground. After a few minutes a crescent moon edged its way through the dark clouds that had built up in the sky, unnoticed by her as she stared out over Brunskill. The faint light made the going easier as she stumbled along the track, arms spread wide to steady herself.

And as she came within sight of the roadway, it outlined the dark figure of the man standing beside her car.

Jane stopped.

The thunder in her breast was audible; she was panicked, alone on the crag, defenceless. The man had heard her approach; he was standing with one hand on the roof of her car, staring up at her as she emerged from the brow of the hill. They stood staring at each other for several seconds. His face was pale in the moonlight, but she could not make out his features at this distance. She stood stock-still and stared at him and after a moment he shuffled, removed his hand from the roof of the car and stood a little way apart from the vehicle. He was still looking dumbly up towards her, a thin, tall figure, dark-clothed in the faint moonlight.

Jane was trembling. Fiercely she muttered to herself, 'Pull yourself together!'

The man raised his hand, turning it slightly, as though he had half-heard the words. He waited. Jane began to walk towards him slowly, fists clenched, the thudding of her heart almost painful as he stood there, watching, silent.

Jane slowed, and stopped when she was just twenty feet from the man. 'That . . . that's my car,' she said. Her voice was husky and dry.

The man lowered his head, peering at her suspiciously. 'What are you doing up here? Are you all right?'

His tone held its own edge of nervousness, but there was something else there too, a tension rooted in suspicion. Jane took a deep breath, and nodded. She began to move forward, hesitantly. The man stood stiffly, watching.

'What were you doing up there at Reivers Crags?' he demanded.

'Dreaming,' Jane replied, suddenly more confident. She began to walk more quickly towards the car, yet carefully, keeping the vehicle between him and her.

'*Dreaming?*' The answer seemed to nonpluss him. He looked past her in puzzlement, up the hill. 'You alone? No one with you? Up here in the dark?'

Jane unlocked the car with a casual air. 'I'm going now.'

He turned, stepped towards her as though there were more questions he wanted to ask. She slid into the driving seat and put the key in the ignition. Her breathing was quick; in the faint light she could see his features were lined, saturnine, his eyes dark-hollowed.

'Funny thing to do, drive here, walk up alone in the dark. Where are you from?'

'Newcastle. I'm leaving now.' She started the engine.

'Newcastle's a fair drive. This is no place to come in darkness, alone. Not if you're just a woman.'

Jane turned on the car headlights. The sandy track seemed white momentarily under the glare and the trees sprang into detail from the dark mass behind. The car engine coughed and then roared as she pressed the accelerator pedal. The man in front of her raised a hand to his eyes.

'Men and women,' she retorted sharply, 'what's the difference? Are you the guardian around here, or something?'

He stared at her, hand still shading his eyes. 'I saw your car parked,' he said. 'I wondered . . .'

When he made no attempt to explain what he was wondering about, Jane put the car into reverse, turned quickly, and without a backward glance drove back on to the road towards Barden village. Her knees were shaking. For the first time in years she thought she would have liked a cigarette.

After the car lights had disappeared down the hill the thin man hesitated, then looked back up towards Reivers Crags. He fished in his jacket for a torch. Reluctantly, he made his way up the sandy track, flashing his torch nervously into the trees as he went. When he reached the top of the hill he turned off the torchlight and walked towards the edge of the crag itself.

He looked down towards the ruins of Brunskill Castle. The breeze was cool on his face and he shivered in the darkness. He waited, and the moon drifted behind the clouds again, and darkness settled about him.

It was then that he caught a flash of light among the ruins of the castle, and he gritted his teeth. He cursed under his breath, an ancient curse that had travelled down the centuries with ritual and decay and death.

Abruptly he turned and hurried back down the track. His car was parked under the trees, some fifty yards past where the woman had left her vehicle. He climbed in and drove back to Barden village.

There was a public phone booth in the narrow main street. He got out of the car and entered the booth. The light had been broken, and the phone book vandalized, but it made no difference.

He knew the number he wanted.

He dialled quickly, his finger stabbing out the numbers with an angry violence.

The phone rang several times, without answer. He rang off, hesitated, then dialled again. This time he waited impatiently, while the phone rang and rang, insistently.

He had almost given up when a voice answered. He recognized it immediately.

'Dimmock?'

'That's right.'

'We've got to meet.'

'Who is that?'

'Weaver. Cliff Weaver. I've just been up at Brunskill.'

There was a short silence.

'What's happened?'

'I found someone up there. We've got to talk. Tonight.'

There was no response for several seconds. He could hear Dimmock's ragged breath at the other end of the phone. At last Dimmock said, 'All right. But not here at the Rectory. I think we'd better meet in the village.'

'The pub?'

'That'll do.' Dimmock paused. 'But for God's sake, Weaver, just calm down, will you? Someone's up at Brunskill, OK. But it's not the end of the world!'

3

It had been a long day.

Arnold didn't care for writing: he was not skilled at turning an elegant phrase and though he knew what he wanted to say when discussing those things that interested him, such as wood and stone, when he tried to express his thoughts on paper they somehow seemed to lack the clarity he needed. Even so, he had all but come to the end of the notes he had prepared on the tower houses, and a final session on the Sunday evening should just about put things right.

He was confident enough about it to break off and do some work in the garden during the afternoon. The fresh air was good for him; it helped clear his mind and as he worked, double trenching the vegetable section of his back garden, his mind remained active, turning over thoughts about John Lewyn and Henry Yvele.

It was clear to Arnold that Yvele had worked on several of the tower houses he had inspected during the previous ten days. John Lewyn's work was well enough known, but he had to admit to himself that it gave him a degree of excitement to think that by publishing his theories in the Tourist Board brochure and, it seemed, in the book to be compiled from it, he would be able to make a contribution to the historical assessment of Henry Yvele. He dug lustily, breathing hard and sweating profusely as the excitement rose in his chest, and he thought of his father, and the long, instructive walks they had taken in the Yorkshire Dales so many years ago. The legacy his father had given him was incomparable: it had shaped Arnold's mature existence.

By five in the afternoon he had had enough. He went inside the bungalow, showered, put on a clean shirt and slacks and returned to the dining-room where he had spread papers out on the table. By seven he had come to the end of his labours: he had written out the brochure material in longhand, corrected it as far as he was able, and it was now just a matter of taking it into the office on Monday morning to get it all typed up.

He toyed with the thought of depositing it on Miss Sansom's desk, as a gesture of confidence, but the thought of her eagle eye and shelf-like bosom dissuaded him. It would be easier, simpler and less stressful to take the material to the typing pool: it was up to the DDMA to give it the priority it deserved. Arnold had been asked to relieve pressure. He had done so—it was the office's task to complete the easing of Brent-Ellis's mind.

Arnold considered he was due a reward, so he fished a glass out of the cabinet and looked for the bottle of Glenmorangie that Ben Gibson had given him for Christmas. It had not yet been opened: this was a good time to do it, by way of celebration.

He poured a little of the golden liquid into the glass, and, guiltily, added a little water. Ben would not have approved. Arnold toasted him silently and congratulated himself, then sipped at the whisky as he settled into his armchair in the sitting-room. He was reaching for the control box to switch on the television and vaguely wondering when he should eat, when he heard the front doorbell ring.

Arnold frowned. He wasn't expecting anyone and visitors to his Morpeth bungalow were few: his list of friends was not large, for he was essentially a somewhat private person. He set down the whisky and rose, went to the door. When he opened it he saw a man standing there. The porch light had been broken some days earlier by youngsters throwing stones in the roadway and for a moment Arnold was unable to make out the features of the person standing at his front door. Then his blood ran cold.

It was Kevin Anderson.

There was a short silence. At last Anderson said, 'Mr Landon . . . can I come in?'

Arnold was at a loss; he did not know what to say. His mind churned with the comments and questions posed to him by Detective-Inspector Culpeper and he stood rooted to the spot.

'Mr Landon? Please?'

Arnold stood aside, gesturing his colleague in. Then, recovering somewhat, he led the way into the sitting-room. Kevin Anderson stood stiffly just inside the door, staring around him.

He was dressed in a dark windcheater and jeans, with scuffed trainers on his feet. Slung across one shoulder was a rucksack: it gaped open at one side and Arnold could see the pattern of a check shirt showing through. The man himself seemed to be in a state of shock. His face was pale, and there were lines of dismay around his mouth. His glance was dull, vacant of intention, concerned with matters inside his head. He hardly seemed aware of Arnold or his surroundings now that he was inside the bungalow: it was as though he had set himself a goal, reached it, and was now overwhelmed by other matters.

After a short silence, Arnold reached forward and helped ease the rucksack from Anderson's shoulder. It was heavy and damp. 'Are you all right?'

Kevin Anderson gazed dully at Arnold. He had light blue eyes but they were dimmed with pain. He frowned,

uncomprehendingly, and Arnold said in a firm voice,
'You'd better sit down.'

Arnold pushed him into an easy chair and left the room.
He hesitated over the Glenmorangie, but there was no other
whisky in the house, so he poured a hefty measure and
brought the glass to Anderson. He pushed it into his hand.

Kevin Anderson stared at it for a moment, then took a
drink. He grimaced, shuddered slightly as the strong liquor
burned his throat, and then he looked at Arnold standing
over him. His voice held an edge of panic when he spoke.

'You've heard?'

He could be referring to only one thing. Arnold nodded.

'I found out this afternoon,' Anderson said in a half
whisper.

'Where have you been?' Arnold asked.

Anderson shook his head as though to clear it. He sipped
more carefully this time at the whisky. 'I've been up to
Oban. I stayed there a couple of nights and then went
walking. I camped out a few times, stayed at the odd farmhouse. But I've seen no newspapers, watched no television
. . . I had to get away, you see.'

Arnold was edgy. He was uncertain what he should do.
He moistened his lips nervously. 'Have you been in touch
with anyone?'

Anderson shook his head.

'Why . . . why did you come here?'

Anderson stared at him blankly. 'Where else was there
to go?'

Something moved in Arnold's chest, a heavy, slow feeling
as he recognized the despair and loneliness of the man
facing him. Slowly, Arnold sat down. 'You want to talk?'
he asked gently.

'I'm not sure.' Anderson seemed confused, disoriented.
'I didn't know where to go. Then I thought of you.'

'I'm hardly a close friend.'

'Maybe that's why. Not that I have any close friends.
But at the office, when you joined the department, I thought

. . . I felt . . .' Suddenly the words came pouring out, things he had bottled up perhaps for months, kept to himself in the dark recesses of his own anxious mind. 'You must understand, there was no one I could talk to. I mean, I knew people in the department, and it's possible they knew about me and Lynne, and what was happening to us, but I couldn't go to them. It was my business. It was private. You were new to the department: we had no relationship; you were undemanding. You seemed sympathetic. I felt shortly after we met that I could come to your office, take coffee with you, and we barely needed to talk. You see, I wanted companionship—I needed someone else there in the room with me, or my mind would churn and churn. But I didn't want questions, I didn't want other people probing into my private business.'

Arnold could understand the feeling. Perhaps he had already recognized that need when Anderson had sat with him. Their conversations had been stilted, inconsequential. He had been aware that Anderson had been disturbed, but hadn't known him well enough to ask why. That had suited Anderson—a private man, like Arnold.

Perhaps Anderson had seen reflections of his own personality in the new man in the department.

There was a silence. Arnold waited as Anderson fidgeted nervously, frowning, twisting the glass in his hand. His fingernails were dirty, the palms of his hands roughened.

'I don't believe it was a mistake, even now,' Anderson rushed on suddenly. 'We were different, Lynne and I: she was effervescent, impetuous, demanding if you like. I'm not like that. But she was like a breath of fresh air in my life, and I believe there was something in me she wanted. Stability. Security. A solid base. She'd run around a bit, you see, had no roots, always seemed dissatisfied with what she had. But when she met me it was as though she'd found what she wanted. We were fine, for a while. For a while.' He stared dully at his whisky glass for a few moments, then lifted it and drained it.

There was a hush in the room. Arnold could hear the ticking of the grandfather clock in the hall, a piece he'd picked up at auction three years ago and had mended himself. With Ben Gibson's help. The glass in Anderson's hands was empty, and he stared at it. Reluctantly, Arnold reached for the glass, went back to the kitchen and replenished it.

'Thank you.' Anderson nursed the glass for a little while, then looked at Arnold. 'You don't mind me talking like this? It helps, you see. Helps to clear my mind, get me thinking straight. Helps me understand.'

Arnold shook his head.

'I realized she was having an affair. Little things. Absences; flare-ups over unimportant things. Working at the newspaper was the excuse she gave for not being around in the evenings—you know, deadlines, unsocial hours, but I eventually guessed there was someone else in her life. After all . . . we'd got on well enough together, sexually, I mean.' He hesitated, not looking at Arnold, glancing around the room almost furtively as though seeking evidence of eavesdroppers. 'But she was always more . . . passionate than I was. And then, it didn't seem as important to her as it had been. It was then that I began to suspect. And I saw her one day, down in Collingwood Street. She was having a coffee . . . with Ben. And I thought it had started up with him again.'

Arnold frowned. '*Ben?*'

Kevin Anderson turned hurt eyes on Arnold. 'You'll have come across him, I imagine. He's well known on Tyneside. Ben Edwards. Director of the Tourist Board.'

Arnold felt cold. He recalled the last meeting he had had with the man. Edwards had not been so much interested in the brochure completion as the whereabouts of Kevin Anderson.

'They were lovers, you see, for two years or more,' Anderson went on. 'They lived together. It was before Lynne and I met. I gather it was a somewhat . . . violent relationship.

Passionate, but violent. Maybe that was why she turned to me eventually. Edwards was too much for her—jealous, possessive, and not above knocking her around.' His mouth twisted at the pain of the memory. 'But she told me the violence could be exciting. That was when we were in one of her rows. But when we quarrelled, I couldn't respond in the way she wanted.'

Arnold feld he was hearing things that were none of his business or concern. He understood Anderson's need to talk, but he was embarrassed by the personal revelations. His own mind was in a whirl about Ben Edwards, also: he felt he was being drawn into a maelstrom of personal passions that were not his concern. Anderson had turned to him before his wife's death and had now come again, for some half-understood reason, for some perceived opportunity of objective sympathy, but Edwards had come to Arnold too, with different motives, and in anger.

'Kevin,' Arnold said quietly, 'do you know the police are looking for you?'

Anderson was silent for a little while, grimacing into his drink. At last he said, 'I read in the newspaper this afternoon. I was on the way back. When I read it I was scared. I didn't know what to do.'

'Don't you think you should get in touch with them?'

'I don't know. I'm confused. Lynne's dead. And this man who was with her. I can't think straight.'

'The police—'

'And I can't really remember what happened, the Friday I left the office. I was upset, angry. You see, I'd discovered . . . I came to sit with you in your office, and then I decided I had to get away, clear my head, come to terms with my own jealousy and hurt. I often used to go fell walking. But I found myself in Oban. I can't remember—'

'You'll have to talk to the police some time, Kevin. It's better you do it right away. They're looking for you.'

Anderson's head dropped. 'You know what Ben Edwards said when he heard Lynne and I were getting married?

"You'll never keep her," he said. I met him at the Eldon
Centre one afternoon, and he said, "I'll see to it you never
keep her," those were his words. And he's right, you see.
She's gone. I couldn't keep her.'
  'Kevin, the police—'
  'Yes. All right. I'll do whatever you suggest. I'm tired.
Very, very tired.'

Arnold had a great deal in common with Kevin Anderson.
Maybe, subconsciously, Anderson had recognized this.
Now, as Arnold watched the young man sprawled asleep
in the easy chair he recognized the trait. When Arnold's
father had died he had been very upset: he had sought relief
in sleep. Arnold had read since that it was a well-recognized
psychological defence mechanism: an escape from the pain
of reality. The Victorians would have called it the blessed
arms of Morpheus. He guessed that it was not that Kevin
Anderson was exhausted: he was simply escaping from the
shock and pain of hearing of his wife's death.
  Or from something else.
  Arnold grimaced. He did not want to think of Anderson's
possible involvement with the double killing at the cottage
in Craster. He wanted to make no judgements, pass no
judgement. He felt sorry for the man, not only for the loss
of his wife, but for the pain and hurt he clearly felt.
  He sat in the easy chair and watched Anderson as they
waited for the police to come, and he cast back over the
occasions when Anderson had come to him in the office.
He could recall little or nothing of their conversations; he
could remember little of his own feelings on those occasions.
Perhaps he had been less sensitive to Anderson than the
young man had hoped; perhaps the bond of sympathy
Anderson had thought existed had never really been there.
A certain guilt welled up in Arnold's chest as he watched,
and waited. He felt that in some obscure way he had let
the man down. It was an unpleasant feeling; irrational,
perhaps, but one he was unable to dispel.

He was not Kevin Anderson's keeper, yet he felt some-how, in some way, he should have been able to help when the man needed assistance. All Anderson had got from him now, even, was a phone call to the police.

Culpeper had been brief. 'Keep him there. I'll be with you in twenty minutes.'

It took him eighteen.

Arnold hear the doorbell ring at the same moment he caught the reflection of flashing blue lights outside his window. He opened the door. Culpeper stood there, with a uniformed constable beside him. He stared at Arnold for a moment, then motioned to the constable to stay outside. He closed the door gently behind him.

'Where is he?'

'In the sitting-room.'

Arnold led the way.

Their entrance disturbed Kevin Anderson. He mumbled something, twisted in the chair and then gradually emerged from the sleep that had overcome him. He did not relish the return to consciousness. He rubbed his left hand over his eyes, then ran fingers through his hair, tousling it. He sat up, staring at Culpeper, and when his glance turned to Arnold there was something almost accusatory in his eyes.

'Kevin Anderson?' When Anderson nodded, Culpeper introduced himself.

'I'm Detective Chief Inspector Culpeper. I work out of Morpeth. I'm glad to see you. We've been looking for you for several days.' The soft, autumn-brown eyes were gentle. 'You'll have heard about your wife. I'm sorry.'

He paused, glanced uncertainly at Arnold as Anderson made no response. Arnold hesitated, then gestured towards a chair. 'Would you like to sit down, Inspector? Perhaps a drink—'

Culpeper looked at the half-empty glass on the small table beside Anderson's elbow. Arnold wondered whether he was going to refuse because he was on duty. He didn't. He nodded. 'One of those would be fine.'

Arnold sighed as he poured a glass of Glenmorangie in the kitchen.

When he returned Culpeper was seated on the edge of his chair, leaning forward, listening as Anderson explained where he had been and why he had not seen the newspapers or television. He had been walking in the hills, camping, living rough. As he spoke Culpeper's face was expressionless, but his mouth was set in a thin line. When Anderson's voice died away, Culpeper sipped his drink. He glanced appreciatively at Arnold and then turned back to Anderson.

'I'm sorry to have to ask you questions at a time like this, Mr Anderson. Clearly, it's been a great shock to you, getting the news today. But I'm not exactly clear why you took your leave so suddenly from the office. I understand from Mr Brent-Ellis that you didn't put in the usual formal request.'

And left your work undone, Arnold thought to himself.

'No. I didn't ask.'

'Why was that?' Culpeper asked gently.

Anderson shrugged unhappily. 'I . . . I was disturbed.'

'About what?'

Anderson shook his head. 'I needed time away from work. I couldn't concentrate. I was bothered, pressures . . .'

'What sort of pressures?'

'Work. You know . . .' his voice tailed off.

Culpeper paused, eyeing the young man carefully. 'Did you know your wife was having an affair?'

Something flared in Anderson's eyes. 'We had a good marriage!'

Culpeper already doubted that but made no response. Instead, he persisted, 'Did you know your wife was seeing one of her colleagues at the newspaper? Lance Stevens?'

'I—I suppose I guessed something was going on.'

'When did you first suspect it?'

Anderson lifted a dejected shoulder. 'Maybe two, three weeks ago. Maybe longer. It's difficult to say . . . things sort of grow. I . . . I felt things weren't right between us.'

'And it was because of this suspicion that you felt pressure, you needed to get away, go walking in the hills.'

'I suppose so,' Anderson said reluctantly.

'When did you know it was Stevens your wife was involved with?'

'I—' Anderson had been about to deny the knowledge. He looked defiantly at Culpeper but the defiance died almost as quickly as it had flared. Miserably he admitted, 'I didn't find out it was Stevens until about a week ago.'

'How?'

'She told me.'

Arnold let out a gust of breath. Culpeper leaned back in his chair, and sipped the whisky Arnold had given him. 'All right, Mr Anderson, how exactly did she come to tell you about Stevens?'

Anderson was silent for a little while as he dredged back over the recent past. He grimaced painfully, and shook his head. 'We had a row. She'd been staying out at odd times. Assignments, she said. And then, she came back one time and there were marks on her . . . her breasts. I asked her about them. We had a row. She told me she was seeing someone. We argued; she told me that life was dull, she needed the excitement. But then she relented, and we sort of made it up. She said she'd give up this man. But the next week, I saw her with a man she . . . she had known before she knew me.'

'Who was that?'

'Ben Edwards.'

'The Tourist Board Ben Edwards?' Culpeper asked in surprise.

'That's right. I was furious. I thought she had gone back to him; thought she was taking up with him again, even though he used to knock her about, treat her savagely.'

After a short silence, Culpeper said quietly, 'Some women like that. But not many.'

'I challenged her about Edwards. She denied it. Said the meeting had been a casual one, unpremeditated. They'd met by accident in the coffee-shop. I didn't believe her. I got angry. We were shouting. I think she finally just got completely exasperated and she yelled at me. Told me I was wrong. Told me it was a man called Stevens, at the newspaper.'

Culpeper was silent, watching Anderson. The young man had reddened with his account, passion had crept into his voice and an anger that seemed uncharacteristic of his quiet, withdrawn nature. Arnold wondered just what it took to turn a man like Anderson to violence, and how deeply the woman had bitten into his soul; Culpeper clearly had similar thoughts on his mind.

'What happened after that?' Culpeper asked.

'I don't understand.'

'Did she move out?'

'No.'

'Was there a reconciliation?'

Anderson shrugged. 'No. She was pretty busy. She'd been working on a series for the *Journal*, and it sent her travelling around the county quite a bit.'

'Ah yes, *Ghosts of Old Northumberland*.' Culpeper had clearly been doing his homework, checking on Lynne Anderson's activities during the last days of her life.

'That's right. So I didn't see too much of her.'

'Were you still sleeping together?' Culpeper asked.

Anderson was silent for a while. 'We didn't seem to see much of each other,' he replied evasively.

'And then?' Culpeper prompted.

'It all got a bit too much for me. I couldn't work. I was unable to concentrate at the office. I had a job on for the Tourist Board, and Ben Edwards's face kept coming up at me. I didn't know this man Stevens, and in some odd way it was Edwards I was getting angry about. I just couldn't think straight. So that Friday afternoon . . .'

'Yes?'

Anderson shook his head. 'I suppose I cracked; it had got on top of me. I was prowling all morning, couldn't get on with my work. I came in to see Mr Landon here. But I can't even remember what we talked about. I was . . . preoccupied. And then I decided. I had to get away, get out, breathe fresh air, clear my lungs and my head. Try to get things straight, see situations in the right perspective.'

'So you went up to Seahouses?' Culpeper asked quietly.

Anderson stared at him. He wet his lips with a nervous tongue. 'I went to Scotland.'

'How?'

'I drove.'

'Which road did you take out of Morpeth?'

'I . . . I can't remember. Coldstream, maybe it was to Coldstream, Jedburgh, then across towards the west coast.'

'Odd way to go.'

'I can't be certain.'

'The Coldstream road—it's not too far out of your way to cut east and head for Craster.'

'I had no reason to go there.'

'Your wife was there. Or going there.'

'I didn't know that.'

'You didn't know Stevens had a cottage at the fishing village? A cottage where he used to meet her?'

Anderson shook his head. 'No. I didn't know where she and Stevens met. As for the day itself . . . I have to tell you, Inspector. My recollections of that day, they're blurred. I've explained I wasn't myself. It had all built up; the pressure, the anxiety, the gnawing jealousy—I admit to it. The whole thing had thrown me out of my stride. I loved her. The thought of her with Edwards—'

'But it wasn't Edwards she was with.'

'Edwards, Stevens, it makes no difference!' Anderson's eyes were hot and wild. 'I couldn't get it out of my mind,

that she was with someone else. I was confused, shaken. I
don't know what I was doing. All I knew was I had to get
away.'

'To the east coast?'

'To Scotland.'

'Why Scotland, particularly? Why not Yorkshire, the
dales?'

Anderson shrugged. 'I've walked in Scotland before. It's
wild country. Isolated. I wanted to get away.'

'But you remember little about your journey. Can't you
even tell me for certain which road you took.'

Sullenly Anderson shook his head. 'No.'

Culpeper finished his whisky thoughtfully. He seemed to
have forgotten Arnold's presence during his interrogation.
Now he caught his eye, as he put down his glass. 'Good
whisky, Mr Landon.'

Arnold hesitated. His own glass was empty. When he
raised his eyebrows at Culpeper the policeman smiled.
Arnold picked up the two glasses, went to the kitchen and
poured two more drinks. He was feeling a little light-headed
as he went back to the sitting-room. Culpeper received his
glass with a welcoming smile. 'Good stuff this, Mr Landon.
Not often a poor copper can get his hands on Glenmorangie.'

He'd recognized the brand, nevertheless, without seeing
the label, Arnold thought to himself.

Culpeper raised his glass in salute, took an appreciative
sip, and then looked back at Anderson. 'Right, well, I'm
sorry to question you like this, but you know how it is. In
a murder inquiry we must leave no stone unturned. Tell
me, Mr Anderson, what do you do for hobbies?'

'Hobbies?'

'I know you go walking, but apart from that what do you
get up to? How do you spend your leisure time? Do you
go to Newcastle races? Do you watch rugby or support
Newcastle? Or even Sunderland? Maybe you're not that
much of a masochist,' he added, smiling.

'None of those,' Anderson replied soberly.

'Dogs, then. Do you go to the dogs down on Teesside? Ten-pin bowling? Or maybe whippet-racing? Pigeons?'

'Chief Inspector—'

'Or maybe you do the odd spot of business up on the moors,' Culpeper said softly.

'Business?'

'Pheasant. Grouse.'

Silence fell. It grew around them, heavy with a new menace as the import of Culpeper's questions came through to both Arnold and Kevin Anderson. The Chief Inspector himself still seemed at ease, leaning back in his chair with his glass half raised, the rim resting against his chin, but his eyes were no longer soft. They were wary, keen in their observance of the man facing him in the easy chair opposite.

'I don't go grouse-shooting,' Anderson said at last, in a strangled tone.

'And you don't have a gun licence?'

'No.'

'So it's superfluous of me to ask if you've ever owned a shotgun.'

Anderson stared at him. Arnold shuffled uncomfortably, wondering how he had ever thought that Culpeper was a sympathetic man. But then, he was only doing his job as he saw it.

'I've never owned a shotgun.' Anderson hesitated. 'Is . . . is that how they were killed? With a shotgun?'

Culpeper made no reply. He was frowning now. He finished his drink, set it down. He sighed deeply. There was an air of dissatisfaction about him as he rose. 'I think I'd better give you a bit of advice, Mr Anderson. Without wishing to be offensive, in circumstances which I know must be extremely painful to you, I'd advise you to think deeply about what's happened these last few days. I'd like you to come along with me now. I've got transport outside.'

'My car—'

'Don't worry about that. I'll get it driven down with us.'

I'd like you to come down to the station at Morpeth, to the Incident Room where we can go over all this again, and in more detail. I'll then be asking you to make a statement, and sign it. After that, well, we'll see. But while we're going down I think you'd be wise to think carefully about what you've told me so far, and do your utmost to fill in the gaps.'

'I've told you all—'

'Most particularly,' Culpeper warned him in a sober tone, 'you'd be well advised to try to remember exactly what route you took north. You should think about times. You should think, try to remember where and when you stopped, who might have seen you, in other words, establish with precision exactly what you were doing, and where you were doing it, when your wife died.'

'You can't suspect *me*! I *loved* her!'

It seemed, from the expression on his face, that Culpeper regarded that as a *non-sequitur*. He grimaced. 'I'd think hard, Mr Anderson.'

'But I don't even know when she died!'

'I can tell you it was some time after you left the office in Morpeth. So a detailed statement would be advisable. Are you ready now, sir?'

Kevin Anderson rose to his feet uncertainly. He glared at Arnold, who sheepishly handed him the rucksack he had discarded. 'I . . . I suppose so. But I need a change of clothes. If it's going to be long.'

'It'll be no problem to stop off at your home, Mr Anderson,' Culpeper said gently. He walked out of the sitting-room and opened the front door. He called in the police constable.

'Mr Anderson is ready to come along with us now. Tell Connors to take Mr Anderson's car; follow us to the station.'

Anderson stared at him and then looked at Arnold. 'I'm sorry,' he mumbled. He seemed to want to say something more but the words would not come. He walked out with the police constable.

Arnold stood just inside the front door but the Chief Inspector seemed reluctant to leave. Culpeper observed Arnold quietly. 'So he *did* come to you after all, Mr Landon.'

'I still don't know why.'

'I think I do.' Culpeper allowed himself a faint smile. 'I'm glad you called us. That was public-spirited of you.'

'You can't really believe he killed them,' Arnold said.

'Most murders are committed by people close to the victim.'

'But I hardly think—'

'It would be helpful if you also could give us a statement. No hurry, of course: tomorrow will do. Just in case he said anything to you, before I arrived, that he didn't repeat to me.'

'We didn't talk much.'

Culpeper nodded gravely, and stepped out into the porch. In the driveway he paused and looked back. 'Thank you for your hospitality, Mr Landon.'

The door closed behind him. Arnold heard the car engine start up, saw the blue light fade away down the road. He went back to the kitchen.

He stared morosely at the half-empty bottle of Ben Gibson's Glenmorangie.

It was not an evening he would want to remember.

CHAPTER 4

1

'So. Is this it?'

Brent-Ellis switched his cigar to the corner of his mouth without using his hands, leaned back in his chair and riffled through the papers that Arnold had presented to him.

'That's the complete material for the brochure, sir. I thought you might wish to have a look at it before I send it on to Mr Edwards.'

'Hmmm.' Brent-Ellis glanced vaguely through the papers, clearly not particularly interested in the contents. Or maybe it was a defence mechanism: if it was known he had approved them in detail, any problems arising thereafter would land on his desk, rather than Arnold's. 'I'm sure I can trust your work, Landon. There's, er, nothing . . . controversial there, I hope?' He glanced up at Arnold, sniffing suspiciously, stroking his moustache in a nervous gesture.

'I'm not aware of anything, sir. I think I told you I visited each site before I wrote the material, and I think my arguments about Henry Yvele and John Lewyn—'

'Who?'

Arnold thought it a waste of time going into lengthy explanations. 'I've included some material on the architects, or master masons, who had a hand in building these tower houses.'

'The peles, you mean.'

'Ah . . . well, yes,' Arnold replied dejectedly.

Brent-Ellis cleared his throat noisily. 'Right. I'm pleased you've hit the deadline anyway. Edwards was blasting away about ten days, wasn't he?'

'That's right.'

'So we're actually early.' Brent-Ellis beamed. Arnold noted the 'we' sourly. Brent-Ellis handed the package back to Arnold. 'Where's the photographs?'

Arnold's stomach churned. 'Photographs?'

'That's right. Edwards wanted sketches and photographs as well as words. You haven't included them in this pile of paper. You got a separate folder for them?'

'I, er, I wasn't aware that photographs were necessary.' Arnold's tongue felt thick. 'Nothing in the brief I was given suggested—'

Brent-Ellis frowned and took his cigar from his mouth. He inspected it coolly. 'It was in Anderson's brief.'

'I found no mention of it.'

'Hmm.' Brent-Ellis tapped his cigar with his index finger. Flakes of grey ash floated down to the carpet. He observed them gloomily. 'You're ahead of the writing deadline, Landon. I shouldn't think it would take you too long to get down to the library, fish out some standard photographs, and stick them in with these papers. Ought to satisfy Edwards.' He paused, frowning. 'Though he's a pernickety bastard.'

Arnold made no response.

'Anyway,' Brent-Ellis continued, 'you better get those photographs added. And talking of Anderson, I hear you had a visit Sunday night.'

The grapevine had been buzzing. Did grapevines buzz? Arnold shrugged and nodded.

'Did you see the paper this morning?' When Arnold shook his head, Brent-Ellis rolled his cigar around his mouth again and said, 'They're still saying Kevin Anderson is helping with police inquiries, but all the signs are that he's going to be charged. It's not good for the department, is it?'

It wasn't good news for Kevin Anderson, either. 'I can hardly believe he killed his wife,' Arnold replied slowly.

'Ah well, worms can turn,' Brent-Ellis said wistfully and looked out of the window with an air that suggested he would not be averse to a bit of wriggling himself.

After escaping the DDMA and negotiating the censorious glances of Miss Sansom, Arnold made his way down to the archives section of the department. The bored young clerk who acted as Cerberus there referred to a formidable lady called Miss Eastwood: she had been a denizen of the archives basement for thirty years, it appeared, and rumour suggested she rarely saw the light. Looking at her tight, stony face, and pallid skin, Arnold was inclined to believe it. She had a morose, despondent look about her and Arnold guessed her gloom was perpetual. Buried among musty papers and books, she seemed incapable of raising enthusiasm about anything.

'You'll not get much out of here.'

'I beg your pardon?'

'First place they cut. Once budgets get into trouble, cut the archives section, they say. Nothing here of any use.'

'There must be some photographs I could use.'

'Peles? I doubt it. Try under "P" over there. We run a logical filing system. "P" for peles and "F" for photographs. Kids they send to me can't spell so we work a phonetic system. And then there's the Victorian collection. That comes under "Q".' She sighed. 'For Queen Victoria. They spent money in those days. Not now.' She ducked her head towards a series of grey filing cabinets, and went back to her laborious persual of *Horse and Hound*. Arnold imagined it would be the lure of open fields, as a contrast to her dungeon confinement here, that drew her to the magazine.

Arnold walked across to the files. He spent twenty minutes looking through the drawers. There were very few photographs there, and nothing he could possibly use.

'Is that all there is?'

'That's the lot, bonny lad.' Miss Eastwood sighed, and flicked over a page depicting a rawboned hunter. It looked something like her, Arnold considered. 'You know you're the first visitor we've had down here in eight weeks?'

Arnold did not express surprise.

Unhappily, Arnold returned to his office. He sat behind his desk for a while, thinking. If he was to keep to Edwards's schedule, he had just one day in which to photograph the tower houses. He couldn't see how it could possibly be done. There was a photographic section in the department. He had already rung them. They would process the prints for him quickly—but he knew they'd never get out to the sites in time to suit him. And he would have to supervise their work, to make sure they took shots of the appropriate parts of the houses.

He doubted whether there'd be anyone there with the right feeling for the periods, and the constructions, to be able to work alone. And he couldn't possibly go along with them to each site. He sat there gloomily, staring out of the window and then gradually he perceived the solution.

He reached for the phone.

'Ben? It's Arnold.'

'Ringing from Morpeth?' Ben Gibson chuckled. 'This is a pleasure and an honour.'

'Have you got a camera?'

There was a short silence. 'I'll have you know, my son, that I was once known as the David Bailey of the North. I have an ancient plate camera which has the most amazing capacity to work in any weather; I have an elderly Brownie, believe it or not, and I have one of those mucky, automatic, do nothing yourself but press the button things, which cost me all of two hundred quid. Never use it.'

'Can you do me a favour?'

'Ask away, my friend.'

Quickly, Arnold explained his predicament. 'So you see, if I could split the work, get someone to lend a hand, maybe I could get the photographs done in time. But I need someone who understands what I'm trying to do; someone who has a feeling for the past, and can get the right kind of shots—'

'The work would be done faster by three rather than two.'

'Jane?' Arnold hesitated. 'Would she be prepared to lend a hand?'

'You know she's always absolutely delighted to help you out in your research,' Ben Gibson purred. 'I'm sure she'd be more than happy to help.'

There was a confused noise suddenly; Arnold could hear Ben speaking, but the words were muffled. Obviously, he had his hand over the mouthpiece. After a short interval, when Arnold seemed to detect a certain argument going on, Ben came back on the phone. There was a smile in his voice. 'As I guessed, Arnold, she'd be delighted. When do you want it done?'

There was an exasperated snort in the background. Arnold swallowed. 'Tomorrow.'

'No problem. We can manage tomorrow, can't we, Jane?'

The hurried way in which he grasped the mouthpiece again suggested to Arnold that Jane was about to be profane.

They had a longer, three-way conversation that evening. Arnold drove down to the bookshop on the Quayside and they shared a pizza and a bottle of wine. Ben suggested Arnold stay overnight rather than return home to Morpeth, so all three could get an early start in the morning.

Arnold was able to brief them on what he wanted. Jane was quiet at first, clearly somewhat miffed at being thrust into this activity by her determined uncle, but as the conversation went on she warmed to the project, and became interested in the linkage that Arnold wanted between the sites themselves and the materials he had prepared. He gave them both copies of the brochure typescript and discussed it with them in some detail.

'So, if we split the sites between us tomorrow, we could meet up later to exchange notes. If you can let me have the films you've used, I'll take them back to Morpeth and get them developed in the department. If Brent-Ellis wants the job completed on time he'll have to put a charge into the people in the photographic section, get them moving. Once the shots are taken, we'll be off the hook.'

'*You'll* be off the hook,' Jane muttered. 'There's no line on us.'

'I'm grateful,' Arnold mumbled.

'Aye, well . . .'

Ben Gibson smiled complacently upon the pair of them. 'So how are we to split up the task, children?'

Arnold spread a map of Northumberland upon the table in front of them. 'I think we should go for a sensible kind of grouping. The sites we need photographs of are Belsay, here . . . Tarset Hall, the Old Rectory at Temple Barden, Dacre House, and then Brunskill Castle—which I've not actually been to—'

'I have,' Jane interrupted. 'And I didn't enjoy the experience.'

'Oh? How do you mean?' Arnold asked.

'She had a *frisson*,' Ben Gibson said.

'I had a bloody fright!' Jane snapped. 'I drove up there, sat on Reivers Crags for a while, and it got dark before I realized it, and then I saw lights at Brunskill.'

'The castle's a ruin,' Arnold said.

'That's right. But there was someone poking around down there. It's silly, I suppose,' she went on a little shame-facedly, 'but it made me shiver a bit. Anyway, I left there in a bit of a hurry—it's an odd feeling, seeing lights in an ancient pile like that, with the darkness around you. Like I said, shivery.'

'It's one of the places mentioned in that series on *Ghosts of Old Northumberland*,' Ben Gibson said.

'The series written by Anderson's wife?'

'That's right.' Ben Gibson wrinkled his brow. 'I seem to recall there was a bit of fuss up there recently, too. About secret societies, black magic, that sort of nonsense. I heard it's one of the sites that occultists tend to use, because of its ancient connotations.'

'What connotations?' Arnold asked.

'Oh, you know, castles built on sites of devil-worship. Bad luck for the de Bohuns, all that sort of rubbish.'

'It can sometimes get serious,' Arnold said ruefully.

Ben Gibson nodded. He knew all about Arnold's involve-ment with the occult and secret societies; he could also appreciate it wasn't something Arnold wanted to dwell on.

'Anyway,' Jane went on determinedly, after the interrup-tions, 'when I got back to my car there was this man.'

Arnold looked quickly at her; she was clearly still disturbed by the experience. 'What happened?'

Jane shrugged. 'Nothing, really. He was standing beside my car in the darkness. He scared me. But . . . He just asked me what I was doing on the crags. Maybe he was a local farmer. I don't know. I just got the hell out of there. He was a bit creepy.'

Arnold hesitated. He stared at the map. 'Well, there's no reason for you to go back up to Brunskill—'

'Hey, I'm not bothered—'

'No, if we group things sensibly, I think it should be Ben who goes up to Brunskill to take some shots. You see, it means we could work it like this. Ben can do Chipchase and Brunskill; I'll do Temple Barden and Belsay; you do Tarset Hall and Dacre. We'll leave Langley out: we don't need to include every tower house mentioned in the brochure. If we cover the ones I've mentioned, we should have plenty of shots to choose from. And if we start in this manner—' he traced his finger across the map—'we'll all end up within ten miles of each other. That means we can meet up here at the Stag Inn, compare notes, you can let me have the films and I needn't come back to Tyneside with you. I can get straight back up to Morpeth and hand the films in first thing in the morning.'

'Makes sense.'

Jane grimaced. 'Tarset Hall, hey? I had a run-in with the owner of that place too.'

'Major Manners? You've been getting around.'

'I don't think he likes women.'

'I believe,' Arnold said slowly, 'he feels he has good reason not to. How did you come across him?'

'In the entrance to his driveway. I was just looking around.'

Arnold stared at her, not understanding. 'If you're bothered . . . Would you rather not go there?'

'Hell, no,' she bridled. 'If Ben has stuck me with this, I'll go through with it. I'm not about to start picking and choosing.' She stuck her thumbs into imaginary lapels and twiddled her fingers. 'You call the shots, feller, and I'll go along. Where did you say we'll be meeting?'

'The Stag Inn. At Hartside. If we said, maybe, four o'clock?'

'Make it five,' Ben suggested. 'The light is still OK till then, and this job might take rather longer than you might think, Arnold.' He smiled suddenly at Jane. 'And who knows? Some of these photographs might help give you background for your next work of fictional consequence.'

Arnold thought he actually heard her growl in her throat.

They left at eight next morning. They went in separate cars, Arnold in his Ford, Jane in her Vauxhall, and Ben in the rather battered VW Passat that he had been driving for some years. They drove north through Newcastle in procession, picking up the motorway that led towards Ponteland and then swinging west, where within a few miles they split up, Arnold heading past Ponteland to Belsay, Jane striking out for Dacre and Ben pottering along in the direction of Chipchase.

There had been a tower house at Ponteland, of course; it had now been converted into a pub, and the one at Cambo now functioned as a post office. Belsay was a different matter. It had become a tourist attraction: the Middletons at Belsay had managed to combine the gardens, castle, manor and hall into a unit which reflected the evolving style of border life over the last six hundred years. One of its principal features was the quarried garden with its exotic plants, an idiosyncratic feature that drew the tourists, but Arnold was more interested in the castle itself. He spent most of the morning setting up the photographs he wanted; the fourteenth-century border tower house had been renovated with new floors and roof but was otherwise largely intact, although little remained of the seventeenth-century manor house.

Well after midday he left Belsay and drove north-west

past the high outcrop of Shaftoe Crags, towards Elsdon. He parked near the eighteenth-century farmworkers' cottages in the village and went into the Bird in Bush Inn for a snack and a glass of lager.

When he came out again, he hesitated at Elsdon Tower: once the rectory, it also was fourteenth-century and incorporated a pele, but it was outside his brief, so he went back to the car, drove through the wooded valley and headed for Temple Barden.

He passed hilltop villages along uncongested roads; he was in the 'debatable' lands that he loved, the area which had endured centuries of skirmishing between English and Scots. The mellow sandstone cottages calmed him; the rich, open farmlands, the wooded valleys and the magnificent sweep of the fells always heartened him. As the road rose and stone walls replaced hedges and he crossed humpback bridges with long views of the Cheviots, his spirits rose. He almost forgot about Brent-Ellis, and the office, and the deadlines that had brought him here to the rugged moorland.

When he finally dropped down towards Temple Barden the sun was shining. It would mean he'd get some good shots of the Old Rectory; it was, of course, peripheral to the tower house theme, but it was mentioned in Anderson's notes and he had continued with the material, so it was as well to include it.

Arnold had no doubt that when Nick Dimmock saw him, he'd want to know what more Arnold might be able to tell him about the painting he had found secreted in the house. Arnold would have to find some way of sidestepping that: the pressure he'd been under from Ben Edwards and Brent-Ellis meant that he had had no opportunity to do the necessary research. At that moment, all he'd be able to do was supply Dimmock with the kind of educated guess he'd already made on the occasion of their previous encounter.

As Arnold approached the village and neared the Old Rectory itself he saw that there were two cars parked outside the house. It meant he had to drive a little further on to find a parking place that wouldn't be a menace to other drivers. He drew his car in under the hedge some sixty metres from the driveway, its front wheels on the grass. He got out and locked the car. Camera slung over his shoulder, he walked the short distance along the narrow road back towards the Old Rectory.

One of the cars was a Japanese-built vehicle with a Newcastle number plate. The other was a nondescript Ford which had seen better days. It was dirty, with mud-splashed sides. Arnold wondered who they might belong to, as he walked towards the front door. With luck, if there was company at the Old Rectory it would mean there wouldn't be the opportunity for Dimmock to cross-examine him on the painting.

As he approached the door he got a surprise. It opened, and framed in the doorway was Detective Chief Inspector Culpeper.

The policeman was as surprised as Arnold. 'Mr Landon! What are *you* doing here?'

Arnold ducked his head. 'It's an assignment. For the department. I need to get Mr Dimmock's permission to take some photographs.'

'Here's the man himself,' Culpeper remarked drily and stepped out away from the doorway. The tall, lean, bearded figure of Nick Dimmock emerged just behind him.

Culpeper glanced at Arnold and then looked back to Dimmock. 'Well, I should thank you for your time, Mr Dimmock. If there's anything else you can remember, anything else you think would be of help, perhaps you could give me a ring.'

'I'm sorry I appear to have been of so little assistance,' Dimmock mumbled. His eyes were down; he was looking neither at Arnold nor Culpeper, and Arnold got the impression that Dimmock would be glad to see the back of the Detective Chief Inspector.

'I'll be going, then,' Culpeper said in a cool tone, and

looked at Arnold. 'And I'll say goodbye to you, Mr Landon. Behave yourself.'

'I always do, Chief Inspector,' Arnold replied with a slight smile. He watched as Culpeper walked past and made his way towards his car. It was, Arnold noted, the mud-spattered Ford. Perhaps it was Culpeper's way of demonstrating Chief Inspectors needed a pay rise, he thought. Culpeper got into the car and started the engine, drew out into the road and vanished around the bend towards the village.

Arnold turned. Dimmock was not looking at him, but was still staring at the space where the Ford had been parked. Arnold was about to speak when a voice came from the passageway behind Dimmock.

'Has he gone?'

Dimmock started, and glared at Arnold. The next moment a man appeared behind Dimmock's shoulder: tall, thin, with saturnine features and dark eyes that seemed withdrawn in hollow cheeks. His hair was carefully brushed, tight against his skull but his skin was dirty in colour, and pitted. He saw Arnold and surprise registered. Dimmock turned his head to glance at him and then swung back to Arnold.

'What is it you want? Have you come about the painting?'

Arnold hesitated. 'Well, no, not exactly. I'm afraid I'm a bit pressed for time at the moment, and I haven't had the opportunity to pursue some of the lines of inquiry I mentioned to you. I'll be able to get on to it later this week. But first I have an urgent assignment to complete—and it means I need to take some photographs. Would you mind if I took some of the external part of the house, and maybe one of the staircase inside?'

Dimmock hesitated for a moment, then nodded. 'I don't see any problem in that. But the painting . . .' His voice died away again, and his eyes flickered towards the roadway, as though he was checking to ascertain whether Culpeper had really gone. 'No, it's fine, you go ahead.'

He stepped backwards, pushing the man behind him into the house and closed the door. Arnold shook his head and walked towards the side of the Old Rectory. The garden there sloped up towards the hill; it should be possible to get some decent shots of the house from there.

There were some stunted apple trees in the overgrown grass and a wild cherry tree near the wall. Arnold stood under the cherry tree and looked down towards the house. He moved around for a little while, seeking the best vantage-point. As he did so he caught sight of the small window at the top of the stairs, on the third floor. He had a glimpse of a white face staring out at him; in a moment it was gone. Someone was either curious about his photographic skills, or was interested to see whether he really was there to take photographs.

For the next twenty minutes Arnold prowled around the house. He managed finally to get three reasonable photographs of the Old Rectory. It was enough. The building was not an important issue in the brochure in any case. He walked around to the front door, and after a brief hesitation, knocked.

He heard shuffling feet in the passageway; the door opened and Dimmock stood there. 'Ah. Mr Landon. You'll want to do the stairs now.'

'If you don't mind.'

It would have been sensible to bring lighting equipment but Arnold had none of his own and it would have been too much of a problem to winkle some out of the photographic section of the DMA. He would have to rely upon the flash on his own camera and hope that the result would be printable as far as the brochure was concerned.

While he manœuvred in the hallway at the foot of the stairs, Arnold was conscious of Dimmock standing just behind him. After a little while the other man arrived as well, silently.

'What's this all for exactly?' Dimmock asked. There was an odd tension in his voice, a nervousness Arnold could not understand.

'It's a brochure for the Tourist Board. I've done the research; it just needs photographs added.'

'You know that man Culpeper?'

Arnold paused, and looked back at Dimmock. 'I've come across him, yes.'

'Has he been questioning you about the death of that woman?'

'No. Not really. He asked me about her husband . . . Is that why he's been here today?'

For a moment, Dimmock seemed disinclined to answer. He glanced at his saturnine, silent companion. 'She came here. Doing that series of articles on *Ghosts of Old Northumberland*.'

Dimmock would have liked that. 'I imagine Culpeper is checking on all her movements during the period before her death,' Arnold replied.

'I suppose so. There was nothing I could tell him, though. She just asked me about the haunting here. I gave her the story. But when I saw you, and realized you knew him—her husband was a colleague of yours, wasn't he?'

'Still is,' Arnold replied shortly.

'He's in custody, I understand.' Dimmock's voice was flat, unemotional. And yet it still held shaky undertones. 'Suspected of killing her.'

'Helping with inquiries,' Arnold corrected him.

'A euphemism.'

'I wouldn't know about that.'

Arnold was very much aware of their presence and it inhibited him. He took two quick shots of the stairs and announced that would do. He turned, and Dimmock and his companion were still standing there, staring at him.

'The painting,' Dimmock said. 'Have you thought any more about it?'

Arnold slung the camera over his shoulder. 'I've studied

the photographs you gave me. And I've discussed it with some friends.'

'What conclusions have you come to?'

'Only tentative ones. I can't do other than guess until I take a closer look at the ceiling upstairs—and I'm afraid that'll have to wait for another day. But there are things about the painting I—or we—found puzzling.'

'Such as?'

Arnold shrugged. 'The trelliswork which is faintly etched in. My friend—Ben Gibson—he has a theory about it. There's the thought it might be in some way a symbolic reflection of the casket in which the Holy Shroud was once housed.'

'He regards it as a link with the Shroud of Turin?'

'A *possible* link,' Arnold replied carefully. 'And to that extent I suppose it helps your own argument.'

'And the Knights Templar?' Dimmock asked huskily.

'We went over the possibility of that link, but it seems tenuous. Temple Barden probably gets its name from the Templar connection with the church but . . . the chances of the Shroud having really been brought to this country . . .'

'It perhaps wasn't the Shroud. It could have been the *sudarium.*'

Arnold nodded. 'I suppose so. But there's no evidence. And the ceiling won't give an answer either. All it will help us sort out is the date when the painting was hidden. On the other hand—'

'Yes?'

'The shield puzzled us. It's very similar to the arms of the de Bohun family.'

'Similar?'

'But not the same. There's something missing. The bars. And yet the strange thing is that there are bars in your painting: faint, hazy, but placed in the background, detached from the shield in a way that's puzzling. Assuming they are connected to the shield.'

'I hadn't picked that up,' Dimmock said slowly.

'It might be of no importance.'

'Perhaps not. You're leaving now?'

Arnold nodded. 'I have a tight schedule. I have a number of shots to take—too many, in fact. I've had to bring in the assistance of two friends—the ones I've discussed your painting with, incidentally. They're doing the rest of the photography for me. We're meeting up later to bring the films together.'

Dimmock paused. 'What other places are you photographing?'

'Tower houses. Dacre. Tarset. Belsay. Brunskill and—'

'Brunskill Castle?' It was the man behind Dimmock who spoke. His voice had a dry rasp to it, the harsh scouring of shingle on a beach.

'That's right. The shots will all appear in the brochure. But time's getting on. I'd better be on my way.'

'Certainly.' Dimmock stepped aside and opened the front door. 'You'll be in touch again about the painting? And you'll call again, to check that ceiling?'

'As soon as I can find time, Mr Dimmock.' He nodded to Dimmock and to his companion and walked out into the roadway. When he glanced back they were still standing there, staring after him. It made the flesh on his back creep.

Arnold turned left to make his way back towards his car. He checked his watch. It was just three o'clock. He was in good time; he needn't have hurried away from the Old Rectory. But the atmosphere there had got to him. There had been an air of hostility, of suspicion, and even of fear. It was nothing he could pinpoint exactly, but he was left with the impression that the two men were worried about something. And his presence had exacerbated it in some way unknown to him.

He reached his car and fumbled for his keys. He unlocked the door and was about to get in when he saw a car coming towards him along the narrow road. He waited, keeping his own door closed until the car had passed.

It slowed, and stopped.

Arnold turned and looked at the driver. It was Detective Chief Inspector Culpeper. He was smiling; it was a rather world-weary smile.

'Well, bonny lad, you keep turning up in the most surprising places. Would you like to lock your car again?'

'Why?'

Culpeper's smile broadened. 'Because I'd like you to keep me company a few minutes. Lock your car, and get in here beside me. I want a word with you.'

2

'So, did you have a canny bit of crack back there with Mr Dimmock and his pal, then?' Culpeper asked, beaming a friendly smile at Arnold, who was not fooled.

'I was just there to take some photographs.'

'I've no doubt. But you've been there before, haven't you?'

'I have.'

'For what reason?'

Arnold hesitated. 'To look at a painting.'

'Why, aye, an art expert now as well! A painting, you say. And was Mr Weaver there then, as well?'

'Weaver?'

'The quiet character who was in the house with Dimmock.'

'I've not come across him before.'

Culpeper sighed. 'Aye, well, he's not the best of company anyway, for you to keep, bonny lad.'

'I keep company with neither of them.'

'That's as may be.' Culpeper stared at him keenly for a moment. 'So you've not come across Weaver before, and Dimmock—'

'Just the once.'

'Hmmm. Did you detect any . . . edge, there today?'

'How do you mean, edge?'

'Atmosphere, like.'

Arnold shrugged. 'I imagine a certain tension always builds up when you get a visit from the police.'

'When it's a friendly chap like me?' Culpeper asked in mock surprise. 'Why, man, I'm gentleness personified.'

'Even so.'

'So you . . . felt nothing.'

Reluctantly, Arnold admitted, 'They were uneasy about something. I guessed it was probably the result of your visit.'

Culpeper winked and nodded his head. He squinted through the windscreen. 'I'm not so certain. Why . . . look there, Mr Landon, our friends are away out.'

A car was leaving the Old Rectory. It was the Japanese vehicle. 'Nissan, built in Sunderland,' Culpeper said cheerfully, as he wrote down the number in a little black-covered book. 'Bonny car. Now I wonder where those two lads are off to?'

'It's a free country.'

'Don't be so surly with me, lad. I'm just a philanthropic observer of Tyneside life.'

'Just exactly what do you want from me, Chief Inspector?' Arnold asked.

Culpeper watched him carefully for several seconds. 'I'm not sure,' he said at last. 'Maybe confirmation. Maybe information. Or maybe it's just that I'm curious about the way you seem to be stepping in and out of this business.'

'What business?'

'The murder of Lynne Anderson and her lover.'

'I'm not in the business at all!'

'How can you say that?' Culpeper's brown eyes were wide in mock despair. 'Her husband is your colleague. The dead woman has visited several places—Tarset, Temple Barden, Langley—and you seem to be following in her footsteps. When her old man gets back after her murder, it's to you he comes first of all—'

'That's all circumstantial, and is easily explained by coincidence. She was doing a series on Northumberland

Ghosts: it's almost inevitable our paths would cross, if I have to finish Anderson's work on the tower houses. Most of these houses are supposed to be peopled with ghosts. And I was recently transferred to the DMA: I didn't *choose* to get involved with Kevin Anderson.'

'That's right. He chose you.' Culpeper looked at him carefully for a few moments. 'I read your statement again. The one you made when you came in on Monday morning. Anderson—he was pretty strong on Ben Edwards.'

'He said he was a violent man. Knocked Lynne Anderson about, before she married Kevin.'

'Seems it checks out.'

'Is Edwards a suspect?' Arnold asked wonderingly.

'Like Anderson, he's a bit vague about his comings and goings,' Culpeper replied.

'And Kevin Anderson?'

Culpeper grunted. 'Oh, he's still our front runner. The only bloody firm one, if the truth were known. But he's consistent in his vagueness. He still can't give us details of his movements.'

'That's bad?'

'It ain't good news for him, bonny lad.' Culpeper was silent for a while. 'Anyway, I suppose I'd better let you go on your way. But I thought I'd better check with you, how well you know Weaver and Dimmock. A piece of advice, Mr Landon. Don't have too much truck with them.'

'I barely know Dimmock and I've never really met Weaver,' Arnold replied. 'But why the warning?'

'Ghosts . . . and old paintings,' Culpeper mused. 'I wonder what they're up to? You see, Mr Landon, those two there, they're a bit . . . kinky? They're tied up in one of these rather unpleasant witch things: you know, midnight rituals, dancing naked around bonfires, swords and capes and black hoods and all that sort of rubbish. We've had complaints; some of the parish churches hereabouts have had gravestones defaced. We're keeping an eye on that pair. And when I was there they were nervous; like kittens on a ropewalk. I'd like to know what's bothering them. It's just that I think innocent lads like you need to keep away from that sort of thing.'

'I couldn't agree more,' Arnold replied.

'I'm pleased you feel that way. So, I'll let you away, hey? Incidentally, how did you first get in touch with Dimmock?'

'An assignment. The painting.'

'Your boss sent you?'

'Mr Brent-Ellis. That's right.'

Culpeper's eyes narrowed. 'The husband of Mrs Brent-Ellis, of course.' He grunted. 'I've heard she rules in that house. And she knows Dimmock.' He grunted. 'Can't see a Committee chairwoman dancing naked around a bonfire, though, can you? But, I suppose more fanciful things have happened.'

Arnold made his way back to his car and watched as Culpeper drove away. He was confused. Culpeper's comments regarding his 'involvement' in the murder of Lynne Anderson and Lance Stevens disturbed him. He didn't feel involved; there was no link between his investigation of the tower houses and Lynne Anderson's ghost stories. The fact that husband and wife had been working on parallel assignments was a coincidence: it had not even been mentioned by Kevin Anderson. It was even possible, given his lack of interest in the work assigned to him, and his anxiety over his wife, that he had not been aware she was travelling to the same sites he was writing about.

Kevin Anderson had, of course, not visited the sites. That was clear from his notes.

As for Dimmock and the saturnine Weaver, Arnold had no intention of courting their company. He had had one brush with the occult already; he did not want another.* The tension in the Old Rectory could be explained: if they were involved in Satanism, a visit from a Chief Inspector

* *The Devil is Dead.*

could be unnerving. Culpeper might well have explained he was calling to investigate the movements of Lynne Anderson before she died, but they could easily have believed there was a hidden agenda. It would have accounted for their nervousness—and even the way they had shot out of the house once he had gone, startled rabbits running from the poacher.

And then there was the painting. It still interested Arnold —the puzzle of the shields, the bars, the trelliswork and the haunted features of the Christ image still fascinated him, but it was an interest he was prepared to put aside if it meant any further contact with Nick Dimmock and his odd companion.

Even if Mrs Brent-Ellis did dance naked around bonfires.

Arnold got in his car and drove off. It was time to meet the other two at the Stag in Hartside.

It was close on five o'clock when he reached Hartside. He turned into a narrow car park beside the squat Norman church and walked across the green, past the stand of beech trees to the Stag Inn. It was a fine old building, an eighteenth-century coaching inn which had served travellers from the Borders through to Newcastle and the south. In those days they had had options thereafter: to continue the rattling coach journey down through York to London or to take ship at the Quayside and make the faster trip down the coast. Options were few now: Hartside itself was a quiet backwater, the nearest railway station was some thirty miles away, and no coaches thundered through the village.

Arnold went into the bar and ordered a half of lager for himself. There were only two other people present: walkers, it seemed by the clothes they wore—cagoules, waterproof trousers, heavy boots. It was too early for the locals to appear.

Jane had not yet arrived and there was no sign of Ben. Arnold installed himself in the inglenook under the great oaken beam and settled back to wait. He thought back over his conversations with Dimmock and Culpeper, but he reached no new conclusions. He was inclined, however, to take Culpeper's advice seriously: he wanted no further contact with Dimmock and his strange companion. Brent-Ellis could find someone else to pursue the matter of the painting.

Jane arrived about fifteen minutes later. She dumped her camera on the table beside the inglenook and puffed out her cheeks as she sat down. 'Drink?' Arnold asked.

'Gin and tonic.'

'You look as if you've had a hard time.'

'Not really. Just this last ten miles. Stuck behind a series of bloody tractors.'

'Penalties of the countryside. You had no trouble with the photographs, then?'

She pulled a face. Arnold rose and walked across to the bar to order her gin and tonic. He brought it back, placed it in front of her and she took a greedy swallow.

'Looks as though you needed that.'

'I didn't stop for lunch, that was the problem,' Jane explained. 'I got rather absorbed, time whistled past, so I had to get my skates on to make it to Tarset Hall and get the work done there.'

Arnold smiled. 'And how did you get on with the rather formidable Major Manners?'

She frowned and sipped at her gin and tonic. 'I'm not sure, really. He's a bit odd, isn't he? When I met him first, the other evening, he just sort of barked at me, went into a reverie, and then drove off as though he'd forgotten something.'

'And this time?'

She wrinkled her nose thoughtfully. 'Well, I don't know. He was . . . inconsistent. I rolled up to Tarset Hall and he met me at the door. I explained what I was about—mentioned your name—'

'*That* would have taken you a long way,' Arnold said ironically.

'Well, I think it gave me credibility, which surprised me,' she flashed back. 'Anyway, I asked him if I could take the shots and he was a bit reluctant but he agreed eventually. What's his problem with women?'

Arnold, slightly taken aback by the abrupt change in tack, replied, 'His wife left him. He was embittered by the experience.'

'The wound?'

'I think that was a contributory factor. My guess would be that there were deeper-seated problems as well. But I wouldn't really know.'

'He was very . . . wary of me. But he's quite passionate about Tarset Hall, isn't he? I think his reluctance to have me poking around was really overcome by his pride in the house itself—he wanted it to be photographed.'

'So you managed to get the shots I suggested?'

Jane nodded. 'I think so. I got the front doorway, and the west wing. I did a pretty good tour of the place in fact, took some extra shots that you hadn't suggested in case they were of any use, and then went around to thank him. He seemed affable enough at that point, if somewhat stiff.' She finished her drink. 'How are you fixed?'

Arnold said, 'I'll get them.'

'Never say that to a feminist,' she retorted smartly and rose to her feet, clutching her glass. 'You drinking lager?'

'Just a half.'

She went up to the bar and came back with the drinks. She had a sandwich. 'I'm starving. I presumed you'd had lunch, so I got you nothing. But if you're peckish—'

'I can manage. You say he was affable up to that point. So what happened then?'

She unwrapped her sandwich with some difficulty. 'Cheese and ham.' She wrinkled her nose. 'Smells a bit elderly. Yes, he was OK up to then so I took my courage in my hands and asked if I could take a few interior shots. He was a bit hesitant but then allowed me in. But he sort of trailed me, you know, and kept interrupting me, asking me questions about the brochure, which tower houses were being photographed, that sort of thing. I told him what I could, of course, and explained how the three of us were working in harness, but I couldn't tell him too much about the brochure itself. He seemed interested in Edwards, asked me a few questions about him, whether I'd met him, and so on. And then the phone rang and he went off to answer it. It was after that he got a bit shirty and agitated.'

'How do you mean?'

'Well, I'd moved on to the sitting-room, you know, taking a shot of the carved fireplace—it's a bit dilapidated, isn't it, that room?'

'I gather he's not sufficiently well-heeled to put the property to rights,' Arnold explained.

'Anyway, he came back into the sitting-room and he had changed completely. He was curt, ill-mannered, and he bundled me out sharpish. I don't know what the phone call was all about, but it seems to me he was pretty upset about it. His whole attitude had changed. No more chat, no more questions, he even seemed annoyed that I was in his bloody sitting-room.'

'That might have been the key,' Arnold murmured.

'How do you mean?'

'The phone call might have upset him. On the other hand, it might have been the fact you were taking shots in his sitting-room. He's a proud man. Taking photographs of the exterior, and structural stuff inside would have been all right, but maybe he wasn't too pleased at you taking photographs in a room he uses personally. As you said, it needs a bit of work on it—it's not exactly *Ideal Home*.'

She shrugged, and munched her sandwich. 'You may be right.' She picked a piece of rind from her mouth and grimaced. 'Sorry. Yes, you may be right. But I felt like a little duckling being ushered from the place after that. He sort of bundled me out like he was in a hurry to see the back of me. He muttered something about an appointment and pushed me out, back to my car, and he got his Land-Rover out at the same time. Followed me down the track. I almost got the impression he wanted to be sure I was really leaving Tarset Hall, and wasn't going to sneak back once he was out of the way. Peculiar feller.'

She pushed aside the rest of her sandwich, and took a sip of her drink. 'I thought we'd be eating later,' Arnold suggested mildly.

'This is only stopgap. Don't worry, I've other corners to fill. Anyway, I left Tarset Hall with camera intact, our friend Major Manners shot off in the opposite direction as I turned towards the Hartside road, and then I got caught behind one tractor after another. You know it's taken me almost an hour to get here?' She snorted. 'How did you get on, anyway?'

Arnold shrugged. 'I had no real problems.' He hesitated about telling her of his conversation with Culpeper. He frowned. 'When you were up at Brunskill, you say you saw lights at the ruins.'

'Uh-huh. Why?'

'And the man who accosted you. What did he look like?'

Jane pursed her lips thoughtfully. 'I didn't get a good look at him: I was a bit scared and wanted to get away from there. But he was kind of tall, thin, lean face, hollow eyes—bit creepy, you know.'

'It could be the same man I saw at the Old Rectory.'

'Really?'

'Can't be sure, of course. But there was another man— named Weaver—with Nick Dimmock. They were rather edgy about something. But then, they'd just had a visit from the police.'

'What about?'

'Just following up inquiries, really.' Arnold sipped his lager and looked around the room. It was beginning to fill up, farmworkers calling in on their way home. 'Tracing Lynne Anderson's last steps, so to speak. She'd been engaged on that ghosts series, so she'd been to the Old Rectory.'

'And this man Weaver?'

Arnold sighed. 'I don't know. But Culpeper—he's the policeman on the case—had a word with me later. Warned me off Weaver and Dimmock. I'd already been told by Brent-Ellis that Dimmock dabbled a bit in the black arts. Culpeper warned me that Dimmock and Weaver were bad news: there've been complaints, it seems, from some of the parish churches. And that made me wonder . . .'

'Yes?'

'The lights up at Brunskill. You said the man who accosted you seemed edgy?'

'He certainly wasn't happy about me being up on Reivers Crags,' Jane replied ruefully.

'From the crags you looked down on Brunskill castle. If it was Weaver, maybe he was worried that you were looking down on his playground, concerned that you were seeing things you shouldn't be seeing.'

Jane stared at him wide-eyed. 'You mean black magic stuff?'

'Ritual. Culpeper reckons Brunskill has been used from time to time because of ancient devil worship connotations.'

Jane snorted. 'I could well believe it of the guy I met up at the crags, Weaver or not. He gave me the shivers.' She glanced at her watch. 'Ben's late.'

'Maybe he's been waylaid by the ritualists.'

'You can't be serious!'

Arnold laughed. 'Of course not! In broad daylight? They're creatures of the dark. And probably quite timid souls, if the truth be known.'

She crumpled up the packet in which the sandwich had been stored and threw it into the grate in the inglenook. 'Well, I hope my dear uncle gets here soon. Time we get back to Newcastle I'll be hungry again.'

Time slipped past slowly. Jane removed the film from her camera and handed it to Arnold. They discussed the shots they had taken, in desultory fashion, for both now were getting uneasy. They decided mutually that more alcohol would be dangerous: each had a long drive ahead, to Newcastle and Morpeth respectively. Arnold bought two glasses of lime and soda and later, Jane ordered two coffees. The noise levels subsided in the bar, and then rose again as a new influx of people came in.

'It's gone six-thirty,' Jane said and struck both hands on the table decisively. 'Ben should be back by now.'

Arnold nodded. He was worried. Ben's recent heart attack had weakened the little man and it could be that the stress of driving out here today and taking photographs at the two sites had been too much for him. It was unlikely, because Ben himself had insisted it would be no problem, but he was certainly late for their meeting.

'Do you think we'd better look for him?' Jane asked anxiously.

'I think so. But there's the chance we could miss him: it's dusk now. I think the best bet would be for you to stay here—'

'No. I can't do that. Sitting around waiting would drive me up the wall. I'll go, or we go, but I'm not staying here.'

'All right,' Arnold conceded, 'you leave your car here— so if he does turn up while we're out he'll realize you at least will be coming back—and then we can both go in my car. I'll leave a message with the barman as well, in case Ben does turn up in the meanwhile.'

Jane agreed. Arnold told the barman that if Ben Gibson arrived he was to be told to wait until their return. Jane was already standing at the door of the Stag Inn when he turned.

They took the road out of Newcastle, west towards Temple Barden and Brunskill. The signposts flashed past: Temple Barden, Barden, the road to Tarset Hall, Reivers Crags. They breasted the rise some four miles from Brunskill and in the gathering dusk they could see, from a distance, the flashing blue lights ahead of them.

'Police car,' Jane said.

And an ambulance.

Arnold speeded up. When he was some two hundred yards from the lights he began to slow: a hundred yards further on there was a police sign in the roadway: ACCI-DENT. Arnold drove carefully on, and then stopped. A uniformed policeman was standing in the road: he waved Arnold forward. When Arnold did not move he walked deliberately towards the car.

He leaned towards Arnold in the driving seat, one hand on the car roof. 'Please move on, sir. There's been an accident.'

'Can you tell me what cars are involved?'

'Just one, sir.' The young policeman hesitated, staring at Jane's anguished face.

'What make is the car?'

'It's a VW Passat.'

There was a strangled gasp beside Arnold. Jane opened the passenger door and got out.

'Miss —'

'I think I know who might be in the car,' she said desperately and ran forward, past the ambulance and the police car. Arnold got out and followed more slowly as the policeman hurried after her.

The Passat was on the wrong side of the road. It was tilted on its side. The nose of the car had ploughed directly into the bole of a massive elm tree. The windscreen was completely shattered, the front of the car buckled beyond repair, and Arnold guessed that the steering-wheel would have been driven into the driving seat.

Jane was crying.

The young policeman turned hesitantly to Arnold. 'Do you know the car, sir?'

'It belongs to a friend of mine. The lady is his niece. His name is Ben Gibson. Short, in his late sixties or there-abouts —'

'We took him out just a few minutes ago, sir,' the young policeman said nervously.

Arnold looked at him silently. There was a cold, empty feeling in his stomach. He did not need to ask the question.

The policeman swallowed hard. 'It would have been quick. Once he hit the tree, he'd have died—he'd have been killed outright. I'm sorry, sir.'

The ambulance was manœuvring away from the edge of the road. Jane turned desperately to the policeman. 'Let me go with him! I'll go in the ambulance!'

'No,' Arnold said quietly, and reached out to take her in his arms. 'There's no point. You'd better come back with me.'

3

The next few days were an odd experience for Arnold. He had been close to his father, and at his death there had been a great emptiness in Arnold's life.

The death of Ben Gibson created a similar emptiness, at a time when Arnold was older, more mature, innured to loss and disappointment. Ben had already had a heart attack, and was nearing the end of his days, but for Arnold the shock of his loss was acute nevertheless. He had been one of Arnold's closest friends—perhaps the closest. It was not that Arnold had known him a long time: the friendship was measured within the last decade. Rather, it was the warmth that had been engendered between them: an undemanding friendship based on humour, good fellowship, an unstated empathy and the kind of relationship that did not demand regular meetings but fed warmly from a regard they held for each other.

Arnold had respected Ben Gibson, and his going left a gap in his life.

The journey back to Newcastle had been harrowing. It was not that Jane had cried extensively: indeed, after her first outburst she sat stiffly in the car while Arnold drove.

She stared straight ahead, saying nothing, and when he dropped her off at Framwellgate Moor she told him she did not need him to stay with her. She was controlled, passive, but he knew that there would be a great tearing inside. She did not want to share her grief: it was personal, and private. The funeral was held at the end of the week. A post-mortem had been necessary but it was apparently unclear whether Ben had had another heart attack before his car had struck the tree. The suggestion was made that he might well have blacked out. There was one matter that was raised, off-handedly, by the police officer who came to see both Arnold and Jane.

'Had Mr Gibson been involved in an accident prior to the crash?'

'I don't think so,' Arnold had replied. 'Why do you ask?'

The policeman had shrugged. 'It looks as though he must have got into some sort of scrape before he hit that tree. But you hadn't seen him, of course, from the time he left Newcastle.'

'No. But I still don't quite understand—'

'It looks as though he might have been in some sort of collision earlier. There's fresh damage to the side of his car. Couldn't have happened in the crash itself for it doesn't seem there was another car involved. But his right offside wing is dented and damaged quite badly—crumpled. Maybe somebody reversed into him at some stage. Or else he hit something himself. Maybe he got dizzy, did some damage to his car, and yet insisted on going on. Till he eventually blacked out and crashed. Was Mr Gibson a *stubborn* man, sir?'

Jane had bridled at that. 'He was a determined man. And if he was stubborn, he was not foolhardy. If he had had a dizzy spell he would *not* have continued to drive.'

The police officer made no reply. He clearly thought the matter of little importance.

The funeral service was held in a small church on the Gateshead bank and there were very few people at the graveside. It was then that Jane told Arnold she was going away for a few days.

'Have you decided what to do about the bookshop?' he asked her gently.

'I'm Ben's closest relative. I believe he left the shop to me.' She averted her eyes for a moment. 'I think I'll just carry it on. I think that's what he wanted.'

'You know that if there's any way in which I can help, you only have to ask.'

Jane looked at him directly. 'I know that, Arnold.' She paused. 'Ben always said you were a good man. I believe that.'

She turned away then, aware that she had embarrassed him.

He had already taken the brochure to the Tourist Board. The films he, Ben and Jane had used had been quickly developed in the department and it was at Brent-Ellis's suggestion that Arnold took the final materials to Edwards personally. It was with a degree of reluctance that Arnold did so.

Edwards's office was surprisingly cramped, a small room on the third floor of an office block in central Newcastle. When Arnold was ushered in, Edwards waved Arnold to a seat. Arnold handed over the materials.

'About bloody time, too,' Edwards growled in a surly, ungracious tone.

He opened the envelope and skimmed quickly through the contents. He grunted—whether it was a sign of content or disagreement was not clear to Arnold. He inspected the photographs and the few sketches Arnold had made. He raised no objection to them, so Arnold presumed they were acceptable.

'You'll be happy to know,' Edwards announced ironically, 'that Miss Savage is still alive—and looking forward to publication of the materials. I phoned her this morning when I was told you were coming in with the package.'

'I hope it will be up to her expectations.'

'It had better be.' Edwards squinted at Arnold in calculating fashion. He bit at his thumbnail, his teeth grinding
unpleasantly.

'Is there anything else? If not—'

Edwards extended a hand, warning Arnold not to leave.
He continued to stare at him for a few seconds. 'I gather
it's *you* I've got to thank for some unpleasant hours recently,
Mr Landon.'

Arnold raised his eyebrows. 'Me? I don't understand.'

'What exactly did you say to the police?'

Arnold was silent. Edwards held him with a steely glance.
'It can only have been you. When they interviewed me they
said that there was a statement about my involvement with
Lynne. That bastard Anderson would have shouted about
it, of course, but I picked up the fact that someone else
had mentioned it. Kevin Anderson gave himself up at your
house, I understand. And you then repeated the drivel he'd
told you.'

'I made a statement, yes. As to your involvement—'

'They've given me a hard time, Landon. You'd have
done better keeping your nose out of things. I make a bad
enemy. People have found that out in the past. You should
have kept your mouth shut.'

'I was asked to repeat what Anderson told me.' Arnold
felt a knot of anger growing in his chest. 'And I don't take
kindly to threats.'

'Who's threatening?' Anderson showed his teeth in a
humourless smile. 'I'm just talking facts. Not that I'm
worried. Looks to me like it's all over bar the shouting,
now. They've charged Kevin Anderson this morning: had
to, or they'd have had to let him go. Circumstantial, I'm
told, since they still haven't traced the gun to him, but he
did have a gun licence years ago, it seems. But I like to
have a quiet life: I don't like snoopers interfering. And I
don't like having to explain my whereabouts to coppers.'

'I gather you had difficulty doing so,' Arnold replied
coldly.

'Don't you worry, my son, I can look after myself, and I'll do whatever explaining is necessary. But you—I understand you got a certain reputation for sticking your nose in other people's business. Well, a word of warning. Our paths have crossed. Let's keep them at a distance in future. I've no desire to see you cropping up in my affairs again.'

Arnold rose to his feet. There was a sour taste in his mouth as he faced the stocky, aggressive man behind the desk. He scowled. 'Mr Edwards, count on it. As far as I'm concerned if we never meet again that will suit me very well.'

Jane had said she was going away for a few days. Arnold was worried about her, so he rang the Quayside bookshop a few times to check if she had returned. There was no answer. A request came through from Brent-Ellis to ask what was happening about the investigation of Dimmock's painting; Arnold replied he was still working on it but had nothing to report. It was a lie. He was overtaken by a curious lassitude: the fact his desk was clear, and that he had little to do bothered him not at all. It was as though he was floating in an empty sea of uncertainty, not knowing what to do or where to go.

He was asked to visit Hadrian's Wall to look at some artefacts they had discovered near Chester's Fort and it roused him from his torpor, but only for a day or so. There was a lecture he attended in Berwick, along with other members of the department: he enjoyed the drive along the windswept Northumberland coast, if not the lecture itself.

But they were interludes.

He was regretting Ben Gibson, and his death, in a way he found impossible to explain to himself. But he suspected that it was rooted in guilt. For if he had not asked Ben's help in taking photographs, the little frog-like man could still have been alive.

Arnold had barely looked at the photographs they had taken. He had made a quick selection, packing them together in the folder for Edwards. They were jumbled together in no particular order. But late in the week he took them out, at home in his bungalow and went through them quietly.

Ben had taken some good shots of Brunskill, and Jane had shown herself no tyro in the way she had photographed her own assignments. Arnold's flash work inside the Old Rectory had not been very successful, whereas Jane's interior work in Tarset Hall was much better.

On an impulse, he reached for the phone and tried her home number at Framwellgate Moor. She answered after the third ring.

'Jane? Arnold Landon.'

'Oh, hi! How are you?'

'More to the point, how are *you*?'

She was silent for a moment. 'I'm OK now, Arnold. I needed time and space. Ben's death was a blow, but . . .' She paused, brightened her tone. 'So, you keeping busy?'

'Not really. But I was just looking at the shots . . . the shots we all took that day. I wondered whether you'd like copies. I know it's a bit crass of me, because it might bring back memories, but on the other hand—'

'Arnold, it wasn't your fault, you know.'

He was silent.

'It could have happened any time,' she said quietly. 'It was nothing to do with the assignment. You mustn't think it was a responsibility you must bear. And there's no reason why you should ring me because of those feelings.'

'That's not why I rang, Jane.'

'Well, if it's to check how I am, believe me, I'm fine. And I'm pleased you thought of me.'

Arnold was silent for a few seconds, struggling to find the right words. 'I miss him, Jane.'

'So do I . . .' She paused. 'But what about these photographs?' she added brightly. 'I hope they all came out all right.'

'They served the purpose. Maybe not works of art—' he smiled—'at least, mine aren't. But would you like copies?'

'I'd like to see them, at least.'

'Perhaps,' he said tentatively, 'I could bring them down tomorrow evening. It's Friday. We could have a meal . . .'

'That,' she replied, 'would be a very good idea.'

He called at her home in Framwellgate Moor about six and they had a sherry and went through the photographs together. At seven-thirty Arnold drove them into Durham City to eat at the County Hotel. Jane looked bright; she was managing to contol whatever emotions she might have been experiencing, mainly, he guessed, for his benefit. They ate well, partook of a bottle of wine, and Arnold thoroughly enjoyed the evening. The shadow cast by Ben's death lifted for a while. He gained the impression Jane enjoyed the occasion also.

'Well,' she said at the end of the meal, 'my place for coffee?'

'If you'd not prefer it here.'

'My place.'

She was silent when they drove back up the hill, past the University and Aykley Heads headquarters, to Framwellgate Moor. As he locked his car she opened the front door. She paused, looked back at him. 'Arnold,' she said quietly, 'it's a long drive back to Morpeth, it's getting late, and I have a spare bedroom with a bed made up. You're welcome to stay.'

'I'm not sure—'

'It means you could have a brandy with your coffee. You don't need to go to work tomorrow. You could have a lie-in. More important, it would give us a chance to talk. About memories. I think we both need a chance to do that.'

He could not disagree, so it was settled.

She made the coffee and brought it into the small sitting-room. 'The brandy's over there,' she said. 'You can pour your own. Ever the genteel host, you see!'

Arnold smiled, and walked across to the drinks cabinet, poured two brandies. 'I take it you want one.'

'I certainly do.'

Arnold turned. Jane was standing beside the coffee table, the tray still in her hands. She was staring down at the pile of photographs that still littered the table. Slowly, she put down the tray on the settee and picked up the top photograph. 'Well, I'm damned!'

'Unladylike,' he reproved her mockingly. She did not smile. 'What's the matter?'

She made no reply. Instead, she turned on her heel and left the room. Taken aback, Arnold waited. A few minutes later she returned. She was carrying a magnifying glass. She inspected the photograph again, under magnification.

'What's the problem?' Arnold asked.

Wordlessly she handed photograph and magnifying glass to Arnold. She left the room again, hurriedly.

Puzzled, Arnold inspected the photograph.

It was a copy of the shot Jane had taken in the dilapidated sitting-room of Tarset Hall, when its owner had been called away to the phone. She'd made a better job of it than Arnold could have done: the flash had picked out the detail in the room remarkably well, including the handsome stone fireplace. But he could not understand what had startled her. It was only when she came back in the room that he realized what it was.

He had been in that room with Major Manners and never noticed it. But then, he would probably have had his back to the fireplace for part of the time. And the Major had engaged him in conversation; he hadn't really looked around, not least because of the scruffy state of the room. The Major, sensitive to the state of the room, would not have appreciated a close inspection.

'The coat of arms,' he said.

It was placed right in the centre of the fireplace, cut into the sandstone, worn, but still recognizable. He could not make out the details, but the shape of the shield was the same and when he applied the magnifying glass, as Jane

had done, he could see enough of the detail to make it
certain.

'The de Bohun shield.'

'No.' Jane was standing beside him, a folder in her hands.
She opened it and took out one of the photographs he had
lent her, of the painting discovered at the Old Rectory. 'No.
Look again. It's the de Bohun shield all right, but with
something missing.'

'The bars.'

Wordlessly, she handed him the photograph that
Dimmock had given Arnold. He stared at it, and compared
it with the coat of arms cut into the stone of the fireplace
at Tarset Hall. She was right. The bars were missing in the
shield in both the painting, and in the fireplace.

'Wait a minute,' Arnold muttered. He riffled through the
photographs on the coffee table and drew out one which
Ben Gibson had taken at Brunskill Castle. 'I didn't send
this in to Edwards. I made a selection, but I wasn't paying
a great deal of attention—I had other things on my mind.
This was one of the shots I discarded.' He peered at it
closely. 'I couldn't make out why Ben would have taken it,
and I didn't take a good look at it, at the time. It's a shot
of one of the walls at Brunskill. I thought he was just running off the end of the roll.'

Jane stood beside him and looked over his shoulder as
he pointed.

'Just a wall, I thought. But I *did* see there was a shield
cut into the stone. I just didn't pay it any attention at the
time: I was preoccupied with Edwards's bloody brochure.'

The photographs had been taken directly against a tall,
crumbling wall. Ben had tilted the camera and had got the
focal length wrong so it was slightly out of focus, but he
had used the zoom lens, and there was an image, somewhat
fuzzy at the edges, of a shield cut into the stone of the wall.

'No bars,' Arnold said quietly.

'The de Bohun shield again?' Jane asked.

'That's right.' Arnold paused. 'Ben saw what we've just

seen. The de Bohun arms, changed as they were on the
painting. That's why he took this photograph. He would
have wanted to show it to us on his return, compare it with
the painting.'

Jane sat down. Arnold picked up his coffee and took the
easy chair across from her. He stared at her blankly. Wild
thoughts chased around in his mind. He was brought back
to reality when she asked, 'What exactly is the history of
Tarset Hall?'

Arnold shrugged. 'The structure, you mean?'

'Yes.'

'The main part of it is fifteenth-century, but there's evidence of thirteenth-century structures there too. It was
originally a tower house which was used as a sort of out-
station to the castle.'

'Who owned the castle?'

'The de Bohun family. As you know, the castle was
demolished in the fifteenth century but the arrangement
prior to that would have been that men-at-arms were stationed in the tower house, and it would certainly have been
in the ownership of the de Bohuns.'

'A sort of lodging-house?'

'Keeping the armed men at hand, but not in the castle
itself.'

Jane pondered for a little while. 'So there's good reason
why the de Bohun arms would appear there, at Tarset
Hall.'

'That's right.'

'What about that fireplace?'

'Certainly not the same time as the gatehouse—which is
the oldest part. I'd say, probably sixteenth-century. Maybe
shortly after the castle was demolished.'

'Did the de Bohuns still own Tarset at that stage?'

'They did.'

She frowned. 'So if the castle was demolished, and they
built the fireplace in Tarset Hall, why did they cut a shield

which was not in fact a replica of their coat of arms, but one which lacked the usual barring?'

'Tradition?' Arnold suggested carefully. There was an odd excitement stirring in his blood.

'What sort of tradition?'

'I'm not sure. But let's think this through. The de Bohuns were a powerful family of ancient lineage. They owned Tarset Castle and the adjoining hall. They would have worshipped in Temple Barden at the Norman church there —it was one of their endowments, and it had Templar connections—and they used as their main residence, originally, Brunskill Castle. They had an approved coat of arms, which they would have used openly. It included the barring we've seen. But for some reason they occasionally showed a different—slightly different—shield. One without the barring.'

'Not in regular usage.'

'I would guess not.'

'That doesn't explain the painting.'

'No, it doesn't.' Arnold considered for a while. 'And we don't know its history. We don't know why it was hidden. We *do* know the Old Rectory would have been part of the de Bohun holdings, and we know that it's an old house. The painting was certainly deliberately hidden, and it contains an image of the de Bohun shield—without the bars.'

'But it also has bars etched into the background behind the Christ head. Why?'

'Your guess is as good as mine.'

Arnold stared at the photograph taken at Brunskill. 'Ben saw something. He took this photograph. It was the last on the roll, yet he took this shot. It's a pity it's so fuzzy. There's something else cut into the stone, just above the shield. It looks like another shield, but I can't really make it out.'

Jane was silent for a while. 'Do you think there's been any contact between the Old Rectory and Tarset Hall?'

Puzzled, Arnold asked, 'How do you mean?'

'Do you think Mr Dimmock has seen the coat of arms at Tarset Hall?'

'I've no idea. But—'

'What?'

'He could well have seen them at Brunskill Castle.'

Jane stared at him with wide eyes. 'Why do you say that?'

'Because he's been up there more than a few times. From what Detective Chief Inspector Culpeper suggested to me, Nick Dimmock and his friends could have been frequent visitors to the ruins of Brunskill Castle.'

CHAPTER 5

1

A mist had risen in the morning fields, lying in a bank in the folds of the hills, drifting and curling at it rose from the valleys to get slowly burned away as the sun rose higher in the hazy sky. From Reivers Crags the patchworked meadows and fields seemed precise and ordered, green and brown and yellow with rape; in the distance the Cheviots were a faded blue, lifting from the mist, the ethereal image from a Japanese print. The crags were a place to gaze from, to think, to contemplate in the silence of the hills.

Arnold stood where Jane had probably sat a few days back. Below him lay the stark ruins of Brunskill Castle. The buildings were in a bad state of decay: the vaulted area at the west gate had collapsed, leaving only two dilapidated arches standing, and the outer walls had been dragged down to erect the dry stone walls that stretched across the farmlands in every direction. It was good building stone for pinfolds and pastures.

The depredations of the farmers and their livestock—for much of the outer walls had been broken down by animals —had nevertheless left the keep largely untouched. But where they had failed, the weather had succeeded and the twin circular turrets had collapsed under the action of frost and storm. Cromwell had done his share of devastation: there had been some battering of the walls by cannon, for a minor Civil War skirmish had been fought here, but throughout all its chequered history the solid Norman tower had largely withstood the ravages of history. Its battlements were broken, the crenellations thrown down, but the tower still reared up proudly to perhaps two-thirds of its original height, its grey stone resisting everything that had been visited upon it. The west wing of the castle had all but disappeared, but there was still a wooden catwalk, erected at the turn of the century for visitors to use, leading into the mound of the keep itself.

Arnold had spent Saturday in the Durham University library, in the shadow of the cathedral and the castle. He'd managed to find an early parking space in the Green and had been one of the first visitors—the students who had drifted in later had stayed only an hour or so before leaving for the river or the rugby field or other social delights. Arnold had settled down in the mediæval section of the reference library: he knew that there was a good local history collection there and he was curious to read about Brunskill and the de Bohuns.

Some of it he knew already. But there was a detailed account of the building of the castle from the date of its original licence: John Lewyn was mentioned, but Arnold noted wryly that the name of Henry Yvele did not appear. Its vicissitudes were noted: its gradual decline; the emergence of a determined de Bohun in the sixteenth century who had attempted to restore it to its former glory, to the ruination of the family finances; the closing of the east wing of the castle as a habitation in the eighteenth century; and its rapid decline thereafter. There were sketches made in 1810 and 1835; a lithograph of 1890, and photographs taken in the 1920s. They showed how rapidly the structure had crumbled in a hundred years of decay and neglect.

It was now, Arnold realized sadly, beyond repair. A designated historical monument, it could be held safe from depredation, but no improvements could be made and it faced a slow and inevitable decline in the face of winter storms.

There were three sketches of the de Bohun arms. Each of them was barred.

And there were four references to the mythical treasure of Tarset. The suggestions made were vague: a 'jewel of immense value obtained from the Saracen'; a holy manuscript 'bound in leather studded with precious stones'; a relic of St Osbert, and 'gold and silver chalices derived from the treasury of Odo of Bayeux'. This last was the nearest any of the accounts got to suggesting an historical provenance for the 'treasure'; its vagueness as to content and history convinced Arnold it was an old wives' tale. There was a comment that the story of the treasure was rooted in the First Crusade, and that a fourteenth-century de Bohun had been given into trust the 'purchase of mankind'—but even that was too slippery a concept to grasp, as far as Arnold was concerned.

The de Bohuns had crumbled with their castle.

Arnold read of their origins, entering France with the Norsemen in the ninth century, and taking part in the swirl of battle and plunder that led to the establishment of fiefdoms in Aquitaine and Gascony and Anjou. By the early eleventh century a de Bohun was making his fortune and reputation in Italy, sweeping down into Capua in 1057 in the freebooting irruption led by Robert le Guiscard, the Crafty. They hacked their way with five hundred horsemen into Calabria and would have taken Palermo had they not been driven back by a plague of tarantulas. De Bohun, Arnold noted wryly, was as human as the rest: he suffered from 'a most poisonous wind, with thunderous farts'—the result, it was assumed, of the tarantula bites.

Whatever the state of his health, it was this de Bohun who laid the foundation of the family fortunes—while one branch flourished in the Angevin kingdom, holding lands in Aquitaine, he left Italy with his retinue and rode north to take part in the papally supported thrust into England in 1066 with Duke William. He was duly rewarded with holdings in the northern lands. The de Bohuns were also prominent in the First and Third Crusades, as Soldier Monks of Christ.

In other words, as Knights Templar.

Arnold checked on Temple Barden. It was, as he had guessed, a de Bohun village, the church established by a dying de Bohun in an attempt to save his ravaged soul, and thereafter continuing with a strong Templar influence which gave the village its name. He discovered also that there had been a de Bohun present at the inquisition of 1312, when the Knights Templar had been overthrown. A footnote suggested that he had not been convicted and executed, but had managed to escape to England.

To Brunskill.

The de Bohun history thereafter was chequered. They seemed not to have been good judges of the political scene: they had a tendency to take the wrong side—Stephen when Matilda was in power, the House of York when Lancaster was at its zenith. Confiscations of family lands were regular, and though usually regained, the great estates were gradually whittled away until it was only Brunskill that remained as a good house, with Tarset Castle in decay in the fifteenth century.

Thereafter, the family dwindled in importance. The last heir had been an Australian who had died in Melbourne in the 1860s. The line was extinct, the holdings dispersed, the achievements of seven hundred years forgotten. And, Arnold thought, the reason for two de Bohun shields lost in the mists that drifted over the valley below.

It was time to go down, and look more closely at the ruins Ben Gibson had photographed.

Sheep cropped the sward that led up to the castle. Arnold parked his car at the gateway, pulling in to the side under the hedge so the car was partly screened from the road. He climbed the gate and walked across the springy grass; on the morning air he could hear the faint sound of church bells, carried up the hill from Temple Barden. The village was probably six miles distant, but the Sunday morning air was still and the bells rang clear and sharp, if faintly.

A hundred yards from the ruins Arnold stopped and stared at the castle. He wondered whether Henry Yvele had had any part in the building of Brunskill. Yvele's West Gate at Canterbury had included external towers circular in plan, and he had repeated the theme at Saltwood Castle in Kent. There were suggestions here of a similar style: the remains of what would have been a tall, circular tower, supported by drum towers and containing a staircase and a chamber above the arch. But he wasn't here to look for such clues.

Arnold drew from his pocket the photographs Ben Gibson had taken of Brunskill before he died. Slowly, he tried to retrace Ben's steps.

The photographs were identifiable as a series: he had probably taken the long shot first. Then he had moved forward to the outer walls, then the gatehouse, then the destroyed west wing. Arnold shuffled the photographs in his hands as he moved forward, trying to follow Ben's route.

At one point he could have diverged: back to the east wing, the vaulted storerooms and the northern of the four stages of construction, or to the south side where he had photographed the Norman tower with its ruined staircase and its six storeys of small chambers, the highest above roof level. Arnold took the first route, then retraced his steps after he had checked off the photographs. He followed on to the south side, slipping the checked photographs into his pocket.

He was left with the main tower.

Tower houses in the Border country tended to be of a pattern: three storeys, which comprised a storage basement vaulted against fire, a first-floor hall, and then the great chamber or sleeping apartment above. But this was not a normal tower house: the Norman tower was older, raised to an original six storeys, Arnold guessed, although it was now no higher than four storeys. The entrance, the ruined newel staircase and half-collapsed chambers on the next three floors could clearly be seen. But where had Ben photographed the de Bohun arms?

Arnold prowled around the site.

He had now discarded all the photographs bar the one, and he was unable to locate the place from which it had been taken. Since Ben had taken a shot only of the wall itself there was no background to identify, which could lead him to the appropriate spot. Nor was the lighting of any assistance: the wall was well enough lit, but Arnold did not know what time of day Ben had taken the photograph. He had used the zoom lens, so it was obvious the carving was above head height, but from ground level Arnold could not make out the section of wall that Ben had photographed.

'Hey!'

Arnold swivelled around. There was someone calling from the gate at the road, sitting astride the wooden gate. Ar arm was raised, waving. It was Jane.

Arnold sat down as she walked forward across the grass towards him. She was dressed in jeans and a light sweater: she looked quite small, and oddly vulnerable. Yet he knew her for a tough, determined woman. She smiled as she grew closer.

'I thought you'd get up here pretty early. Did you find out much at the library yesterday?'

Arnold nodded. 'Quite a bit. But most of it useless, though interesting. Very few references to the shield, and they were all barred. But I'm having trouble now finding just where Ben took his photographs from.'

'It's a lot of stone,' she commented, looking around her, hands on hips.

'I've wandered right around it, but I can't pick up his

vantage-point. I don't think he can have taken the shot from down here.' Arnold squinted up towards the tower. 'And I can't see him trying to climb up that ruined staircase.'

Jane laughed. 'You'd be surprised. He was a tough old bird. And stubborn. He would never admit that he needed to slow down after his heart attack. And he would never admit to his age. I wouldn't have put it past him to climb up there: and I don't think he was bothered with heights. Me, now—well, the crags are one thing, but I wouldn't fancy climbing up that rickety structure.'

'It's stronger, and probably safer, than it looks,' Arnold observed.

'It looks damned crumbly to me. Anyway, I can't stay. I thought I'd take a drive out, see how you're getting on, and it's a pleasant morning. But I've got some work I want to do at the bookshop.' She was looking away from Arnold, her face averted. 'I just wondered whether, when you were through here, you might like to call back at Newcastle. Tell me how you've got on. Maybe we could go have an Italian in Grey Street.'

It was not what Arnold had intended. But he knew what was behind her question. They had talked well into the night on Friday. She had told him a great deal about Ben, about their relationship, about the many little ways in which he had shown his affection for his niece. She missed him badly. So did Arnold. But for her it was worse: the house on the Quayside would echo without him. Her loss was more acute than Arnold's because she had been used to seeing him every day, being the butt of his mischievous affection, being aware of his kindly presence each day in the bookshop, and in the evenings, long chats over a cup of tea or a drink, when the Quayside was quiet. It would be the evenings she was finding difficult to face right now.

It would get better, but this was the hard time.

'I've no idea what time I'll finish here,' Arnold said

quietly. 'But I can't see me being here much after lunch-
time. If you want a hand at the bookshop—'

'That would be good,' she said simply.

'And an Italian would suit me fine this evening.'

'That's settled, then.' She flashed him a quick smile.
'Good hunting.'

He watched her walk away, climb over the gate, and he
heard her start her car. In a little while he saw the flash of
sunlight on its windows as it climbed the hill above Reivers
Crags.

He broke off at midday, frustrated.

He had brought some sandwiches with him, so he walked
across the field to the winding stream that ran its course
between high grassy banks some three hundred yards from
the castle. He sat down on the bank and stared at the water:
the stream would probably have been much closer to the
castle five hundred years ago; it would probably have
served as a latrine for the occupants, taking discharges from
the garderobes. The water was still far from pristine: cattle
upstream had muddied it, and it would hardly be a pure
haven for the trout and stickleback that no doubt still
flashed under its banks.

As he munched on his sandwich he looked back to the
castle itself. He tried to think what would have been in
Ben's mind. Arnold himself had not tried to climb the castle
walls: the stairs were ruined and dangerous, and he could
hardly believe Ben, in his state, would have essayed the
climb, whatever Jane might say. What would he have been
thinking of as he came to the end of the roll of film?

A vague idea began to formulate in Arnold's mind. Ben
had been a man of a romantic turn of mind. A watchmaker
all his life, he had been used to dealing with detail, but in
turning to run a bookshop, he had allowed his idiosyn-
crasies full play. He had stocked his shop with antique
books, old prints, elderly biographies; he held no fiction
and stocked no modern works beyond the 1950s. He had

held a view of the past which had been similar to Arnold's, and one which Jane also shared, in fact. It was a romantic view, but not tarnished with sentiment: it harked back to the realities and harshness of life centuries ago, but it attempted to recreate the feeling of what it had been like to live then. For Arnold it was the way men had worked stone and wood, the manner in which they had carved and built and created; for Ben Gibson it had been different—his world had been books, the words men had put down to explain their feelings, to tell of their experiences, to prove that they had really existed. The two attitudes—Arnold's and Ben's—had been complementary. Yet Arnold could not now get inside Ben's head.

What would he have wanted to do with the last shot on the roll, when the work was done?

Arnold stood up and looked back at the castle. The tower stood out dramatically, outlined against the hills beyond which lay the valley leading down to Temple Barden. The sun had broken through the haze now, and the last vestiges of mist and disappeared from the hill slopes. To the right the Cheviots rose, blue and distant, and high above his head Arnold could hear a lark singing lustily.

But this wasn't the best view of the castle. Its most dramatic backcloth would be the stark hill crowned by Reivers Crags, with the dark forested slopes beyond. Thoughtfully, Arnold walked towards the castle . . . If Ben had wanted a last, romantically dramatic shot—not of detail, but of the broad sweep of the meadow beyond the tower, with Reivers Crags in the background he would have had to climb not the dangerous tower steps but the broken wall above the vaulted storerooms.

It was not a difficult scramble: perhaps ten feet high, the ledge could be approached by a pile of broken stone. And from the ledge above the vaulted basement he could have got a fine shot of the tower walls, the meadow, and the hill and crags beyond.

Arnold climbed over the broken masonry at the foot of

the wall. As he had guessed, it was easy enough, a series of large ashlared stones that provided adequate support. The pile of stones gave him an easy staircase to the top of the wall: quite within Ben Gibson's capabilities. And the view was what he had expected—and what maybe Ben had been seeking for his last shot.

Arnold shaded his eyes against the glare of the sun. He was staring directly at the wall of the Norman tower, in the foreground. He put his head back, looking upwards, and then he took another look at the photograph Ben had taken.

He scrutinized the wall again. Ben had used a zoom lens, tilted the camera so it had been somewhat out of focus. Arnold looked higher, and raised his glance further.

It was then that he saw it.

The shield was etched into the wall some fifty feet above ground level. He could not make out the detail, but above it he could see a second shield. It was here, from this vantage-point above the ancient storerooms that Ben had taken his photograph.

Arnold made his way back down from the ledge, dropping the last few feet from the wall to the grass below. He walked towards the Norman tower. If he was going to take a closer look at the shields on the tower wall he would have to try climbing the ruined staircase.

It was unprotected on one side: the wall had crumbled away centuries ago, and the steps themselves were broken, great gaps appearing to expose rubble and infill of the most precarious kind, if he were to climb up there. But he had no choice, if he was to inspect the shields.

The first fifteen feet were easy enough. The staircase had been protected from storms by the outer wall of the tower itself and by the projecting angle turrets that would have been built there. The drum towers that had been built at the angles gave further protection but as Arnold scrambled higher the stairs became more worn and broken, where the right-hand wall had collapsed inwards, exposing the staircase to a thirty-foot drop into what would have been the chapel area below.

He paused, breathing hard at the exertion. He looked around him. Reivers Crags menaced from above but in the other direction the valley was already opening up and Arnold began to realize more clearly how the tower had given a commanding view of the meadows and fields and river in ancient days. It would have given the de Bohuns a strong and strategic position, with only Reivers Crags offering an overlooking height, but too distant to pose a military problem for Brunskill.

The old master masons had known where to build, in times of military necessity.

He scrambled upwards, leaning against the outer wall, and holding on to the smooth stone where he could. He was now above the first two storeys, and it was here that the great chamber would have been, the sleeping apartments with windows into a light-well placed centrally. This too was now gone, as the stark outlines only of Brunskill Castle remained.

He looked upwards. The shields would be on the right-hand wall, some twenty feet across from the staircase. It would mean traversing a ledge about ten feet wide; it was probably safe enough, the remains of the floor that had been largely timbered but buttressed at this height with masonry. Looking down from this height, he could make out the general layout of the castle below him: the vaulted storerooms, the buttery and pantry, the chapel, the oriel and the chambers leading off from the great hall. In its day, Brunskill had been an impressive building.

Arnold reached the ledge.

He stopped again, looking carefully at the masonry. It seemed solid enough. It led to the right-hand wall of the Norman tower: there the masonry was ten or twelve feet thick, it seemed, the drum tower curving outwards and probably containing a lookout position, a guardroom with a commanding view of the valley across to Temple Barden.

Carefully, Arnold walked across the ledge, keeping one hand on the stone wall to the left, pausing at the narrow mullions of the window opening half way along. A jackdaw flew off suddenly, disturbed at its nest, violent in its cawing protest: the sound was taken up from the belt of trees down near the river, as the warning was given and starlings rose in a black cloud across the fields.

He reached the far wall, stood just beside the drum tower and looked up. Two feet above his head was the carving he sought. It was cut clearly into the stone: the de Bohun shield. Except that it lacked the bars.

It was a replica of the shield in the painting that had been discovered in the Old Rectory at Temple Barden.

Arnold inspected the second shield. It was placed some two feet above the first one. Once again, it was the de Bohun shield. With a difference. This was the formal, heraldic shield as it had appeared in full colour in the books Arnold had inspected at the Durham University library. It included the bars.

Arnold frowned, considering the situation.

The original heraldic shield of the de Bohuns would have been used from the time the family developed it, probably in the ninth century as they moved south with the Norsemen. At some time the shield had appeared in a second version, with the central bars on the shield omitted. That version had been cut into the fireplace at Tarset Hall— owned by the de Bohuns—and again here, under the original version of the shield. And that second version had also been painted.

And if the painting had been created at some time in the fifteenth century, or earlier, it must help date the appearance of the second version of the heraldic device.

But to what purpose? And why, Arnold wondered, had both shields been cut into the stone, up here on the Norman tower? There had to be some significance to it, but it escaped him. He stood, staring at the two devices for several minutes, as the noise of the starlings settled below him and then he edged himself into the corner of the tower and sat down on the warm stone of the ledge. The sun was pleasantly warm on his face and he put his head back. He closed his eyes.

And he thought about the de Bohuns, and the painting, and the bloody, clashing years of the fourteenth century.

2

He dozed for a while, sitting there in the sun as the afternoon advanced. He dreamed lightly, his mind preoccupied with thoughts of mediæval castles, and lumbering horses carrying iron-carapaced men addicted to murder and rapine, yet fearful of the hereafter. His dreams were scarred with the violence and terror of the times, the religious persecution, the widespread feeling of the day that man's time had run its course, that Hell loomed and decay and destruction beckoned.

He came to his senses and he felt groggy, as he always did when he catnapped in the middle of the day. He frowned: there had been something in his dreams that he should get hold of, think over further.

Religious persecution.

Why should a portrait of a Christ head be hidden from sight at the Old Rectory in Temple Barden? It should have been an object of veneration—a symbol of Man's belief in God and Christ. Yet it had been placed secretly above a fourteenth- or fifteenth-century false ceiling. Why?

As far as he was aware there was nothing in the painting at which the priesthood and the established order in the church could take offence. What heresy could be there, in a Christ head, which was similar to so many portraits of Christ painted from the nineteenth century onwards?

But Ben Gibson had talked that evening of symbolism. Arnold wondered whether there were any symbols in the painting that might have caused problems in the mediæval church. There was the trelliswork—but that appeared in a number of triptyches in the fourteenth century and he was not aware that it had occasioned any religious dissension. There was the shield: Arnold could see no problem there, for it could be merely a sort of signature, to demonstrate that the de Bohuns had commissioned the painting. Removing the bars from the shield and placing them elsewhere in the painting was puzzling, of course—but he could see no reason why that should cause offence and bring about the need to hide the painting from public gaze.

Religious persecution could have been the reason for hiding the painting in the first place, but it didn't seem to fit.

He teased at the problem, turning the issues over in his mind. If hiding the painting was not the direct result of religious persecution, what other reason could there be? Obviously, it had been hidden to prevent the painting being looked at.

Or read.

He sat upright. Looking at the painting, taking it at face value was one thing. Reading it was another.

He recalled Victorian paintings—how a bird, a discarded glove in a set scene was intended to have meaning for the onlooker, provide an explanation for the scene which filled in the detailed background in a way the activity of the people in the painting could not. The onlooker was expected to read Victorian paintings, recognize the symbolism of the discarded glove . . .

There were symbols in the mediæval Christ head painting. They were there to be read. But the painting had been hidden . . . *in case the symbols were interpreted by the wrong people.* That could have been the reason for its secretion above the false ceiling. It had a message to give, but one that should not be seen by the wrong eyes. But the message escaped Arnold.

He closed his eyes again, tightly, and when he opened them after a few minutes bright flashes blinded him momentarily. When the sight steadied he was staring at the wall of the half-ruined drum tower to his left, and he could see the clawmarks in the stone, left by masons more than six hundred years earlier.

He stared at them, suddenly puzzled. It was something that should have attracted his attention before now.

In the early days of masoncraft everything was done with the axe—even circular work such as shafts and mouldings. At the time of the Conquest the axe was superseded by the bolster—a form of wide chisel which in time came to be used for all purposes connected with freestone dressing. The bolster tended to mark lines across the stone as the mason drove his tool over the face of the stone: throughout the thirteenth century the bolster marks—or 'toolings'—could be seen running vertically as a series of parallel grooves.

But as knowledge of masoncraft improved the clawtool was developed—a bolster with a serrated edge. At the same time, masons became lazier—they held the bolster differently so that the lines of tooling ran diagonally instead of vertically across the face of the stone.

Arnold could date stonework by observation of such toolmarks. The pre-Conquest axed stonework left rough, deeply scored marks; masonry in the tenth and eleventh century showed vertical tooling; the use of the claw produced a spotty appearance in late mediæval masonry, and in the thirteenth century the lines of tooling ran diagonally, carelessly, across the face of the stone.

Yet none of this evidence would have helped Arnold date the section of stonework at which he was staring. On the four great stones he was staring at, built into the wall of the drum tower, the lines were horizontal. They were not vertical bolster marks, nor were they diagonal clawmarks.

They had not in fact been cut in the ordinary process of dressing the stone at all. They had been deliberately etched into the blocks at a later date.

They were the missing bars in the de Bohun shield.

Arnold stood up. There was a tight feeling in his chest. He stood there for several minutes, staring at the wall and then he moved back towards the section that held the two shields of the de Bohun family. An idea crawled turgidly in his head, as he thought of the painting, and the shields, and the conversation he and Jane had had with Ben Gibson, that evening in the Quayside bookshop before they had gone out together for a meal.

Symbolism, Ben had said. But he had talked of religious persecution too, of a kind. The Monks of Christ. The fourteenth-century purge of the Knights Templar.

The mythical, mysterious, treasure of Tarset.

Slowly, trying to control the excited hammering in his chest, Arnold inspected the drum tower. It looked normal, the usual kind of construction he would have expected to find in a Norman building. On the next floor there would have been a guardroom, no doubt, for lookout purposes, and on the floor below, a chamber with sleeping apartments running off, and garderobes attached. But what had this floor held? Probably, again, a series of chambers with wooden partitions, where castle inmates might sleep.

If so, where was the garderobe?

Arnold stood there, thinking. The problem was, on this broken ledge he was unable to walk where he wished, make a proper inspection. Reluctantly, he turned and began to make his way back down the broken staircase, leaning against the sound wall, careful of his step as he went. The fifty-foot drop yawned below him, culminating in a pile of broken rubble. A false step here and he would never survive the fall.

He breathed more easily when he reached the ground. He walked around the north side of the Norman tower. Looking up, he could see the drum tower where he had been standing. He inspected it closely, shading his eyes with his hand.

The monasteries had been the pioneers in sanitary arrangements. The reredorters of the monks had been well-planned, usually a privy wing at the end of the dorter or dormitory, often at right angles to the dorter and sited wherever possible over or near a stream. There was a good example at Fountains Abbey, Arnold recalled.

When the mediæval kings built their castles they had been influenced by such arrangements; the masons who worked on the monastic buildings also built the castles, and they had developed the concept, including vaulted drains on occasions, sometimes running into chambers that could be cleared if there were no nearby stream. Arnold stared up at the drum tower.

The buttréssing on the outside edge of the drum was designed just like a garderobe: it ran the height of the tower itself, providing latrines on each floor. It would have served the floor below the one he had been standing on, and probably the one above.

But not the floor where the shields appeared for up there he had seen no garderobe entrance—merely a blank wall. Etched with the shields and bars of the de Bohuns.

Arnold sat down. His legs felt suddenly weak, and he was shaking slightly. He tried to calm himself, but his mind was in a turmoil of excitement. He thought back to some of the houses and castles he had visited over the years. Garderobes were functional constructions, designed for a definite purpose. But they had also, traditionally, been used for other reasons.

In the sixteenth century, religious persecution had led to the construction of priests' holes: Nicholas Owen had been famous for his constructions for Catholic priests. At Harvington Hall in Worcestershire Arnold had seen a splendid example: secret access via a garderobe to a shaft concealed by a false wall. The shaft contained an oak pulley which worked the spit in the adjoining kitchen. The pulley wheel could also be used by a desperate man seeking escape, for in the floor of the shaft was access to a lower chamber, with an exit on the edge of the moat.

Twelve-feet-thick walls could be used for a multitude of purposes. But as he stared at it, Arnold guessed that the drum tower had not been constructed to provide means of escape.

Arnold craned his neck to stare upwards. The existence of the garderobe and its shoot on three floors was clear, yet where the etched shields were located there was no garderobe access, and no shoot.

Arnold went back thoughtfully to his car.

He glanced at his watch. It was almost two o'clock. He'd told Jane he'd be leaving Brunskill Castle shortly after lunch, to return to the Quayside. But his discovery of the etched bars changed things: it was too important to leave, with the theory buzzing in his head, he had to try to test it.

He opened the boot of his car, and was angry with himself. When he went walking the hills at weekends he often took tools with him: a hammer, a chisel, some general stone-working implements. When he investigated sites they often came in useful. But on this occasion he had left them behind. He clucked his tongue thoughtfully. He hunted through the back of the car, until he found the standard toolbox issued with the vehicle. There was a wheel jack there, a screwdriver. And an iron handle for use with the jack.

Its end was shaped like a chisel, presumably for springing off the wheel hubcaps. It was the nearest thing he had to a suitable tool. Arnold removed it, slammed the boot closed and turned back towards the ruins of Brunskill Castle, and the staircase rising fifty feet to the ledge fronting the Norman drum tower.

He was perspiring freely in the warm sunshine, even though he had taken off his jacket. Shirt-sleeved, he dug away at the ancient mortar between the massive stones. The horizontal lines that had been cut in the four stones were his markers: taking the top left-hand stone he dug at the mortar, scraping it away from between the closely fitting blocks.

It had been good workmanship, and that in itself was

interesting. The Norman tower had been built in the eleventh or twelfth century, yet these stones had been dressed with care, finely, and then the etched lines had been drawn into them. But the mortar was old and crumbled fairly easily: much of the castle had collapsed under the elements, and this wall also shared in that decay. Even so, it was warm work. Once he had cleaned the first stone he moved to the second, then the third and fourth.

He was left with four loosened blocks of stone—an area of three feet square.

Arnold paused at that point, and sat down again. His head was throbbing, not so much with the exertion as the nervous excitement. The painting, the shields, the etched marks in the stone, they all provided a progressive theory that seemed logical to him, and yet, excited as he was, there was also the fear that he was on a wild goose chase, that the walls of the drum tower were solid, that there was no sealed garderobe behind those blocks of masonry. But he would not find out the truth by sitting there. When his breathing calmed, he went back to work.

It was more difficult now.

It was one thing to clear the mortar from between the stones: it was another to try to ease them out of the wall by using the iron jack-handle as a lever. The stone was unyielding as he pulled and tugged, and thrust the lever into the aperture.

But it moved.

When he could get his fingertips to obtain purchase on the stone he tried to draw it out. After several minutes of pulling, his fingertips were raw and bleeding, and he was forced to stop. The jack-handle was the only answer: it would take longer, but he would have to display the necessary patience. He scraped and pulled away at the stone, and gradually it inched outwards, a solid block of masonry that had been placed there perhaps five hundred years earlier, and undisturbed since.

When Arnold had moved the heavy stone block out from

its resting place to a depth of perhaps three inches, he paused. He looked around him: the sun glinted on the river and sheep grazed peacefully on the sward below him. A faint haze of woodsmoke rose in the air above the hills towards Temple Barden and he could almost imagine himself as a retainer in the de Bohun castle, taking his watch in the drum tower, awaiting the return of the baronial cavalcade. He rubbed his hand over his sweating face, and returned to his work.

Slowly he inched the stone outwards from its place. The margin he had to work with was small with this first stone: the second stone would be easier, he knew, because he would have more room to drag it sideways. When he had pulled the block out perhaps six inches he paused again and looked down at the stone ledge under his feet. It seemed solid enough: he wondered whether he could risk dropping the block, rather than lifting it down, for it would be heavy, perhaps too heavy for him to manage.

He thrust the jack-handle into the narrow aperture again, easing the block outwards. Inch by inch it moved, and his eyes were stinging as sweat dripped down from his forehead. The stone was now eight inches out of its cavity, and he was able to obtain good purchase on it: his biceps strained as he grasped the stone with both hands and pulled steadily. With a grinding of ancient mortar, stone on stone, the block moved outwards. He had pulled it out a good twelve inches, and he had the feeling now it was balanced, the surrounding blocks still holding it in place, but with only a couple of inches to go. He pulled, and pulled again, vigorously, and the stone suddenly moved, came out unexpectedly and Arnold staggered backwards.

The movement had caught him off balance, and the block was too heavy for him to hold. His hands slipped on the dressed edge of the stone and it fell from his hands, striking him on the thigh, scoring a long weal along his shin, before it crashed on to the ledge. There was a shivering movement under his feet and Arnold swore, hopping on one foot, holding his shin and hissing with pain. He rolled up his trouser leg and saw the broken skin, the thin welling of blood along the line of his shin. Hobbling, he leaned against the wall and screwed up his eyes against the rising dust. He took a deep breath, and slowly, deliberately, rolled back his trouserleg. The injury was unimportant. He turned back to the drum tower wall, and the aperture caused by the removal of the heavy block.

There was another block behind it.

Arnold stared. He was dumbfounded. An immense disappointment washed over him, a cold ache in his chest. He had expected to see an opening, a dark space, the way into the interior of the drum tower and the secret of Brunskill. But there was only rubble, and another stone block. It would be impossible to move it with his improvised tool; it was set fourteen inches deep into the wall, and he knew now there was no guarantee that beyond it there would be anything other than more solid wall.

His theory had been based upon a false premise: there was no garderobe entrance and no secret chamber. For some reason the drum tower on this floor had been constructed of solid stone, even though garderobe had been created above and below this floor. There would be a linking shoot of course, on the exterior wall of the drum tower, connecting with the floors above and below, but that was all.

Yet that didn't make sense.

There was no architectural reason why the drum tower should have been sealed as a solid construction at this level. It served no purpose as a buttress, or as a support to the tower extension above. He frowned, puzzled. He stared again at the etched bars in the remaining stones. He was sure they were there as a signal, as a pointer to anyone who had read the symbols in the painting and guessed them correctly.

He wondered whether his disappointment was an overreaction. He picked up the jack-handle again and attacked the second stone. This was easier to move: by forcing the jack-handle into the aperture to the right of the stone, where we had cleared out the binding mortar, he was able to force it sideways into the space left by the stone he had already removed. Vigorous jerking with the handle pushed the block sideways and he was soon able to get a grip on the stone with his bleeding fingers.

He paused for a few moments, to gather his breath. A sudden irritation caught at him: he pulled violently at the block, angry that he had discovered nothing behind the first one but solid wall. He dragged at the heavy stone, pulled it sideways until it was half out of its space. He thrust a hand behind it, pressed his shoulder against it and then pulled backwards, bracing his legs to take the weight.

The block was poised, ready to be drawn out. Arnold stretched his fingers deep into the aperture, praying he would find space, an emptiness. Instead, he touched mortar again, crumbling drily under his hand. Then another solid block. There was no entrance to a sealed garderobe behind the etched blocks. His theory was wrong; his reading of the Christ head painting was a romantic folly.

The sudden anger of a moment ago was now exacerbated by his disappointment, and he felt a surge of adenalin in his blood. It was uncharacteristic: he was normally a patient man, careful in his approach to ancient stone and wood, wary that if he moved impetuously he could destroy evidence, reach wrong conclusions. But the de Bohuns were in his mind, and it was as though they were mocking him, these long-dead Normans. They had etched their shield on this wall, and cut a second shield minus the bars, and they had then caused the patterns to be shown in the painting, before eventually hiding it above a false ceiling in their hall in Temple Barden. They had placed their clues, but those signs ended in a black wall. Angrily, frustrated, Arnold dragged at the second stone carelessly, and it suddenly surged out of the wall. He was unable to hold it and it crashed down to the ledge at his feet as he stepped wildly back to avoid it crushing his feet.

The effect was instantaneous. The stone of the ledge beneath him shattered; as it did so, part of the wall of the drum tower, where it was supported by the ledge, collapsed. With a thunderous roar the ledge gave way, the wall at the base of the drum tower opened cavernously and Arnold slid forward, into the drum tower wall itself, and crashed downwards, striking his head on the stone wall as he fell.

He came to rest, painfully, in a cloud of dust that half choked him, but there was a singing noise in his skull and his senses were fading. There was a rumbling all about him, ancient stone settling, disturbed after centuries, and rubble and mortar crumbled and fell about him. The noise seemed to continue for an age, but it could only have been a matter of seconds before the black mist stole over his mind and he drifted into a dark, unconscious pit.

3

The tomb enveloped him.

Arnold had no idea how long he had been lying there unconscious: his wits were still muddled, his senses vague. He pushed with his hands and there was no resistance in the darkness above his head. His skull throbbed, his breathing was painful and the dust clogged his throat and nostrils, stung his eyes as he struggled to open them in the darkness. He coughed, and felt the bile rise in his throat, thick with the dust of centuries.

Arnold shuddered and tried to open his eyes. They were gummed: he rubbed his hands against them and there was something wet crawling slowly across his face. His fingers traced the trickling wetness upwards and explored his scalp; he felt a thick mess there in his hairline. Its stickiness suggested it was his own blood: he had struck his head when falling, and a wound had opened in his throbbing skull.

He tried to move and pain shot through his back, and

his shoulder. He stretched his arms more slowly and flexed his muscles: the pain came again momentarily, sharp. He groaned. The sound came back to him, sepulchrally, and he blinked, clearing his eyes and his mind. He looked around him, squinting against the dust, peering in the dimness.

In spite of the sunshine outside, the light in here was poor.

He was in a low-roofed chamber. It was perhaps six feet square. It was half piled with rubble: and as he looked about him he could see that a mass of mortar and stone had fallen in with the collapse of the wall above the ledge and was almost burying him. The pile lay across his legs and lower body, and the dust still hung thickly in the air, making it difficult to see his surroundings.

He tried to move his legs, but he was pinned down.

Arnold struggled for a short while as an unreasoning claustrophobia seized him. He tried to twist, turning his body sideways and dragging at his legs. The sweat ran down his face, mingling with the slower, thicker mass of blood seeping from the wound in his hairline and the sharp stabbing pain came again in his back, a muscular tear down his left side.

Arnold stopped. It was necessary to calm himself, get rid of the feeling of pressure that had built up in his mind. He flexed the muscles in his back, easing them. He stopped twisting and lay still. Deliberately he slowed his breathing, calming the unreasoning panic that had arisen in his chest. It was a matter of patience: taking each step slowly.

He was lying on stone, the rubble pressing into his back. He struggled to sit upright: he could manage a half-sitting position, but then the stone that had crashed down as he fell and slid into the chamber was covering the rest of his body. The blocks were heavy, but he was able to flex his toes and his knee so he knew he had not been seriously injured. It was simply a matter of taking things slowly.

He reached forward and took hold of the nearest block

of stone. It was heavy: he pushed hard, levering it away from him and after a few moments it tilted and rolled over sideways. Dust rose and danced briefly, then hung in the dimness, a grey, misty haze.

For the next few minutes Arnold repeated the process, taking one stone block at a time, shifting it, pushing it sideways away from his body, and as he worked he realized how fortunate he had been. He was sore and bruised, but the sharp pain in his back had eased. There was blood running from a cut on his head and his hands were badly torn, but he had suffered no major injury, and even the stone that had pinned him to the floor was not crushing him: the blocks surrounded him but placed no great pressure on his body, probably because some heavy masonry had fallen beside him and was supporting the later material that had collapsed into the chamber.

After a few minutes' exertion he lay back and rested, sweat streaming down his face, mingling with the drying blood. He touched his head gingerly: a thick sticky mat was now encrusting the crown of his head. He wondered how long he had been unconscious. He craned his head backwards and looked up behind him. The sunlight seemed less bright through the aperture some ten or twelve feet above his head. He peered at his watch. The face was shattered, crushed in his fall.

He returned to his labours, taking one piece at a time, calming the anxiety that still touched him. Gradually he felt the weight lessening on his lower body and he managed to free his hips, dragging himself to a more upright position. After a while he felt iron under his hand: the jack-handle, which had fallen into the chamber with him. He picked it up, used it to prise away some of the blocks and ease his stinging fingertips. It made the work easier: the strain on his waist and back as he leaned forward to clear the rubble from his lower body was far less.

He got his right leg free, then finally his left. He rolled sideways on the hard stone, the dust still thick in the air, and he lay back for a moment, exhausted momentarily with the effort and the relief of his freedom from the crush of rubble and stone.

He knew now his theory had not been wrong in its entirety.

He had assumed that the bars etched in the wall of the drum tower had proclaimed the entrance to what might have been planned originally as a garderobe, but which had functioned eventually for quite a different purpose. His disappointment when he had discovered solid wall behind the etched bars had been premature: the etched bars had certainly been pointers, but his guess now was that the entrance to the drum tower chamber had lain not behind the bars themselves, but lower down, where the floor of the ledge on which he had been standing abutted on to the tower wall itself.

The old masons had been adept at providing entry systems for such chambers as this. In many cases it was by way of a subtle balancing of stones, requiring no pulley arrangement. In this case, Arnold guessed, access had been made more difficult deliberately: there was to be no accidental discovery of the entrance. It would always have been necessary to lift the stones at the base of the drum tower, directly below the etched bars, to find the entrance to the chamber. But the centuries had weakened the wall and the ledge, and when Arnold had carelessly allowed the heavy block to drop it had cracked the stone ledge, the wall and the entrance stone had given way and the chamber had been exposed.

But it was not like a garderobe attached to a sleeping chamber. This was more secret, dropped below floor level, lying behind and below solid stone between the two floors of the drum tower. Arnold had come across priest holes no bigger than this—indeed, some had been smaller. But this had not been intended for such a purpose, he was sure of that. This was no hiding-place for a man. The half-formed thoughts in his mind suggested other reasons for the existence of this chamber in the drum tower.

And now he was free of the rubble and stone, he could test his theory about the painting, and the shields and the bars etched in the stone wall of the drum tower.

He stood on the rubble, forced to stoop under the low roof of the chamber immediately above his head. Behind him the roof was higher where the wall had collapsed at the entrance, but here it was no more than six feet. The dust was still thick, hanging in the air, and the light was dim. He squinted, his back to the faint light that entered through the narrow aperture above and behind his head, and looked around him.

Gradually, he made out the dimensions of the chamber, and saw the narrow ledge that ran along the length of the far wall. It was about two feet wide, and lying on it was a formless mass, perhaps three feet by two. Arnold was still, but he could hear the thudding of his heart as he stared at the bundle.

Slowly, Arnold stumbled over the rubble, moved towards it, crouching under the low roof. He peered at it, leaning over to inspect it more closely. The light was too dim to allow an identification of the object, but when Arnold reached out his fingers touched a coarse woven cloth.

He hesitated.

The cloth would be old; it felt crumbly to his touch. If he unwrapped it now he could damage it, and would not know what he was destroying. Yet a desire burned fiercely inside him: he remembered the old accounts of what might lie in the hands of the de Bohuns: a fabulous treasure, the ransom of kings, the purchase of the world.

His fingers trembled slightly as he reached out and lifted the bundle. Inside the coarse cloth was something firm, and heavy. But not heavy enough to be gold, or silver, or jewels. Arnold smiled in the darkness: he thought now he could guess what might lie inside these wrappings. Not the specific item, perhaps, but its general nature. He turned, glanced back at the aperture.

There was no hurry now. He could leave the bundle here for collection later. It would be time then to satisfy his curiosity. The fact that he had found the treasure of Tarset, the secret of the de Bohuns, was enough. The first imperative was to release himself from this tomb-like chamber. Then, later, he could come back and retrieve the bundle, and have it properly investigated.

He turned away. His foot struck the jack-handle, where he had dropped it. He picked it up and placed it on the ledge beside the bundle, then he walked forward to the edge of the chamber.

The low roof had collapsed at that point. The aperture through which he had fallen was some twelve feet above him. A narrow chimney of solid stone gave him the possibility of escape, if he could reach the lip of the opening. It was not going to be difficult: it was simply a matter of building a mounting-block, a staircase of stone.

The de Bohuns, when they built this chamber, would probably have used a wooden ladder to get down into the chamber below floor level. Arnold had no ladder, but there was plenty of broken stone about that he could use to build the necessary platform. He cleared a small area of rubble to give himself a solid base, and then he began to lift the heavy squared blocks, one by one to build a mounting-platform that would enable him to reach the aperture.

The dust rose again, choking him as he worked. The light also was fading: he realized he must have been unconscious for some time, before he had set himself to the labour of clearing the stone that had pinned him to the floor. It would be dusk outside, but that was no problem: within the hour he would be out of the chamber and back to his car.

Then, tomorrow, he could return and collect the bundle. He smiled to himself in the darkness: this would cause ripples of excitement in the Department of Museums and Antiquities and make the DDMA open his eyes.

It was then that he heard the sound of footsteps on the ledge above his head.

Arnold stopped.

He opened his mouth to call out, relieved that someone would be out there to help him. But no sound came. For suddenly, the relief was replaced by anxiety as warning bells rang in his head. He could not explain his sudden concern: it might have been the care with which the footsteps moved on the walls above him. It might have been other, vaguer thoughts that had been with him for some days.

He recalled what Culpeper had said to him. Dimmock and Weaver were suspected of using these ruins, with others, for occult meetings. Culpeper had warned him away from them. Arnold was silent.

'Hello?'

The voice rang out, echoing against the deserted walls of Brunskill Castle. The voice was distorted by the walls, bouncing back, skittering down into the drum tower, whispering unrecognizably in the dark corners of the chamber.

'*Hello!*'

Arnold made no reply. He stood frozen, waiting. He could get out of here by himself; he needed no assistance. And he was reluctant to expose his presence. He could not explain why, but he felt nervous, and his heart was thudding in his chest.

The footsteps stopped. There was a long silence. It was only one person, of that Arnold was certain: Dimmock would not have brought his coven with him. Arnold kept still, and waited. The steps began again, walking away towards the stairs, and then they stopped, as Arnold held his breath. There was a long, frozen silence.

The steps came back, slowly, a measured stride, confident.

Arnold looked up. In the aperture he could see the form of a man, dark outlined against the sky. He was staring down into the chamber constructed by the de Bohuns.

Arnold heard a long, strangled sigh, almost of relief.

'Is it you, Landon?'

Arnold was silent for a moment. 'Yes.' He hesitated, not certain what to say. 'The floor collapsed when I was up on the ledge. I'd be careful, if I were you. I've been trapped down here for a while.' He cleared the dust in his throat. 'I'm just making my way out. Maybe you can give me a hand.'

'Are you hurt?'

'No. I'm pulling stone blocks, so I can climb out. I'm almost finished. If I reach up then, perhaps you could pull me out.'

The man was silent. Arnold peered upwards. 'I just need a few more stones. I—'

'Did you find it?' the man interrupted.

Arnold stared. He was unable to make out the man's features, but he thought he knew the voice. 'Find what?'

'Don't play silly games with me,' the man replied quietly, but with a menacing coldness.

'Who are you?' Arnold asked nervously.

'We've met, Mr Landon, we've met.'

Arnold was certain now, and a cold fist hardened in his chest.

The man above cleared his throat. 'I repeat: have you found it?'

'I don't know what you're talking about.'

'Come on, Mr Landon, don't treat me as a fool. You're an intelligent man. Pay me the compliment of assuming the same about me. You need to accept that I've been looking for the same signs that you have—though maybe for longer.' He paused: Arnold could hear his steady breathing. 'I know why you're up here. I know what you're looking for. You saw the shields, and you guessed their importance. It's the same thing that that bloody woman saw up here—and maybe the old man too!'

'Woman?' Arnold was startled. He frowned, stared up at the man above him. Then the realization came to him, and his blood ran cold. '*The old man?*' he repeated thickly.

The man on the ledge grunted. 'It's ironic, isn't it?' He was silent for a while, mulling over his thoughts. 'I've been coming up here for a year—ever since I saw the painting, and realized its significance. I found the etched shields on the drum tower six months ago, but I could make no sense of it. And then that damned woman, she came to me about her bloody stupid series. She'd been up to Brunskill before she came near me, but then when she was talking to me, looking around, I saw the sudden light in her eyes—the excitement. She couldn't get out of the house fast enough, and I knew she'd found something I hadn't.'

'Lynne Anderson,' Arnold almost whispered.

The man paused, and there was something like a deep growl in his throat. 'She left me, and she came straight back here, to Brunskill, up to this ledge. And from her excitement, I knew she'd worked out something I'd failed to do. I was angered—I couldn't let her steal it from me. So I followed her.'

'Lynne Anderson,' Arnold said slowly. 'You killed her—because she had seen the shields—'

'It's no matter,' the man interrupted impatiently. 'How did you find the chamber? She saw something up here. I came back—but still it escaped me. Perhaps it was all too familiar to my eye: I could make no connection. But she did. What did you see up here that's escaped me for six months?'

'You mentioned an old man,' Arnold said slowly, a dull ache in his chest.

There was a short silence, then an exasperated sigh. 'I was told he'd come up to Brunskill to take photographs. I came after him, as soon as I heard. I didn't know what he had seen. But at this stage, I couldn't take a chance. There was too much at stake. I saw him from the crags, taking his last photographs. He was looking up towards the drum tower. I waited till he left, drove past me. I drove behind him. It was easy enough.'

'You forced him off the road,' Arnold said wonderingly.
'It's no matter. What have you found down there?'
'Nothing.'

In the silence that followed the man's breathing was
harsh and unsteady. 'You're lying.'

'This was an accident. The floor collapsed. There's just
an empty chamber down here.'

'No. It can't be. The painting at the Old Rectory, the
shields etched here—I know I'm right! The de Bohuns
planned this, secreted the treasure somewhere here at Brunskill. And you've found the chamber. It has to be here.
You're lying! But it makes no difference. I can find out for
myself. You'll not be leaving this chamber, anyway.'

There was a sudden movement. Arnold caught a glimpse
of something long and dark being pushed down into the
aperture. For a second he was frozen in surprise, and then
he leaped backwards, striking his head against the low roof
of the chamber, falling backwards, half-stunned, over the
pile of stone, as the thunder crashed in the room and echoed
madly inside his head.

There was second explosion and flash of violent light, the
firing of a second shell, and the sound roared and reverberated around the narrow chamber until Arnold felt his head
was almost bursting. Half deafened, he lay on his back on
the rubble as the silence returned. He lay still, his mind
spinning.

After a moment he heard a clicking sound, the shotgun
being broken, new shells being inserted.

'Landon?'

Arnold lay still.

'Are you still with us?'

Arnold made no reply.

The man above seemed uncertain momentarily. 'That
was just a warning. I've no reason to want to hurt you. I
just want what you've got down there.'

He was lying and they both knew it. It was impossible
for him to allow Arnold to leave Brunskill alive. The silence

gathered around them, the dust settling thickly in the chamber. Above, the man shuffled impatiently, still uncertain. 'Are you able to talk to me? That was just a warning. Just to tell you I'm serious. But you've got to give me what you've found down there.'

He wasn't certain whether Arnold was alive, or injured or dead. But to come down into the chamber was risky: he knew nothing about its dimensions, it was getting dark, and Arnold could be waiting for him, ready to attack him as he came down unsteadily into the chamber.

'There's enough in this for both of us, Landon. I'm not greedy. I'll share it with you. You know what's been said about it over the centuries. The ransom of kings. Bring it out with you, or hand it up to me. We can do a deal. We both keep quiet about what's happened. We split the proceeds. We go our separate ways.'

Arnold was amazed that he could even contemplate the thought that Arnold would be persuaded. There could be no deal with this man. It was a measure of the obsession that gripped him that he thought he could talk Arnold into exposing himself. He could think only of what was in the chamber. And yet he held all the cards. Arnold was trapped in the drum tower room. All he could do was wait: the man up there had the shotgun. On the other hand, his assailant couldn't safely come down into the chamber until Arnold was dead.

As long as Arnold stayed still, and out of range of the shotgun, he would be safe. He could wait it out. Someone was bound to come to Brunskill eventually. Jane would surely be wondering what had happened to him. She had already come out to Brunskill once today: she knew he was here.

If he failed to turn up at the Quayside she'd ring his home, get no reply—it would probably occur to her some accident might have happened out at Brunskill. She'd come looking for him.

And when she arrived, up there would be the man with

the shotgun. A man who had already killed twice in his obsessional search for the treasure of Tarset.

Arnold was in a dilemma. If he moved, he could die. And if Jane came looking for him, they could both die. He hesitated, not knowing what to do.

In a few moments the matter was resolved for him. Arnold heard a scuffling sound, a harsh, grating noise as something heavy was dragged towards the aperture leading to the chamber. Next moment there was a curse as a heavy stone thundered down into the chamber. The solution for the man on the ledge was simple: he was going to seal the chamber.

The first stone had fallen in. Arnold could hear him grunting as he dragged at another block on the ledge littered with fallen stone. He would pull it towards the entrance, block it, seal the chamber. By the time Jane, or anyone else arrived, it would be too late. The chamber would be sealed; there would be no sign of Arnold. She would assume he had left: it was unlikely she would climb the ruined staircase to this height, and the thick walls of the chamber would muffle Arnold's cries.

The chamber would be unsealed later, and the bundle removed.

When he was dead.

'All right!' he shouted suddenly. 'All right! Let's do a deal.'

Arnold rose and made his way towards the ledge where the bundle lay. There was a short silence, and then footsteps clumped back towards the entrance. He was aware the man would be peering in, shotgun probably levelled into the aperture. 'So you are still alive. But not for long, my friend.'

'There are people who know I'm here. They'll come looking for me.'

'They'll not find you.'

'But they might! They could get here before you finish! Even if they didn't, they could cause you problems. Police crawling over the site. You don't want that.' There was no reply for several seconds. 'We can do a deal,' Arnold said desperately.

The man with the gun hesitated. 'Talk to me,' he growled.

'There *is* something down here.'

The man hissed between his teeth. 'What is it?'

'It's wrapped in cloth. I haven't looked. I think there's a box inside.'

There was a short silence. 'Hand it up here. Let me see it.'

'Not until we've done the deal.'

'The bundle—'

'I don't want any part of it. You can keep it. As long as you let me out. Put the gun to one side. Let me out of here. I can't breathe. I'm claustrophobic. *I've got to get out of here!*'

Arnold had injected panic into his voice, but for a long while there was no reply. The minutes dragged past. 'Well?' Arnold asked, raising the tone of his voice, simulating terror.

'I've got to see the bundle first.' The man's voice had a nervous, shallow ring. He was suspicious. He knew that Arnold must guess his continued existence would be a threat to him. But he could not be certain help was not on the way, as Arnold claimed. It would be better if he could get his hands on the bundle immediately. He could not afford the risk of inquiries, searches up here for Arnold. But essentially, his greed to see the bundle was paramount. 'All right. Pass it up to me,' he said at last, 'and I'll let you go.'

Arnold's heart was hammering in his chest. 'This is a deal, isn't it? If I give you the bundle, you'll let me out.'

'It's a deal,' the man lied. 'You can trust me. Pass it up here.'

'Put the gun down first.'

There was a short silence. The calculation was being made. If the gun was put to one side and the bundle was passed up there would still be time to pick up the gun, discharge it before Arnold could get even his head through the aperture. There was little or no danger. Arnold heard the clatter of the shotgun as it was put down.

He took a deep breath.

'I've put it to one side,' the man above growled. 'Pass the bundle up here.'

Arnold's fingers were on the coarse cloth. Then they slipped past, closed around the cold iron of the heavy jack-handle. He stepped carefully towards the entrance, stooping under the low roof until he was under the aperture, looking up to the dark, towering figure of the empty-handed man above him.

'Pass it up,' the man exclaimed harshly.

Arnold knew he had just one chance, one opportunity only. He gritted his teeth, gripped the jack-handle firmly. Then he swung his arm behind him in a long arc and with all the strength he could muster hurled the iron jack-handle upwards, straight into the face of the crouching man above.

There was a dull thud and a flurry of movement, a cry of pain. Arnold saw the man stagger, stretch upright, and then reel back. Footsteps broke unevenly on the ledge and there was another, more desperate cry. Arnold leaped on to the rubble in a desperate attempt to drag himself through the aperture but he could not reach its lip. He heard the crashing of stone as something above gave way, he himself fell backwards to the floor of the chamber, and then there was silence. It extended, grew, filled the chamber.

Arnold waited, but there was no sound. There was no one on the ledge above him and the night outside was still.

At last, wearily, choked with dust, Arnold began to finish the mounting-block of stones.

Five minutes later he crawled out of the aperture. The evening was dark: no stars shone in the cloudy sky. He could make out the shotgun lying on the broken ledge. He picked it up and looked around. There was no one else on the ledge. He walked carefully to the edge and looked down. There was a huddled shape broken on the pile of stones fifty feet below. Arnold felt sick. He sat down, and calmed himself. A breeze rose, lifting the damp, blood-crusted hair on his forehead.

There was the sound of a car engine on the hill. Headlights swept over Reivers Crags. Arnold waited, and after a little while he saw the lights up at the gateway. A car door slammed; someone climbed over the gate, flashlight in hand, and began to walk into the field.

'Arnold!'

The call came echoing eerily towards the ruins. It was Jane. She had come to look for him, as he had suspected. He knew now he had been right to take the chance he had. Had he not acted, she would have had to face the man lying on the stones below. He called her name, and began to pick his way slowly down the broken staircase.

When he reached the base of the Norman tower, she was standing near the wall. He came forward and she shone her torch in his face. 'What on earth have you been doing up here all this time? I thought—*my God!* What's happened to you?'

He made no reply. Wearily he took the flashlight from her and picked his way over the pile of rubble to the front of the tower. She stood behind him as he shone the flashlight on the crumpled form on the masonry. He heard her draw a sharp breath; the torchlight rose, played on the face of the man lying there. The head was at an odd angle, the back twisted and broken: the torchlight picked out the indentation in the forehead where the jack-handle had struck him and the harsh, purple scar that had destroyed his face in the aftermath of the Falklands.

'Major Manners!' she said with a gasp. 'What on earth's happened here, Arnold?'

He shook his head. 'I'll explain later.'

He took a deep breath. Explanations later, but there was something that had to be done now. If he left now, he would never be able to return to Brunskill and the chamber in the drum tower, to relive the horror of the last half-hour. He had to do it now, rather than leave it for another. He took the flashlight from Jane's hand.

'Wait here.'

Wearily, carefully, his bones aching as he climbed the ruined staircase of the Norman tower, Arnold made his way back up the ledge from which Rodney Manners had fallen. The aperture at the foot of the drum tower yawned blackly at him. He placed the flashlight on the ledge and eased his aching limbs back into the chamber. His feet found the mounting-block; he crouched, made his way back to the narrow ledge that held the bundle Manners had sought.

He came back to the entrance, climbed the block, placing the bundle on the ledge above and climbed out. A few minutes later he was rejoining Jane. She was silent and shaken. She was curious, but she asked no questions. She took his arm and led him back to the car.

He had difficulty climbing the gate. His whole body seemed to ache, and his legs and arms were stiff. She opened her car door and he climbed in. 'We'll pick your car up later,' she said, and got into the driving seat.

Only then, as she looked at him clutching the bundle in his arms, did she ask. 'Just what is it you've got there?'

The coarse woven cloth had fallen away, shredding and crumbling as he had carried the bundle to the car. There was no reason now why he shouldn't open the box that lay inside.

'Shine your torch on it,' Arnold said.

The box was of dark hardwood, richly carved with a trelliswork pattern and inlaid with thin beaten gold and silver. It flashed under the light of the torch, gleaming brightly after its six-hundred-year interment.

Arnold lifted the lid and Jane shone the beam inside. 'What on earth is it?' she asked.

Arnold grunted wearily. 'It's the treasure that Major Manners mistakenly thought would enable him to restore Tarset Hall. The mythical treasure of the de Bohuns.'

'But . . . but it's just a piece of old cloth!'

It lay there in its ornate, protective box. Unlike the wood and the silver and the gold, it had not survived the centuries intact. The threads were fraying, the linen crumbling to dust almost as they watched.

'No,' Arnold said wearily. 'It's not just a piece of old cloth. It is—or more likely, was reputed to be—the cloth the Templars spirited out of eastern Turkey and brought to England in secret. An object of veneration for the Templars, the cause of their trouble with the Church in the thirteenth century. To them, a treasure beyond price.'

'I don't understand.'

Arnold sighed, despondently. 'It's the *sudarium*. The linen cloth that had once been soaked with His sweat and His blood in the tomb.'

4

The bluetit tapped on the window, imperiously. It was clearly accustomed to being fed. Arnold and Jane sat silently in Culpeper's office, staring at it. They had said nothing since the Chief Inspector had left the room with their signed statements. The bluetit was cocking its head on one side, peering into the room. Arnold wondered how long Culpeper had been feeding it, and whether it ever came into the room.

The door opened behind them and Culpeper walked in. He saw them looking out of the window and he grunted. 'Bloody pest!'

He sat down behind his desk and took from the drawer a small packet of birdseed. He opened the window carefully: unruffled, the bird hopped to one side and waited as he spilled some of the seed on the window ledge. 'You can trust birds,' Culpeper remarked as he turned back to face Arnold. 'They have behaviour patterns they stick to. People, now . . .' He did not finish the sentence.

Arnold waited. Beside him, Jane too was silent.

Culpeper sighed. 'Well, I've gone over your statements

and I think they help clear up most things. It means we can release Kevin Anderson—' He stared at Arnold thoughtfully. 'You never rated him as a wife-killer.'

'No.'

'Gave me problems, too. Ben Edwards, now, he was another matter. But he's off the hook as well, and is no longer helping us with our inquiries.'

So he could concentrate on his bloody brochure, Arnold thought sourly. 'Did you take a statement from Nick Dimmock?' he asked.

'Aye, from him and his stablemate Cliff Weaver. That was the guy you saw up at Reivers Crags, Miss Wilson.'

'He frightened me,' she said quietly.

'And you worried him! It seems Dimmock and Weaver had been using Brunskill for their coven meetings—too much fuss when they used parish churchyards. They thought they were well enough isolated at Brunskill. But they got worried when they realized someone was poking around there at night, flashlights, that sort of thing. They thought they were going to be harassed—and my visit to the Old Rectory didn't help, either. When Weaver met you at the crags, he thought you were part of some surveillance team and he got scared.'

'But it was Major Manners who'd been investigating the ruins,' Arnold said.

'That's about the size of it. Ever since he was led there by Lynne Anderson.' Culpeper looked at Arnold thoughtfully for a few seconds. 'You understand it all now?'

'Not really.'

Culpeper sighed. 'Well, the way I've pieced it together, it looks to me like Manners has always wanted to find this so-called treasure—'

'He wanted to rebuild Tarset Hall.'

'Aye, well, it was a sort of obsession with him. And he'd been shown Dimmock's painting two years ago. He made the connection between the shield in the painting and the one etched into the fireplace in his own home—but that's as far as he got. He couldn't make sense out of it.'

'Until Lynne Anderson visited him, doing research for her newspaper series?'

Culpeper took out his pipe and began to fill it. 'That's right. He wasn't all that keen on helping her, but he allowed her into the house, I guess. When she saw the shield etched into the fireplace she must have got excited. She'd worked on her series, read about the treasure of Tarset, seen the old drawings of the de Bohun arms, and had seen the shields up at Brunskill when she was researching her ghosts series. She was a sharp lady. She made the connection. The same connection you made.'

'Eventually,' Arnold said grimly.

'Manners must have seen the excitement in her face and was furious—he knew she'd discovered something he hadn't. She left Tarset and must have hurried back to Brunskill to check, and Manners followed her. He then realized the clues led to Brunskill, but he was afraid she'd blow the story before he could look for the treasure himself. If she wrote about it in the newspaper, Brunskill would have been crawling with treasure-hunters. He couldn't allow that.'

'So he followed her and killed her.'

Culpeper tamped the tobacco thoughtfully. 'It wasn't difficult. She was high—the barman in Craster testifies to her subdued excitement. Sexual—but heightened by her discovery. The cottage door hadn't been locked when they went in. Manners waited until midnight or thereabouts, and killed them both.'

'Which unfortunately, with her husband's disappearance, pointed the finger towards Kevin Anderson.'

Jane coughed slightly. 'The first time I met Major Manners he drove off in a hurry from Tarset. I think now he must have been going up to Brunskill again.'

Culpeper nodded. 'There were too many strangers hanging around. He was getting nervous—anxious to crack the secret of the treasure. And then, when you actually entered his house and photographed the fireplace, he realized you might notice the shield in the stonework and he bundled you out quickly.'

Jane was pale. 'It was I who told him that Ben was up at Brunskill, taking photographs.'

Arnold touched her arm carefully. 'There was no way you could know.'

But he realized there would be an image in her mind of Ben happily driving back from Brunskill with a job well done, and Manners driving murderously behind in the Land-Rover that would force Ben off the road to his death. Both Jane and Arnold would have their secret torments, now.

Culpeper scratched a match and lit his pipe. He looked nervously at Jane for a moment but she made no comment. He sighed. 'What doesn't come out in your statement, Mr Landon, is how you found that hidden chamber.'

Arnold shrugged. 'I realized what must have happened centuries ago. The Templars had been suppressed. They used the Shroud and the *sudarium* for secret religious rites. But when they were overthrown by papal fiat both Shroud and *sudarium* were spirited away. The Shroud was hidden in France. The de Bohuns brought the *sudarium* to England: they probably still used it for secret services at Temple Barden in the fourteenth century. But when things got too hot they decided to hide it. They walled it up in Brunskill. And they caused the painting to be made.'

'As a reminder to later generations of Templars?'

'That's right. But the persecution was severe. So they secreted the painting above a false ceiling, in order that unholy eyes should not discover the clues placed there. The shield of the de Bohuns—without the bars. The trelliswork, which pointed to the traditional background to the Holy Cloths. The bars themselves, floating in seemingly aimless fashion in the painting of the Christ head.'

'I still don't follow—'

'The complete de Bohun shield denoted Brunskill Castle

—the home of the de Bohuns,' Arnold explained. 'The Christ head pointed towards the link with the Holy Cloths. The shield without the bars, in the painting, was the signal, the pathway to the hiding-place: the bars themselves stated where the hiding-place was actually located. The trick was to find all three in one location: complete shield; shield without bars; the bars themselves. But in the end this secrecy was self-defeating.'

'How do you mean?'

'The Templars collapsed as a movement. The de Bohuns gradually died out. The existence of the painting was forgotten. The clues were not understood. All that remained were vague rumours—a "treasure worth a king's ransom"; the "purchase of the world".' Arnold grunted. 'And so it was, to the Templars, a treasure beyond price. But four hundred years later the secret had been lost.'

'But when you saw the two shields on the drum tower at Brunskill—' Jane murmured.

'All I had to do was look for the bars. And they almost escaped me—as I imagine they'd escaped Manners, and Lynne Anderson and Ben too, for that matter. It was merely that, when I looked . . .' His voice trailed away. He thought suddenly of his father, and the enthusiasms he had nurtured in Arnold all those years ago.

Culpeper sucked at his pipe. 'It'll all make the painting famous. Dimmock could make a packet out of the publicity.'

'He wants to refurbish the Old Rectory,' Arnold said.

Culpeper shook his head. 'Support his bloody occult society, more like. Still, that's his business—until he starts messin' about in parish churches again, like.' He puffed blue smoke ceilingwards. On the window-sill the bluetit was tapping again, insistently.

In the car park Arnold walked Jane to her car before going to his. He held the door open for her. As she got in, she said, 'What about the *sudarium*? What'll happen to it now?'

Arnold shrugged. 'It's in a poor state. And it's an object

of curiosity only. It's just a mediæval forgery, of course. But it's of some interest, and I imagine there'll be a battle now between the National Trust—who own Brunskill—and the finder.'

'But that's *you*!'

Arnold laughed. 'I've agreed with the DDMA I was actually working for the department when I found it, acting in the course of my employment—so it's my employers who'll reap the benefit. If they win the argument. It makes little difference either way—if it doesn't go on display in some National Trust museum, it will in Northumberland.'

'They might put a little blue plaque underneath it, with your name on,' Jane suggested mischievously.

'Somehow I doubt that,' Arnold said, grinning widely. 'I doubt that very much!'